I0782428

THE RANCHER'S UNEXPECTED BRIDE

SECOND CHANCES IN HARMONY SPRINGS ~ BOOK ONE

LAURALYN KELLER

Copyright © 2025 Lauralyn Keller

All rights reserved. No portion of this book may be reproduced or transmitted in any form or by any means - photocopied, shared electronically, scanned, stored in a retrieval system, or other - without the express permission of the publisher. Exceptions will be made for brief quotations used in critical reviews or articles promoting this work.

The characters and events in this fictional work are the product of the author's imagination. Any resemblance to actual people, living or dead, is coincidental.

Unless otherwise indicated, all Scripture quotations are taken from the Holy Bible, Kings James Version.

ISBN-13: 978-1-963212-22-8

To Christine: thank you for always being a sounding board and encouraging me in this writing journey. It's always fun talking story with you!

CHAPTER 1

FEBRUARY 1887

*A*riella Mountbatten's heart pounded in her chest as she hurried through the dark streets of Boston, her sister at her side. Sludgy gray snow covered the boardwalk. Cold wet seeped into the skirt of her navy traveling dress. The added weight slowed her down, a reality that only heightened her anxiety. She had to get away before anyone noticed her absence. Under the layers of clothing, her body pulsed with pain, a reminder of the reason she needed to flee. Shivers shook her, a combination of cold and nerves.

"They've likely noticed we're gone by now." Tori's voice stayed low. "Hopefully, no one thinks to check the train station at this hour."

Ella gripped her sister's hand. "I worry about you going back home alone."

Determination lifted Tori's chin. Her brown eyes glittered. "I've hailed carriages at night before. I'll be fine."

Ella's hold tightened. "Are you sure you don't want to come with me?"

"You know I need to finish my schooling. If things get bad, I'll stay with a friend." She squeezed Ella's hand. "Don't worry about me. Let me worry about you for once."

Tori was stubborn. Mother said it was a product of her fiery red hair. Right now, Ella was thankful she possessed that quality.

The two of them hastened along in silence. Ella had chosen to pack a single carpetbag and to walk rather than use a carriage, knowing the servants would alert Father and Mother if she asked for it.

They arrived at their destination minutes before the midnight train was to depart. Relief poured over her. *No one will be able to stop the train.* Ella paid for her ticket, receiving a cursory glance from the sleepy ticket master as he shoved a ticket across the counter. She took a deep breath. Her fingers trembled as she picked it up. She turned to Tori, fighting tears. "This is the only way," she said, more to herself than anything.

Tori wrapped her in a fierce embrace. "I will miss you." The whispered words hung heavy in the air. "Godspeed, Ella. I love you."

"I love you too." Ella kissed Tori's cheek, her throat so tight it hurt.

"Go." Tori gave her a firm push, the word a mere whisper above the train's whistle.

Ella hugged her sister once more, then hurried to the train before she could change her mind. As she boarded, the train lurched forward. Ella rocked on her feet, gaining a tentative balance.

A conductor shuffled toward her. "Ticket, miss?"

After she gave him her boarding pass, he showed her to her seat. She threw her bag on the space beside her, then pressed her nose to the window to find Tori. The younger woman caught Ella's gaze and waved. Tears streamed down her cheeks.

Only eighteen months apart in age, they had never been

separated for more than a day. How was Ella to bear life without her sister? She had no plans to return home. Tori was the only one who knew she was leaving, but even she didn't know where Ella was going. It was safer that way.

A sharp pain pierced her heart. She watched Tori until the train turned a bend. Ella trembled with the gravity of what she'd done. Her hands clenched. She stared out the window as everything familiar slowly vanished from sight. Tears poured from her eyes. Scared and alone, she muffled her sobs with a handkerchief as the train picked up speed and carried her away from Boston.

⁓

HARMONY SPRINGS, MONTANA TERRITORY

A shrill scream split the air. Cody Brooks jerked awake. Another cry sounded, this one softer but no less painful.

Addie.

He threw the covers aside. As his feet hit the floor, he sucked in a sharp breath. The chill that seeped into his feet bit hard.

Addie wailed again. Cody hurried out of his room and down the hall. Pushing open the door to the children's room, he strode in. His six-month-old charge flailed in her crib. Blankets tangled around her body in disarray. The dim light of dawn illuminated the tears streaking her face. Poor girl.

He reached into the crib and picked her up. She cried harder. He held her to his chest, at a loss what to do. *I'm no father.*

Just three weeks ago, his best friend died in a riding accident along with his wife. Their children passed to Cody. *Why'd Jake and Harriet choose a gruff, unmarried rancher like me to be their kids' guardian?* He couldn't puzzle that out. He had no experience caring for children. Little ones made him nervous. Yet he now found himself in possession of three, all under the age of six.

Addie's breaths came in hard gasps. He shifted her, hoping the position was a comfortable one. How, exactly, was one supposed to hold a baby? Not for the first time, he wished he'd accepted one of Harriet's many offers for him to hold Addie when he visited their home.

The little girl screamed again. All at once, her breathing hitched. Her mouth remained open, but no air passed in or out.

Panic slammed into Cody. "No!" He laid her over his arm and slapped her back. "Breathe!"

She lay rigid. He hit her back again, desperately praying she'd take a breath. Amid his hazy focus, a small, angry voice sounded from the bed.

"What are you doing to my sister?"

He only had time to register Isaiah's voice before he slapped Addie's back once more. An angry growl sounded behind him just as the baby gasped, inhaling precious air. Seconds later, she wailed.

Releasing a sigh of relief, Cody lifted her upright. His relief was short lived as little fists pummeled his legs.

"You hurt her! You hurt Addie!" Isaiah screamed and pounded harder.

Addie cried louder.

Worried that he might drop the baby, Cody gripped both of the boy's hands in one of his. "Enough!" The single word, unintentionally snarled, made Isaiah glare back at him.

The little boy struggled for his freedom. He kicked with everything in him, his foot connecting hard with Cody's shin. Sucking in a breath, Cody struggled for control of his own temper. Anger burned in his chest. He couldn't give these children what they needed. The last three weeks proved that depressing fact.

A sound of dismay hit his ears. Amidst the kicks and screams, Jonah huddled in the bed, tears streaming down his cheeks. The three-year-old hadn't spoken since his parents died, but his face revealed his emotions better than words could. Cody's heart clenched. For a child that small to wear such a desperate look of pain...it smote him more than anything else.

Despair consumed him. He couldn't do this. There was a reason two people shared the responsibilities of parenting. To try it alone felt insurmountable.

He sank into the rocking chair beside the crib. Addie's cries mixed with Isaiah's sobs. When did he start crying? The boy finally stopped kicking him, and he buried his little face into his hands. Cody rested one hand on Isaiah's back. With the other, he bounced Addie up and down as gently as he could. She hiccoughed as her cries faded. Jonah remained in bed, silent tears making twin trails down his cheeks.

Cody's stomach turned. *I'm a failure.* How could he give these grieving children the life they needed? He couldn't even provide enough comfort to stop their tears.

Isaiah sniffled, lowering his hands. "You hurt her."

"She couldn't breathe. I had to do something." He turned Addie toward her brother, voice rough. "She's fine."

The boy's lower lip trembled.

Cody raked a hand through his hair. "Do you want to hold her?"

"Yeah." Isaiah took Addie, holding her close. He eyed Cody as he rocked the baby in his arms, looking far too old for his five years.

The sun crept over the horizon, lighting the room. Cody pushed himself up. "You kids want pancakes?"

Jonah climbed out of bed. He rubbed his brown eyes before nodding.

Isaiah shrugged, face impassive. "Guess so."

"Then let's rustle up some pancakes."

At least he could manage that.

~

Four days after she escaped Boston, the train pulled into Ella's destination. She glanced out the window. A large sign hung by the platform, welcoming travelers to the town of Harmony Springs. People bustled about, wrapped in warm coats as they trekked through a layer of fresh snow. Wooden buildings lined the main street. Bold signs proclaimed the services of each business. She made out a mercantile, bank, and blacksmith near the station.

Ella picked up her bag, ignoring the ache in her ribs. Drawing in a deep breath, she straightened her shoulders. "I can do this."

The words sounded flat. She stifled a sigh, then shuffled her way to the exit. Anxiety crawled through her gut. She'd come here on a whim. What if her plan backfired?

A humorless chuckle left her lips. *Plan? What plan?* Reaction motivated her flight from Boston. Nothing had been set except her destination. She didn't even have a trunk with personal belongings. Her only possessions in the world were stuffed in the carpetbag she clutched close to her side.

Ella stepped from the train onto solid ground. Cold air nipped at her cheeks. She shivered, her nerves fraught.

Upon exiting the train station, she glanced around. As in other towns they had passed through, the building appeared to be located at the edge of town. The main street stretched before her, long and welcoming, but unknown. Her vision grew hazy and her head began to pound. Dark spots danced in her line of sight.

Her back stiffened. She might be in a strange place, but she would not faint. Never in her life had she resorted to the ridiculous tactic employed by many young ladies in society. She wasn't about to start now. Head held high, she marched down the street. Her gaze swung from building to building, reading the signs and looking for the one she needed.

The morning sun provided a bit of relief against the winter chill. With a start, Ella realized she had forgotten to bring a hat. Her mother's stringent voice echoed in her head.

A young lady never goes about in the sun with her head uncovered. Especially not with your coloring. You will gain horrid, unsightly freckles.

Ella tugged at a strand of her auburn waves, then turned her face to the sun, eyes closed, in direct defiance of her mother's vain demands. Maybe a few freckles would give her face character.

"You all right, lady?"

She opened her eyes with a start. A young man stared at her, brows raised. Ella cleared her throat. Her cheeks burned. "Yes, thank you."

He shot her a dubious look but nodded and continued down the road. Ella stifled a sigh. People were going to think her addled in the mind if she wasn't careful.

A happy squeal made her turn in time to see a young woman launch herself at another lady. Ella's breath caught. *They look like sisters.*

All the emotions she'd suppressed over the last four days overwhelmed her. Tori's face flashed through her mind. Her heart squeezed in her chest. Loneliness gripped her stomach. The one person she'd been able to count on for love and support was hundreds of miles away.

Tears spilled from Ella's eyes. Unable to stop them, she

hurried into a small alleyway between two buildings. She ducked deep into the shadows, away from curious eyes.

Once the tears began, they flowed in torrents. Her throat constricted painfully. Deep sobs wrenched from her belly. Her entire body hurt with the physical pain of loss. She sank to her knees, heedless of the snow that soaked into her dress. Doubts crept in, whispering that she'd made a big mistake.

What have I done?

CHAPTER 2

Cody urged his horse into a gallop as he left his ranch. Wind whipped against his face, chilling him to the bone. Preston responded to the pressure of his knees and flew over the prairie. Straw-like grass stretched as far as the eye could see. Within a couple months, the vast landscape would be green, dotted with bluebells, larkspur, and buttercups. For now, winter held everything in its cold grasp.

A tremor went through him as he took in the number of dead, rotting cattle laying frozen in the fields. Last month, the worst blizzard in recent memory swept the plains. Every rancher in Harmony Springs and beyond took significant losses in livestock—some up to three-fourths of their herd.

He'd been more fortunate than most. Cody thanked the Lord that he'd had the foresight to store up as much hay as possible over the last few years. It saved a good portion of his herd after the blizzard. Even so, the cattle he lost would make money tight this year.

It would have been hard with only himself and the ranch to support. Now he had three children to care for.

The children. He sighed. Yet another morning had passed

that proved he had no business being a father. As he was preparing to head to town, all three kids had meltdowns. As usual, Isaiah started things. His stubborn nature made him defy Cody at most turns. The ensuing temper tantrums were enough to upset his younger siblings. This morning, the catalyst was Cody bundling Addie in a green blanket rather than a pink one. Cody couldn't figure out why the color choice bothered the child. He'd screamed and thrown himself onto the floor in a flurry of arms and legs. Addie started wailing soon after, and Jonah stood nearby sniffling and holding back tears. Cody's babysitter, Miss Hattie, showed up in the midst of it all. He could imagine what the older woman thought of his parenting skills.

Hattie took one look at the distraught children and shooed him out of the house. "I'll take care of them, young man," she'd said.

A pang had gone through him. He'd looked at the kids, his throat working.

Hattie's eyes had softened. She'd patted his arm. "It'll get easier, Cody. They just need time."

Time. He uttered a bleak laugh, his breath puffing white in the freezing air. How could he possibly give them the time and attention they needed when he had to be out on the range? Most days, he worked from dawn to dusk. He'd have to work extra this year to plant a larger supply of alfalfa since his reserves had been depleted after the blizzard.

A sigh rose from deep inside his chest. Answers eluded him. He needed advice, and he knew where he could find it. Though he was headed into town to buy some supplies, it wouldn't hurt to pay a visit to his sister and brother-in-law as well.

According to the position of the sun, it was nearly ten o'clock. Maybe he would find Cassie first. She owned the only café in town, and the breakfast rush would be over. They'd have a reasonable amount of privacy to talk.

It didn't take long to reach Main Street. But when he neared the café, it became clear a train had recently pulled into town. People milled around the boardwalks, meeting family members or waiting for the train to depart to its next location. He reined in Preston outside the small building and considered his next move. A glance inside the café window confirmed his sister was bustling about, placing plates of steaming food in front of her customers. He should find Travis first. His brother-in-law was the local sheriff and shouldn't be too busy at this hour.

Cody turned his horse toward the opposite side of the street. Travis's office was close by. He'd nearly reached it when a strangled sob sounded nearby. Cody pulled Preston to a stop once more. The cry came again.

He spotted an alley between the millinery and the barbershop. Were the cries coming from there? Another broken sob sounded, raising his protective instincts. He dismounted and made his way to the alley. Looking around the millinery, he peered into the shadows. Nothing other than buildings and dingy snow. But as his eyes adjusted to the light, he saw a woman kneeling on the ground. Her hands covered her face, muffling her sobs.

He moved forward, determined to help. "Ma'am?"

Her head whipped up so fast, he worried she'd smack it against the wall. Losing her balance, she tumbled onto her side in the snow. Cody hurried toward her, but her red-rimmed eyes grew large. Panic plain on her face, she scrambled back until the wall stopped her progress. She cried out, raising her arms to shield her face...as if expecting a blow.

Cody halted. Her reaction screamed of more than fear of a stranger. He held out his hands and spoke in the soothing voice he usually reserved for calming spooked livestock. "It's all right. I'm not going to hurt you."

Her hands slowly lowered. Wary green eyes met his. Her face was red and mottled, as if she'd been crying for a while.

His heart twisted. He stepped forward again, then crouched to be on her level. "Can I help you?"

She shook her head. Her lips trembled, and she looked down. He took in the large wet patches on her dress. The entire lower half was soaked. How long had she been kneeling in the snow? She would catch her death out here if she remained in that state. He'd seen too many people succumb to frostbite in the winter months. This lady would not be another victim if he had anything to say about it.

He inched forward. Her head snapped up again. A whimper left her lips. She stared at him, frozen in place, as if he was a rattler posed to strike. What had made this young woman so skittish? From her delicate cheekbones and heart-shaped face, he guessed her to be in her early twenties. Her clothes looked fancy, as though she came from wealth. What was she doing in an alley in the snow?

A dark thought whispered through his mind. Harmony Springs was a safe town, but people came through all the time on the train. Had she been robbed? That would explain her distraught countenance.

"You need to get somewhere warm." He rose, holding out a hand with his palm up. "Why don't you let me take you to see the sheriff? He's always got a pot of coffee on. Maybe you could tell him what's wrong."

She looked him fully in the face for the first time. When she spoke, it was a degree above a whisper. "The sheriff?"

"Yes, ma'am. He's a good man. He'll make sure you're safe."

She swallowed. Her teeth chattered, and her body shook. Her wet clothes must have her chilled through.

Alarm ran over him. "Please, let me help you."

She eyed his extended hand, uncertainty written all over her face. It was clear she didn't trust him. Not that he blamed her. He was a stranger, and her reactions told him she'd suffered some kind of mistreatment at the hands of a man. But they didn't have time to dally. If she didn't get warm soon, she could get sick. Or worse.

He reached out and grasped her hand. "I promise I won't hurt you."

The woman's eyes widened into saucers, but he ignored it and pulled her to her feet in one fluid motion. He overestimated her weight. She flew toward him, gasping as she landed with a thud against his chest. He could feel her heart beating rapidly through the layers of her coat. A tiny, frightened mew left her lips. To his horror, her eyes rolled back, and her body went limp. He caught her up in his arms as she fell, dismay pulsing through his veins. A woman had never fainted on him before.

A pang smote his belly. If he'd scared her that much, he owed her reparation, no matter how well-meaning his actions had been. Silently cursing his impulsivity, Cody lifted her into his arms like a baby and cradled her close to protect her from the wind.

There was no way to escape the eyes of the townspeople as he walked from the shelter of the alley. Many of them stopped and stared. He heard whispers, but he ignored them. His only concern was getting the young woman to safety.

⁓

Warm darkness surrounded Ella. Something pressed down on her, a heavy weight holding her limbs still. She cracked her eyes open. Bright sunlight streamed through a nearby window. Glancing down, she took in the stack of blankets laid over her. She blinked. Looking up, she found herself in an unfamiliar room. Panic seized her. Where was she, and how had she gotten here?

Memories of the tall, intimidating man from the alley crashed down on her, his face indiscernible in the shadows. Though he spoke with a kind voice, it held notes of gruffness. He'd insisted he wanted to help her, but then he jerked her toward him, and the terror...

She shivered despite the layers of blankets. Why couldn't she remember anything after that? Closing her eyes, she tried to fit the pieces together. Within moments, it clicked. Ella sucked in a sharp breath. She'd fainted! The one thing she promised herself she'd never do had happened because of another overbearing man who thought he knew best. Another man who tried to make her bend to his wishes. Another man who...

Ella cut the thought off by squeezing her eyes shut. "No!" Speaking the word out loud helped her calm. The man in the alley had been trying to help. Perhaps she judged him too harshly. Just because men had proven false time and again in her life didn't mean this man was bad.

Did it? He'd said he wanted to take her to the sheriff. She let her gaze roam the room. This bright bedchamber was decidedly not an office of law enforcement. It was clean and comfortable, decorated in good taste, with dainty blue curtains at the windows and an ornate vase on the nightstand. Had he taken her to his home?

Panic threatened again, but a cheerful, feminine voice cut it short.

"Oh, good. You're awake."

Ella turned her head as a blond woman walked into the room. A smile graced her face, making her blue eyes twinkle. She came to a stop beside the bed. "You had us worried there for a bit. A good portion of your dress was horribly wet. Cody was afraid you might take sick or have frostbite. He wasn't sure how long you'd been in the cold."

"Cody?"

"My brother. He's the one who found you. I'm Cassie." She plopped in a chair beside the bed. "You're not from around here."

"No." Ella pushed back some blankets and struggled to sit up. Her ribs ached in response. She grimaced, falling back against the pillow.

Cassie stood at once. "Let me help you." She slid an arm behind Ella's back and helped her into a seated position.

The ache soon subsided. Ella gave the woman a small smile. "Thank you."

Cassie sat again. She chewed on her lip for a moment before blurting out, "Is it the bruises?"

Ella froze. How could Cassie know about those? She looked down, noting that she wore a nightdress that didn't belong to her. A gasp left her lips. "Did you change my clothes?"

Cassie nodded. "You couldn't stay in that wet dress. You needed warmth. But I saw..." She trailed off, glancing at Ella's arms. "Well, I saw your arms. And your sides." She looked up, meeting Ella's eyes, compassion lighting her own. "What happened? Cody thought someone might have attacked you as you left the train station." She frowned. "But I didn't think bruises formed that fast."

"I...I..." Panic set in again. She swallowed, trying to fight it.

Understanding flashed over Cassie's face. "It's all right. You don't have to say if you don't want to."

Ella slumped against the headboard. "Thank you."

Cassie reached out to cover her hand. "Would you like me to get in touch with anyone for you? Was Harmony Springs your destination, or are you headed somewhere else?"

"This was my destination."

"Then who are you here to see? I know everyone in this town. Maybe I can reach out to your friends."

Trust didn't come easily to Ella, but she sensed in Cassie a friend. "I only know one person in town, but he doesn't know

I'm here. He once told me if I ever needed a fresh start, I could come to Harmony Springs, and…" They'd been out of touch for so long. What if he had moved on from this small town?

"Was he a sweetheart of yours?"

That elicited a laugh. "Oh, no. Not at all. He was like a brother to me. We were friends back in Boston." Ella clamped her lips shut. She hadn't meant to divulge her city of origin. But Cassie perked up as soon as she heard the word.

"Boston?"

Ella bit her lip. Too late to deny it now. She nodded.

A smile bloomed on Cassie's face. "There's only one man here from Boston. Travis Doyle. He's the sheriff."

Relief coursed through Ella's body. He was still here. "Oh, thank God." Her hand went to the simple cross hanging around her neck. Perhaps small miracles still occurred, after all. If Travis was here, he would help her.

Cassie's smile widened. "That must make you Ella Mountbatten. He told me all about you and your sister. Victoria, was it?"

Ella blinked. "Yes—Tori. He told you about us?"

"Yeah. He's my husband."

Ella's mouth dropped. She shook her head, a small laugh escaping. "He was so set against marriage when he was in Boston. I'm happy to hear he found love. You seem like a sweet woman." A smile tugged at her lips. "Taking care of a stranger and all."

Cassie chuckled, waving a hand. "I'm the lucky one. We had something of a bumpy road to get to our happily ever after, but we got there." She tilted her head, studying Ella for a moment. "He hated to leave the two of you behind, you know. Especially you."

Ella's lungs constricted. She pressed her lips together. "He had no choice. My parents made sure of that." Tears stung her eyes while guilt smote her conscience.

Cassie's gaze slid to Ella's arms, as if seeing the bruises underneath the sleeves. "He said you were trapped in a bad relationship."

Her throat burned. All she could do was nod.

Cassie's eyes softened. "Is that why you left Boston?"

Again, she nodded. Her throat felt tight, keeping any words from leaving. The terror of her last night at home tried to take over. She pushed it aside. Howard was not here. Her parents were not here.

She was safe.

Cassie patted her hand. "My brother went to find Travis. They should be here soon." She stood. "Until then, why don't I make you a cup of tea?"

More tears pricked her eyes. "Thank you, Cassie. That sounds lovely."

In his final letter, before Howard forced her to end their correspondence, Travis made Harmony Springs sound like a haven, a place where new beginnings were possible. A small smile curled on her lips as her eyes drifted shut. Maybe Travis was right.

Maybe.

CHAPTER 3

Cody rode through town, finally finding Travis near the livery. His friend smiled in greeting. "I didn't expect to see you here."

Travis's words carried a hint of the accent that denoted his Irish heritage. He patted his horse before swinging into the saddle.

Cody nodded. "I've been looking for you."

"Are the kids all right?"

"Depends on what you mean by 'all right.'" Cody rubbed a hand across his eyes. "We both know I'm struggling with them. But that's not the reason I searched you out. I came across a young woman crying in an alley. She fainted, so I took her to Cassie. My sister got her changed into some dry clothes, then told me the woman had bad bruising along her arms and sides. Cass thinks she was attacked."

Travis growled low in his throat. "I'll never understand how a man can harm a woman." They nudged their horses into a walk. "Did you recognize her?"

"No. She had a carpet bag. I think she was a passenger on the train, probably passing through. Her clothes looked fancy, and I couldn't find a purse when I went back for her bag. She must have been robbed."

"That would explain why she was attacked."

They rode in silence for a bit. When Travis spoke again, his words were blunt. "You look tired."

"It's that obvious?"

"Yeah. How're you holdin' up?"

Shaking his head, Cody sighed. "I'm not, Trav. I barely get by each day, and I don't know the first thing about being a parent. What am I gonna do when I've got to work? Hank and the boys have taken on more than they should because I'm trying to figure out fatherhood. Those poor kids need more stability than I can give."

"You know Cassie and I would be happy to…"

Holding up a hand, Cody cut him off. "You two are as busy as I am. That café is Cassie's dream. I won't ask her to give it up because her big brother can't manage his own problems."

"Have you considered the orphanage?"

A pit formed in Cody's stomach. Unhappy memories threatened to surface. "You know I can't."

"I figured you'd say as much." Travis drew in a breath before leveling a look at Cody. "I have another suggestion, but I doubt you'll like it any more than the others."

Cody cocked a brow when his friend didn't continue. "Well?"

"If you plan to keep those kids, you need a wife. I'd recommend a nanny, but you can't afford one after your losses this winter."

A lump formed in his throat. "I have no intention of loving again. Not after Liza."

"I know. But you need help, and those kids need a mother. You keep saying you can't do this by yourself. Logically, that means getting married."

"You realize I don't have time to court, right? And even if I did, there's a shortage of available women in this town."

"You could advertise for a mail-order bride."

Cody winced. His stomach knotted into a hard rock. "And invite a stranger into our lives?"

Travis shot him a sympathetic look. "I know it's not what you want. But you don't have many options."

The lump in Cody's throat grew. "No kidding."

When they reached the house, they dismounted. Travis clapped a hand on Cody's shoulder. "Pray through it, my friend. Perhaps a solution will show up where you least expect it."

"I hope so." Cody scratched his jaw as he followed Travis up the porch steps. That was something he'd consider later. For now, they had to figure out what happened to the young woman resting in the Doyles' guest room.

As they stepped inside, Cassie met them with a huge grin. Both men stopped in their tracks. Travis gave his wife a puzzled look. "I thought this was a serious situation."

Cassie grabbed his hand. Cody could almost see the excitement radiating from her. "You'll never guess who's here, Travis!" She dragged her husband into the house and up the stairs to the stranger's room. Cody followed, confusion burning inside. When he left, Cassie had been hovering over the woman in concern. Now, she bounced with glee.

His eyes landed on the woman he'd carried here. She was awake and sitting up in bed. Her auburn hair had been plaited into a neat braid. Her fair skin was smooth as porcelain, no longer mottled from crying. But what arrested his attention were her eyes. They were a unique shade of green, one he'd never seen before. He stared into them, his mind working to label the color. Only when she fidgeted did he realize his gaze made her uncomfortable. He immediately shifted it to Travis, who also stared at the young woman, mouth gaping open.

"Ella?"

She smiled. It didn't quite reach her eyes. "Hello, Travis."

Travis wasn't often at a loss for words, but he floundered before finding his voice. "What're you doing here?"

Uncertainty crept over her features. "You said if I ever needed a fresh start..." She fiddled with the covers. "That is, I thought...I thought..."

The poor woman looked at a loss. Cassie took charge. She stood in front of Travis, hands planted on her hips. "Travis McKenna Doyle, get a hold of yourself! Your friend is here, and she needs your help."

A smile crossed Travis's face. "Yes, dear." He chuckled, pressing a kiss to Cassie's cheek. "What would I do without you?"

Her eyes softened. "Thankfully, you don't have to find out." She slipped to his side, motioning to Ella. "Now, you were saying?"

He chuckled. "Forgive me, Ella. It's a shock seeing you here. But a happy one." He took a step forward. "Things got that bad, did they?"

Tears welled in her luminous eyes. She nodded, then stared down at the covers, twisting them in her hands.

Cody cleared his throat. "Ma'am, could you tell Travis who attacked you? Were you robbed?"

She blinked, her eyes moving up to meet his. "Robbed?"

"I didn't see a purse, and Cassie said you had bad bruises..."

Before he could continue, Ella shook her head. "I was not robbed, nor was I attacked."

It was Cody's turn to blink. But the bruises? How did she get them? He shifted his gaze to Travis. His friend watched Ella with a thoughtful expression but didn't say anything. Cody continued. "But you were so distraught, you almost froze in the snow."

Her cheeks turned pink while her hands resumed their

mutilation of the covers. "Yes, I was distraught. I missed my sister."

Cody waited for her to continue, but it seemed that was the only explanation she planned to give. Anger flared. "You nearly gave yourself frostbite because you were *emotional*? Do you realize you could have died out there?"

The words came out harsh and loud. Ella flinched. Her cheeks went white, and her body shook.

Cassie glared at him. "Quit growling, Cody. You're scaring her." She sat on the bed and slipped an arm around Ella's shoulders. "Don't mind him, honey. His bark is worse than his bite. I promise. He doesn't mean to sound so menacing."

Travis laughed. "He has some bear-like tendencies, but underneath that gruff demeanor, he's got a heart of gold."

Cassie chuckled. "A big softy. That's what he is."

Cody gaped. "A softy...!" He couldn't even finish his sentence, the idea was so preposterous. Clamping his lips shut, he crossed his arms and glared at his sister and friend. That just made them laugh harder.

Ella looked between the three of them with utter confusion on her face.

Cassie stopped laughing and pierced him with her blue gaze. Her brow hiked up near to her hairline.

He knew exactly what she expected of him. Cody suppressed a sigh, rubbing a hand over his jaw. "My apologies, ma'am. I didn't mean to frighten you...again."

Ella tilted her head, a question in her gaze.

He scratched his ear. "In the alley. I scared you into that faint, didn't I?"

Roses bloomed on her cheeks. She ducked her head. "You were trying to help. I should have realized that."

Cody frowned, taking a step closer to the bed. "Why'd I scare you so bad?"

Ella swallowed. Her hands moved to rest on either forearm while her throat worked.

Cassie's glance slid over her arms. "The bruises. Who gave them to you, Ella?"

A tiny moan sounded from Ella's lips.

Travis stiffened beside Cody. "Howard."

The single word was a statement, not a question. It also held unmistakable venom.

Ella sniffed with a small nod.

Cody watched in amazement as Travis's face turned red with rage. "If I was still in Boston, I'd..."

Cassie shot him a warning glance.

Ella huddled over, bent in on herself.

Travis dropped to his knees beside the bed. Cody stood back, feeling like an intruder, knowing he could do nothing to help. He had no history with this woman. Travis did, and Cassie had already made friends with her. They would be able to do something. He fidgeted, hating the helpless feeling as he watched a silent river of tears slide down Ella's cheeks.

Travis spoke quietly. "It's all right, Ella. We'll keep you safe. You're free from that monster."

She sucked in a breath. "Am I? What if he finds me? He won't rest until he possesses me, Travis. He's obsessed with my money and...and with me. My parents will try to find me too. They won't take kindly to the rumors that are sure to develop with my sudden absence."

Travis gently took her hands while Cassie rubbed her back. "We'll think of something," he said. "I promise."

Ella relaxed. Her tears soon dried up. A wobbly smile touched her pink lips. "You always were a good friend."

Travis whispered something to her, too low for Cody to hear. He shifted from foot to foot.

Cassie glanced his way. She stood and came to him. "Why

don't you get your errands done? Travis and I will take care of Ella."

Cody looked at the young woman. Ella would probably feel more comfortable with him out of the house. He'd already scared her twice. He didn't want to do so a third time. "Good idea."

$$\sim$$

The next morning, Ella smoothed the front of her green dress, then braided her long hair. After a full night's sleep, she felt more like herself.

Heavenly aromas of savory bacon and warmed sweet fruit wafted from the kitchen. Ella made her way downstairs. Travis and Cassie worked side by side. When Ella entered the room, Cassie beamed. "Just in time! We're about to have breakfast. Please, sit."

Travis held a platter of food in each hand as he walked to the table. "I hope you're hungry. We've got a real feast this morning."

On cue, Ella's stomach rumbled. She pressed a hand against it with a shy smile. "I am."

"Great." Travis placed the platters on the table, then held a chair for her. He did the same for his wife, then took his own seat and held out a hand to each of them. "Let's pray."

He blessed the food, his prayer simple but heartfelt. When he finished, they passed the platters around the table. Travis hadn't exaggerated when he called the fare a feast. There were eggs, bacon, fluffy biscuits with gravy, and stewed fruit. Coffee rounded out the meal. Everything tasted divine.

Once she felt pleasantly full, Ella leaned back with a second mug of hot coffee. She took slow sips of the strong liquid, lightened with cream. It felt like a tiny slice of heaven.

Travis rested his elbows on the table, a mug of his own in

hand. Ella looked between him and Cassie. "How did you two meet?"

They both laughed. Travis winked at Cassie, his grin wide. "You tell her."

Cassie's blue eyes swam with amusement. "I was walking to the café, minding my own business, when a man decided to steal my reticule. There was a substantial amount of money inside, enough that I didn't stop to think. I ran after him, shouting he give it back. He was surprised. I don't think he expected a woman to chase after him." She turned a sassy look on her husband. "Of course, I would have caught him if not for a handsome, charming Irishman who stepped in my way."

"Stepped in your way?" Travis repeated, barking out a laugh. He gave Ella an amused grin. "By 'stepped in her way,' she means I got off the train."

Cassie smacked her hands together. "He got off, and I ran straight into him. Knocked us both over."

With a chuckle, Travis took up the story. "We stared at each other for a few moments. I couldn't breathe. Didn't know if it was being flung to the ground or instant attraction to the lovely woman who'd thrown herself in my arms."

Riveted, Ella leaned forward. "What happened next?"

Cassie laughed. "I yelled that the man was getting away. Travis jumped up and raced after the thief." Her eyes glowed with pride. "He caught him too. Arrested him on the spot."

"It turns out I'm a knight in shining armor." Travis grinned. Cassie lightly punched his arm.

Ella smiled. "What a meeting."

Travis sat back, holding his wife's hand. "It was. She certainly made an impression on me. I was hooked at once, though it took a bit of convincing to get her to agree to a courtship."

Cassie waved a hand. "I was busy getting my café started,

with no time for a relationship. Or so I thought." Stars in her eyes, she turned to her husband. "Thankfully, I was wrong."

Ella's heart squeezed in her chest. *To think I used to dream of a love like that.* She stifled a sigh. Now, she'd be happy just to survive on her own.

Cassie's voice broke into her thoughts. "Ella? Are you all right?"

Ella shook herself. Both Travis and Cassie were scrutinizing her, concerned expressions on their faces. She forced a smile. "What a wonderful story."

Husband and wife exchanged glances. She pretended not to notice.

Travis cleared his throat. "Are you thinking about your previous relationships?"

How'd he read her so well? Ella swallowed. "Yes."

Sympathy shone from his eyes. "I'm sorry you've had bad experiences in love. But..."

The hesitation in his voice caught her attention. "But what?"

"Things had been bad for a long time. What happened to make you leave home?"

Her throat tightened. Some memories were better left buried. "I'd rather not talk about it. It's in the past."

He studied her. She sensed those hazel eyes saw more than she wanted to reveal. Ella looked down at the table.

To her surprise, Travis's large, rough hand covered hers. "Someday, I hope you heal enough to bring whatever darkness you experienced to light. For now, we'll respect your wishes."

Tears burned her eyes. Compassion and understanding were not things she encountered often. "Thank you."

Cassie patted her other hand. Ella appreciated the silent show of support even as Travis continued. "Did you tell anyone where you were going when you left?"

She shook her head. "No one. Not even Tori."

"It must've been hard leaving her."

An ache in her heart, Ella whispered, "It was."

Travis blew out a breath. "At least your family can't pry your location out of her."

A spark of hope lit within. "Do you think I'll be safe here?"

"Montana territory is vast. We're a long way from Boston. It's possible you could remain in Harmony Springs undetected. But your parents are very influential people with strong connections. They aren't likely to give up. And Howard..." He squinted, anger tightening his cheeks. "If I read him right, he won't let you go easily." Travis thrummed his fingers against the table. "Do any of them know where I settled after leaving?"

"I...I'm not sure." Dread seized Ella as a realization crawled through her mind. "Your letters...they were in my bedroom desk. I didn't think to take them with me." Her heart raced. "Do you think they would make the connection if those letters are found?"

Travis pressed his lips together. His eyes told her all she needed to know.

Cassie stood and rounded the table. Sitting by Ella, she slipped an arm around her shoulders. "You have us now. We're your friends, and we'll protect you however we can."

Ella smiled, but it felt weak. Friends notwithstanding, if her family discovered her here, they would find a way to drag her back to Boston. Of that, she was certain.

CHAPTER 4

*L*ife in the West was harder than Ella expected. Comforts she had taken for granted in Boston had no place in Harmony Springs. Indoor plumbing did not exist in this small town. The first time she made her way to the small outhouse in the freezing cold, Ella gagged at the stench inside. The dusty roads made washing more often a necessity. And while she was thankful to gain independence, doing her own chores instead of relying on servants was an adjustment.

Her bruises faded, the marks of her past vanishing in welcome relief. She spent her days with Cassie at the café. Her new friend graciously taught Ella how to cook—at least in a passable manner. Nothing Ella created tasted as good as Cassie's dishes, but she took solace in the fact that she was able to make anything at all. No one allowed her to set foot in the kitchen back in Boston.

One evening, a week after her arrival, she prepared her first solo dinner for the Doyles. Since she made roasted chicken several times under Cassie's watchful eye, Ella thought that might be a good choice. While the chicken cooked, she boiled potatoes to mash and opened a jar of canned peas to serve alongside.

The chicken turned out drier than it should, and the mashed potatoes were lumpy. Even so, Travis and Cassie complimented her on her attempt.

"It's not easy learning to cook." Cassie slathered more gravy over her potatoes. "You're coming along great, Ella."

"Thank you."

"Would you like to learn to make caramel cake tomorrow?"

That request seemed oddly specific. Ella took a bite of chicken before answering. "That would be nice. But why that particular cake? I've heard caramel is difficult."

Cassie speared some peas. "Cody always comes for dinner on Sundays. Caramel cake is his favorite. I thought it might be nice for him to have something he likes, since things have been rough lately."

The thought of Cassie's brother made Ella want to squirm in her chair. He'd been so stoic last week, and when he raised his voice in anger, it terrified her. Despite both Cassie and Travis assuring her that Cody was a good man, she found him intimidating.

"Ella?"

She brought her attention back to Cassie. "Yes?"

"Are you all right?"

The concern in Cassie's eyes helped Ella relax. "I'm fine. It's just...the thought of seeing your brother again is a little frightening."

Cassie gave her a sympathetic smile. "I know you didn't get off on the best foot. But I promise, he's a good man. He would never hurt anyone."

Visions of Howard marched through her mind. She shoved them away. "It's nice to know there are some decent men out there."

"No doubt." Cassie propped an elbow on the table, resting

her chin in her hand. "So what do you say? Would you like to help me with the cake before church? Be honest. I don't mind if the answer is no."

Ella's shoulders relaxed. She hadn't even noticed the tension there until it was gone. "I would be happy to help."

"Wonderful. It should help having another adult around when the children are here." Cassie shook her head, her eyes shifting between amused and troubled. "They can be a handful."

Curiosity festered in Ella's mind. "What children?"

"Cody's, of course."

She blinked. "Your brother has children? I didn't realize he was married."

"He's not. A few weeks ago, he became the guardian of three little ones after their parents died in a tragic accident. The poor man is in over his head, but he's determined to care for them the best he can."

Ella let that information sink in. She hadn't expected that of him. "It must be hard raising children alone. Has he considered an orphanage?"

Cassie's eyes shadowed. "No." She pushed some potatoes around her plate, not meeting Ella's eyes. "Cody and I grew up in an orphanage. He vowed not to let Jake and Harriet's children face that fate."

Something squeezed in Ella's chest. She'd visited a few orphanages in Boston over the years. The children always seemed sad, even in the institutions that boasted enough money to properly care for them. Reaching out, she put a hand over Cassie's. "I'm sorry. That must have been hard for you both."

"It was. The people who ran the institution were not kind. They were poor substitutes for our parents. Cody made it his mission to protect me. He gave me portions of his food, defended me from bullies, and even did many of my chores. My brother has always been a protector. It's his nature."

A protector. Ella's heart softened a little toward the man. He'd even protected her, a complete stranger. He tried to save her in the alley—though he could have gone about it in a different manner.

"It sounds as though your brother is a rare man."

Cassie smiled softly. "He is."

They resumed their meal, and only then did Ella realize Travis hadn't said a single word during her conversation with Cassie. Ella peeked at him. He poked at his food, looking distracted. A sudden sense of foreboding washed over her. "Travis?"

"Hmm?" He glanced her way. "Yeah?"

"Is something wrong?"

He coughed, stabbing a bite of chicken. "What do you mean?"

Ella set down her fork. "You're avoiding my question. What aren't you telling us?"

Lips pressed in a tight line, Travis shook his head. "I'm sorry, Ella. I didn't want to worry you."

Worry was the least of her concerns. She gripped the napkin in her lap, twisting it with her hands, begging him with her eyes to continue.

"I got a telegram from Boston. Your father demanded to know if I'd seen you. It seems he found our letters and thinks you might have come here."

Her heart dropped to her stomach. "What did you tell him?"

"I haven't responded."

So much for her secrecy in leaving. "He knows. He knows I'm here." It only took a week for her father to figure out the puzzle.

Cassie's hand covered hers. "You don't know that. He might be grasping straws."

"You don't know my father. He's likely to come to Montana himself to find me. Even if Travis tells him I'm not here, Father won't believe it." Ella pushed back from the table. Her stomach protested the lack of food, but the steel vice gripping it made eating impossible. "Excuse me."

Once in her room, Ella paced back and forth in front of the fire. Her escape had been for naught. Father would come, and he would take her back to Boston.

Which meant she would be forced to marry Howard.

Despair crept over her, stealing her breath. She clutched her head in both hands. How long before she lost her freedom forever?

~

On Sunday morning, Cody managed to get all three children dressed and ready for church in a timely fashion. Isaiah didn't fight him but appeared sullen and withdrawn. Cody kept an eye on the boy as they departed the house. He couldn't shake the feeling that something must be wrong.

They made it to church just as the traveling preacher took the pulpit. Cody settled into a back pew, Addie in his lap and a boy on either side. As soon as he relaxed, the baby began to fuss.

He stifled a groan. Lifting her to his shoulder, Cody bounced her up and down, hoping the motion would calm her. It only seemed to make things worse.

With a glare at Addie, Isaiah clamped his hands over his ears. "Make her stop."

People stared. Cody's neck flushed hot under his collar. He

jiggled Addie more urgently, but she only cried louder. For a moment, he felt paralyzed.

A gentle hand landed on his shoulder. Cassie slipped into the pew with them. "Take her outside," she whispered, nodding to the baby. "I'll watch the boys."

Cody mouthed a thank you, then hurried out of the church. He paced back and forth across the yard as Addie's cries increased in volume. She'd eaten and been changed before they left. Why was she crying?

Minutes passed like hours. Nothing he did helped. Addie wailed as if in pain. Cody hated feeling helpless, but he had no clue what to do.

Behind him, the doors to the church opened. To his surprise, Ella Mountbatten descended the steps, wrapped in one of Cassie's winter shawls. She took halting steps toward him. Wariness shone in her eyes, but determination did as well. She came to a stop beside him.

An awkward silence ensued, broken only by Addie's cries. Ella drew in a breath and held out her arms. "May I hold her?"

Surprise rendered him mute. He nodded and held out the baby.

Ella accepted the precious bundle and cradled her gently. "Hello, little one. What's the matter?"

Addie paused, apparently surprised to find herself in a stranger's arms. Seconds later, she resumed her wailing.

Ella looked up at Cody. "Has she been fussy a lot?"

Still unable to find his tongue, he nodded again. Ella studied Addie's face, then stuck her finger inside the child's mouth. Cody blinked at the unexpected action. Addie stopped crying and began to chew frantically. Her little hand closed over Ella's finger as if she wanted to keep it there.

"She's cutting a tooth."

Cody's brow furrowed. "A tooth?"

"It can be quite painful for babies." Ella shifted Addie in her arms. "Would you mind fetching a bit of clean snow?"

He shot glances at her as he did her bidding. The church yard was packed with wagons, but he found a nice patch of snow under a tree. He created a loose ball in his hands before returning to Ella's side. "Here."

"Thank you." She withdrew her finger from the baby's mouth, covering it with snow before putting it back against Addie's gums.

Blessed silence filled the yard. Cody let out a breath. "You're a miracle worker, ma'am."

Her lips curled into a small smile. "You just have to know what to look for." She gazed down at the baby. "What's her name?"

"Addie."

"That's lovely. Is it short for anything?"

"Adelaide. It was her mother's middle name."

Ella ran a finger over Addie's cheek. "What a wonderful legacy your mother left you, sweet girl."

"How'd you learn that snow trick?" Cody asked, unable to help himself. This woman came from high society. He doubted what he'd seen was something taught in finishing school.

She shifted. "I used to take baskets of food to immigrant families from Ireland on a regular basis. They had many children, and I would teach them to read and write, or if the mothers felt overwhelmed, I cared for the infants and younger children. Those mothers gave me a lot of advice on ways to help little ones. Snow or ice for teething babies was one of those tips. A wet cloth to chew on will do as well."

It was so simple, but brilliant. He never would have thought of such a solution. For that matter, he wouldn't have guessed Addie was cutting a tooth. A tired sigh left him. There was so much about parenting he didn't know.

"I'm surprised a fine woman like yourself spent time

teaching immigrants." Blast it all, he sounded accusatory. Clearing his throat, he sought to clarify. "I mean, you must have had other things to do."

She chuckled. The sound was sweet and musical. "I understand your surprise. It doesn't fit the image of society life, does it?"

At a loss, he shook his head. "Not from what I've heard, ma'am."

"You've heard right. It's not typical. But I couldn't bear to spend my days in frivolous pursuits. I spent time with immigrant families because it gave me purpose. They were far more joyful and loving than anyone else I knew, even if they were poor as church mice. They shared what they had with others, and they did so without reservation." She let out a quiet breath. "I had planned to open a school for those children."

"What happened?"

Her eyes hardened into mossy green rocks. "My fiancé found out. He told my parents, and they put an end to it." Her shoulders slumped. "They dashed my dream before it even began. Claimed it wasn't proper for a society miss. I tried to go ahead with the school, anyway." She sighed. "That was a mistake."

"Why's that?"

Ella's throat convulsed. "They retaliated in a way I didn't see coming. You may have heard the story."

He frowned. "Why would I have heard it?"

She glanced at him side-eyed. "Travis didn't tell you why he left Boston?"

Cody rubbed his neck. "Travis did tell the story, but I was a bit rattled at the time because he was interested in my sister. All I caught was that city life wasn't for him and that he wanted a new start out west."

Ella's eyes softened. "There's no doubt he always had a spirit of adventure. But that's not the only reason he left. My parents were furious that he was helping me with the school. They smeared his reputation, accusing him of horrible things. Travis was fired, and it was my fault for going against my parents' wishes." Tears swam in her eyes, but she ducked her head.

Cody placed a hand on her arm. When she flinched, he withdrew it. "I'm sorry, Ella. But that doesn't sound like your fault."

She huffed, swiping at her cheek with a free hand. "If I hadn't rebelled, Travis would still have a sterling reputation amongst Boston society. As it is, his name has been dragged through the mud. He was forced to leave his home."

"And if that hadn't happened, he never would have come here and married my sister."

Ella blinked up at him. A tiny smile appeared on her lips. "I suppose you're right."

Addie had fallen asleep. She rested in Ella's arms, looking for all the world as though she belonged there. Cody nodded at the baby. "Thanks for your help. I've been at my wits' end lately."

"Taking care of children is hard." Ella brushed back some of Addie's fine hair. "Your sister told me you took them in. That was kind of you."

A compliment? He cleared his throat. "I didn't have much choice."

She studied him for a few moments, her clear eyes seeming to see straight to his soul. "We all have choices."

The direct gaze didn't last. Ella flushed and lowered her head. Cody frowned. The move looked subservient. For some reason, it left him uneasy.

Ella spoke to the ground. "She's quiet now. Perhaps we should take her inside."

He nodded. Ella made no move to return the baby. Instead, she climbed the stairs, leaving Cody to follow behind. He entered the pew after her, then sank into his seat. Jonah climbed into his lap. Isaiah eyed Ella, suspicion in his gaze, but he stayed silent.

Cody tried to listen to the sermon. Even so, his attention strayed to Ella. She held Addie close, rocking her gently while listening to the pastor. The baby looked more peaceful than she'd been since her parents died. His throat closed on itself. Travis's advice on taking a wife came back to him. He'd thought about it off and on but hadn't come to a decision. Now, watching Addie being cared for by a woman, he saw firsthand the benefits of giving his children a mother. While he didn't like the idea of a stranger coming into his home, it would be in the best interests of Isaiah, Jonah, and Addie.

He held Jonah a little closer. His breaths came in shallow spurts. A sense of peace mixed with fear in his heart, and he wasn't sure which was stronger.

It was time to take a wife.

CHAPTER 5

$\mathcal{E}$lla snuck glances at Cody throughout the meal. Their interaction in the church yard had been surprisingly amiable. She'd seen the vulnerability in his eyes while he tried to calm his new daughter. There'd been no hint of the gruff demeanor from before. It had put her enough at ease to share things with him that she hadn't intended to.

"Hey! That's mine!"

The childish shout was piercing. Ella's gaze turned to Isaiah. He had a spoon clenched in his fist, his eyes shooting daggers at his brother. Jonah quivered under Isaiah's anger, a light whimper indicating his distress.

Cody heaved a sigh. "What's the matter?"

"He took my spoon!"

"Your spoon is in your hand."

Frowning, Isaiah stared at the utensil. Jonah whimpered again. Ella slipped an arm around him. "It's okay. There was just a misunderstanding."

The child blinked at her for a moment, then crawled into her lap. She froze. Jonah laid his head against her chest and stuck his thumb in his mouth.

Hesitating only a moment, Ella wrapped her arms around him. Her gaze met Cody's.

He gaped a full thirty seconds before collecting himself. "Jonah never goes to strangers."

With a chuckle, Travis mopped up some stew with his bread. "Ella has always been good with children. It's one of her God-given gifts."

Warmth surged through her cheeks. "It's nothing, really."

Cassie touched her arm. "That's hardly nothing, Ella. Children have an intuition about people. I'd say Jonah's trust in you is a great sign of your character."

A rush of warmth went through her as Jonah looked up at her with big brown eyes. "It's okay, sweetie," she murmured. He rewarded her with the smallest of smiles. Adorable. She'd always loved children, always wanted to be a mother. Not that that was likely anymore—but the maternal instincts remained. She pressed a soft kiss to Jonah's head.

Cody still stared. Ella fought the urge to fidget. The rest of their meal finished in an uneventful manner, the attention finally diverted from her and Jonah. When Cassie brought out dessert, Cody's eyes lit up. "Is that caramel cake?"

His sister smiled. "It is indeed. Ella helped me make it."

He darted another look at Ella. Her cheeks grew warmer. Cassie served the cake. Between bites of her own dessert, Ella couldn't help peeking at Cody. His genuine smile softened the rugged planes of his face. "Thanks, ladies. This is delicious."

Isaiah poked at his cake in a listless manner. Ella's gaze traveled over a flush on both his cheeks. They seemed unusually bright. She discreetly elbowed Cassie and nodded toward the child. "Is he all right?" she whispered.

Cassie studied Isaiah, then stood. "Isaiah, would you like to lie down in our guest room?"

Eyes drooping, the little boy nodded. He didn't put up a fight when Cassie took his hand and led him from the room.

Cody's shoulders slumped. "He's sick, isn't he? And I missed the signs."

Travis clamped a hand on his arm. "Don't beat yourself up. You're new to parenting."

A struggle tightened Cody's forehead and jaw. His gaze flitted from the doorway to Jonah to Addie. He swallowed hard. "Trav, I think you're right. I need a wife."

Jaw dropping, Ella stared between the two men.

Travis, however, looked unfazed. Her friend nodded with a sympathetic smile. "That couldn't have been easy to admit."

Cody shook his head. The gruffness returned to his voice. "I don't like it, but I have to think of the kids. Can you help me place an ad for a mail-order bride?"

A stifled shriek came from the door. Cassie stood there, eyes wide and arms akimbo. "Cody! You can't possibly be serious!" She came into the room, sinking into the chair beside Ella without removing her eyes from her brother.

He ran a hand through his blond hair. "I don't have any other choice, Cass."

"But...a mail-order bride? You could end up with anyone."

Travis reached for her hand. "Cassie, we'll make sure he finds a good woman. Cody can correspond with potential candidates for however long he feels necessary."

Cody shifted, fiddling with his fork. "That's the problem. I don't have much time. These kids need care now. I have to be on the range. A few women are able to watch them now and again, but every day?" He shook his head. "The kids need stability. They need a mother."

Cassie bit her lip, staring between her husband and brother before turning abruptly to Ella. "Will you please talk some sense into these men?"

Ella reared back. "Me?"

"You're a woman. Explain to them that a marriage of convenience is not something we want." Cassie's gaze begged her to comply.

"Well, actually…" Ella cleared her throat, pulling Jonah closer. "That doesn't sound all that bad."

Cassie's mouth fell open. "What?"

Ella strove for a calm she didn't feel. All eyes were fixed on her. She took a sip of her tea to fortify herself. "Mr. Brooks is in dire circumstances. He's right that his children would benefit from a mother. I've heard mail-order brides are common here in the west. Maybe it would be good for everyone involved."

Cody jerked his head in a nod. "That's my hope. Thanks for your opinion, Miss Mountbatten." He turned to Cassie. "Whoever I marry would gain some benefit as well. While the loss of cattle this winter set me back, I make a good living, and my wife would have the protection of my name." He continued, his voice fading into the background as his words danced in Ella's mind.

The protection of my name.

That was an option she'd never considered in her flight from Boston. If her father came to find her, he had every right to take her back…unless she was married. Then he would have no power over her. Neither would Howard.

Her gaze darted to Cody again. For the first time, she saw deep lines etched on his face, signs of exhaustion and stress. He needed help as much as she did.

Travis's voice broke into her thoughts. "It's settled, then. We'll write up an ad this evening, and I'll send it to the papers tomorrow. With any luck, you'll be married within a few weeks."

Cody's shoulders fell further. "Great."

The look on his face—at complete odds with his comment— touched a deep part of Ella's heart. Instead of relief, he seemed defeated. A cry split the silence from the other room. Addie must be up from her nap. Jonah snuggled closer to Ella, wrapping one arm around her neck. The warm feeling returned, pushing away some of her fear. The children needed a mother. She needed protection. There was a solution that would help them all.

Cody pushed up from the table, likely to get the baby, when words came tumbling out of Ella's mouth.

"What if you married me?"

~

$\mathcal{H}$e couldn't have heard her right. Cody stared at the young woman across from him. She looked like a deer caught in a hunter's trap. Even so, she held his gaze without flinching.

Addie cried again.

Cassie shot up from her chair. "I'll get her." She smiled at Ella, and Cody thought he saw relief on his sister's face. Was she pleased with Ella's shocking question?

Travis considered the woman in question steadily. "Are you sure about that, Ella? I don't want you to make a hasty decision you'd later regret."

Cody agreed with Travis. While he needed a wife, that didn't mean the skittish Ella Mountbatten had to volunteer for the job.

Ella caught her bottom lip between her teeth. Cody's gaze automatically followed the movement, but he snapped it back up to her eyes. There was no reason for him to look at her lips. Ever.

"My father will try to find me, Travis. If I'm married, he'll have no hold on me." She lifted her chin. "This is not a selfless offer. I need that protection Mr. Brooks mentioned as much as he needs a mother for his children."

Cody frowned, wondering yet again what happened to

make Ella leave her home. Not just leave home but offer to marry a near stranger to escape her family for good.

"Hmm." Travis leaned back in his chair. His glance flicked between them. A slow smile spread over his face as he settled on Ella. "That's a good idea. I've been wracking my brain for a solution to your problem. This fixes everything."

"Well, perhaps not everything, but it would be mutually beneficial." Ella glanced at Cody before returning her gaze to Travis. "You trust him, right?"

Travis gave a firm nod. "With my life."

Ella relaxed into her chair. "That's all I need to know."

Travis turned to Cody. His brows quirked. "You haven't said anything, my friend. What're you thinking?"

Cody pursed his lips. "I don't know what to think. This would help, but it could also be a terrible idea."

Ella's cheeks reddened.

Travis crossed his arms. "What do you mean?"

Though his friend asked the question, Cody directed his answer to Ella. "I mean, being a rancher's wife isn't easy. The house is a decent size, but nothing compared to what you must have known. It's hard work from dawn to dusk. You'd be responsible for all the household chores and cooking, not to mention watching the children. I don't know how you were raised, Miss Mountbatten, but I'm betting maids and cooks were involved."

She stared down at Jonah. "They were."

Her hands trembled. Blast it, he'd frightened her again. He forced himself to take on a soothing tone. "Ma'am, it's not that I think you can't learn. I'm worried that you'll find yourself overwhelmed."

Ella squared her shoulders, meeting his eyes. "I assure you, Mr. Brooks, a life on your ranch would be preferable to what's waiting for me in Boston should my father find me. And he will. Travis had a telegram from him yesterday. I'm running out of time."

Cody studied the little boy curled up in Ella's arms. Jonah had fallen asleep, much like Addie had earlier. It was clear both children trusted her. That was miraculous. If he sent for a mail-order bride, there was no guarantee the children would like her. With Ella, two out of three did. And Isaiah hadn't been outright rude to her—at least not yet.

Travis chimed in. "I hate to be the bearer of bad news, but this is a decision that needs to be made fast. The preacher leaves tomorrow morning, and we have no idea when he'll be back. It's been two months since he was last here."

Dread crawled through Cody's gut. Things were moving far too quickly. Ella's face had gone white. On impulse, he rounded the table to sit in the chair beside her. She looked up at him, eyes widening. "Miss Mountbatten..."

"Ella."

Surprised at her interruption, he stared for a moment. "What?"

"Call me Ella." Her mouth turned up in a faint smile. "If we're going to marry, we might as well be on a first name basis."

"All right...Ella." Her name felt strange on his tongue. "Are you certain this is what you want?"

She swallowed. "It's not so much what I want. It's what I need. It's what you need. What other option do we have?"

She was right. Their options were limited. This opportunity had presented itself in a providential way. But to commit the rest of their lives together? That would be stepping into unknown territory. He knew as much about being a husband as he did about being a father.

What do I do, Lord? Is this the answer?

No audible answer came, but peace settled in Cody's soul. Maybe that was answer enough. He didn't like that there was no time for discernment, but Travis knew Ella and wasn't objecting. That spoke to her character.

"I can't promise you love."

Now where had that come from? It was the truth, but to blurt it out like that?

Ella didn't flinch. "That's fine. Neither can I."

At least they were in agreement. He nodded slowly. "We're actually doing this?"

"We are." Once again, she lowered her eyes.

It might not be a conventional marriage, but the least he could do was propose properly. He got down on one knee, eliciting a look of surprise from his bride-to-be. Reaching out, he took her free hand. "Ella, will you do me the honor of becoming my wife?"

Her surprise melted away, replaced by a look he couldn't decipher. She blinked at him for several long seconds before a wry smile tugged at her mouth. "Yes, I'll marry you...Cody."

The hand he held felt soft, unused to hard work. How long would it be before calluses roughened her smooth skin? Shaking the thought aside, he rose to his feet. "I'll go rustle up the preacher."

A flicker of fear danced across Ella's face. The look sliced through him, remaining in his mind as he left to find Pastor Richards. Neither one of them knew what they were doing. This might be an answer to their problems, but what if it was a disaster in the making?

Cody lifted his eyes heavenward and sent up a silent prayer. *Please help us.*

*In short order, Ella found herself sitting in Cassie's room, dressed in a silvery white gown borrowed from her friend.

"It was my wedding dress," Cassie said, arranging Ella's hair into a braided crown. "Hopefully, it helps you feel like a part of our family. This might be a quick wedding, but you deserve to look stunning."

"Thank you, Cassie. For everything." If nothing else, she'd gained a sister from this unconventional bargain.

Cassie pinned a final piece of hair in place. She met Ella's eyes in the mirror. "I know this is scary. You're about to become a wife and a mother, and there's a lot you'll have to learn. But Cody will take good care of you. If you two trust each other, I think you'll get along fine."

"I hope you're right."

Cassie helped her stand. "I must admit, I'm relieved you're the one marrying my brother. The thought of him having a mail-order bride didn't sit well with me." She reached around Ella's neck to clasp a strand of pearls. "There. You're ready."

Ready? No, she wasn't ready. How did she prepare herself for marriage to a man she barely knew? Her only comfort came from Travis and Cassie's glowing opinions of her future husband. If they trusted him, she could trust him—eventually.

Male voices murmured downstairs. Ella's stomach pulsed with butterflies. "I think I'm going to be sick."

"Take some deep breaths. I'll get you a glass of water."

Cassie hurried for the pitcher on the nightstand while Ella inhaled. She downed the contents of the glass Cassie brought her and felt a little better, even if the prospect of walking downstairs to her sudden wedding made her want to fall over.

"Let's check on Isaiah before we meet the men, shall we?"

A distraction sounded perfect. "Yes, let's."

They made their way to the guest room. Little Isaiah slept with one hand under his cheek, curled into a ball. His face showed splotches of red.

"He still looks sick." Ella brushed a hand over the boy's soft hair.

Cassie tucked the covers over his shoulders. "He might not have been sleeping well, or perhaps his body is fighting off some illness. We'll know more in the morning." She glanced at Ella. "Well, you'll know more."

A sense of panic tore through her. "I don't know anything about doctoring children."

Cassie put an arm around her shoulder. "He should be fine, Ella. If he's still unwell tomorrow, Cody has plenty of willow bark tea. That will help with most anything that ails the boy."

Still, Ella hesitated. "If you're sure."

"I am. Now, let's get you married."

The anxiety inside increased, but Ella allowed Cassie to lead her downstairs to the parlor. Jonah slept on the settee, while Addie was awake and alert in Cody's arms. Travis stood with the preacher. Cassie led Ella to Cody's side, then tried to take Addie. The little girl squawked, burrowing closer to Cody. He put a hand on his sister's arm. "It's all right, Cass. I'll hold her."

His voice sounded gruff, but the way he held Addie belied his tone. The child rested her head on his shoulder, looking content. That had to speak to his character, didn't it?

The preacher opened his prayer book. "Miss Mountbatten. The men tell me you've agreed to this marriage?"

With a hard swallow, she nodded.

"Very well, then. Are we ready to begin?" The man glanced between her and Cody.

Ella felt frozen in place. Could she truly do this? Was it the right choice?

Oh, Lord, am I making a big mistake?

"Hey."

The warmth of Cody's hand surrounded hers. Looking up, she met his blue eyes. He used the same voice he'd used in the alley. "You don't have to do this if you don't want to."

Even with the preacher before them, he gave her the choice

to change her mind. The contrast between him and Howard yawned like the Grand Canyon. She bit her lip, remembering Howard's last words to her.

You will marry me, and that's final! I don't care what it takes to make that happen!

Cody regarded her with a calm look. Her panic dissipated. She kept her hand in his and moved closer. "I'm not going to change my mind."

He gave her a half smile, then turned to the preacher. "We're ready."

Ella barely heard the words of the ceremony. Her mind whirled as she spoke vows to a man she'd now be tethered to forever. When it came time to exchange rings, Travis stepped forward with two bands. Ella briefly wondered where they came from before Cody slid one onto her finger.

"With this ring, I thee wed."

The words jolted her out of her reverie. She lifted her head to look at him. He gazed back, solemnity written all over his handsome face.

Handsome? She blushed, trying to banish the thought.

Addie babbled something, patting his cheek. His eyes broke from Ella's for a moment, giving her time to breathe. She took the ring Travis offered her and placed it on Cody's finger.

The preacher smiled. "I now pronounce you man and wife."

And just like that, they were married.

CHAPTER 6

Cody stole glances at Ella throughout their silent drive to the farm. She sat ramrod straight on her seat, Addie held secure against her chest. This woman—his *wife*—possessed a curious ability to get through to his children. She'd been the one to carry Isaiah from the guest room to the buggy after their wedding, and Cody noticed the little boy snuggle closer to her even in his sleep. Jonah and Addie both fell asleep on her. It seemed they already trusted their new mother in some capacity. Time would tell if it continued.

His gaze grazed the golden band on his finger. The preacher had a stash of wedding rings for cases just like these. Apparently, he'd done more than a few last-minute weddings here in the west. The ring felt foreign on Cody's hand. It might take some getting used to—just as it would take time getting used to being married.

Frigid wind blew over the land. Ella shivered, her cheeks red. Cody placed the reins on the seat beside him, holding them in place with his thigh, and lifted the blanket from his lap. Without a word, he wrapped it around Ella and Addie. His new wife clasped her hand around it, holding it firm against Addie's back. "Th-thank you."

He nodded in response, taking up the reins again.

"Won't you be cold without it?"

Cody's legs already tingled, but his first priority was making sure she and the children were warm. "I'll be fine. It's only a few more miles."

After another couple minutes of silence, Ella spoke again. "Why are there dead cows everywhere?"

"It's been a harsh winter. Lots of ranchers ran out of cattle food near the end of the year. Then in January, we got a nasty blizzard that wiped out a lot of livestock. There wasn't enough food to go around. Most of us are struggling."

She tilted her head, studying him. "Including you?"

"Yeah." He snapped the reins, urging the horses to pick up their pace. "Things might be tight, but I like to be prepared. My cattle fared better because I had plenty of food stored up."

"And now?"

"Now…I pray we have a plentiful crop of alfalfa this season."

Ella fell quiet. That suited him just fine. He didn't know what else to say to her, anyway.

They crossed onto his land and rumbled toward the house. He pulled Preston to a halt. After jumping down, he rounded the wagon to help Ella out. She stood, letting the blanket fall in a heap, and eyed the descent. With a baby in her arms, it wouldn't be easy. Cody reached for her. His hands encircled her waist as he lifted her and set her on the ground. Her wide eyes blinked up at him. Once again, he felt her shiver. Only then did he realize he still had his hands around her waist. He let go and turned his attention to getting the boys.

Jonah had awakened and was rubbing his eyes, but Isaiah slept on. Cody helped Jonah down before taking Isaiah in his arms. Was it his imagination, or was the child more feverish?

When he turned again to face the house, Ella stood studying it. He surveyed his home, trying to see it through her eyes.

The log house was two stories, with plenty of windows to let in the light. He'd built it with the goal of providing a nice home for Cassie after he brought her back from the orphanage. A porch wrapped around the front of the house, where the two of them had spent many evenings together reading or talking. It wasn't anything fancy, but they'd made it a home after being bereft of one for so long.

"It's not much." Especially not for someone used to Boston society.

Ella glanced his way. "It's lovely."

For some reason, his back straightened in pride. He nodded to the door. "Let's get the kids inside. I'll show you around right quick, but then I need to care for my horse."

"All right."

They walked into the house. Isaiah never stirred. Jonah stayed close to Cody's side. He paused in the small foyer. "Let's start with the kitchen." He turned left, leading the way. "It's nothing grand, but it's got a stove and some tables for getting food ready. We've got a small cellar and pantry in the corner. And here's the table we eat at."

Ella ran a hand over the stove. "It's nice."

Nice was generous, but he didn't contradict her words. He led her back through the foyer and to the right. "This is the parlor. The kids have their toys in that box by the window." What else could he say about the room?

"You have books?" Ella went to the single shelf holding his small collection of novels. She ran a hand over them, her eyes lighting up.

"Read any you like." Why was his voice so gravelly as he said the words?

Ella stepped back from the shelf. "Thank you."

"Over here's my office." He pointed into a small room off the parlor. "It's got just enough room for a desk and some ledgers."

His wife peeked into the room. Her gaze roamed it before looking back over the parlor. "It's cozy. I like it."

It'll feel even cozier with five of us. He didn't pretend the house was a good size for a family of five. At some point, he might have to expand it.

"I'll show you upstairs." As he led the way up the steps, he glanced back to find that her eyelids were drooping. "It's been a long day. You're probably exhausted."

"I'm fine." She yawned. A sheepish smile pulled at her lips. "But I am tired."

They went to the children's room first. Cody laid Isaiah on the boys' bed and covered him with a blanket. The child didn't stir. He showed Ella where the nightclothes were, then prepared to change the kids. When Ella's gentle hand touched his arm, he turned.

"I'll put them to bed. You said something about your horse needing care?"

"Are you sure?"

She gave him a timid smile. "Yes."

"All right. Holler if you need anything."

She nodded. He headed for the doorway but paused to look back. Ella already had Addie on the bed, looking very capable as she unpinned the little girl's diaper. Yes, she had things in hand. Cody walked down the stairs, relief flooding him.

He was no longer alone in parenting these children. The burden he'd been carrying for weeks lifted. Sure, it had been replaced with new concerns—such as how he and Ella were going to live and work together—but that felt less complicated than single parenting.

After securing the wagon and taking out Ella's carpetbag, Cody turned his attention to his horse. When Cody locked Preston in his stall, the stallion nickered. "You're tired, too, aren't you, boy?" He reached out to pet the horse's nose. Preston pressed into his hand with a snort. "Looking for a sugar cube?" Cody smiled and pulled one from a box by the stall. "Here."

Cody glanced toward the house, where he had one more room to show his new wife.

The other bedroom. *Their* bedroom.

A shiver went down his spine, and he swallowed. They hadn't talked about room situations before getting married. To be honest, he'd forgotten that little detail. But now it presented itself with all its awkward implications. How could he have neglected to remember such a thing?

Preston nudged his back.

Cody cleared his throat. "What? I'm not dawdling."

His horse didn't look convinced.

"I suppose I need to face her, don't I?"

Preston nickered.

Cody chuckled. "Thanks, boy. Leave it to me to get a scolding from a horse." He patted Preston once more, then hoisted Ella's carpetbag and carried it to the house.

Utter silence met him as he walked inside. He climbed the stairs with a growing sense of trepidation. When he reached the top step, he heard someone singing. The sound was so foreign, he stopped in his tracks. Moments later, reason caught up. It was his new wife singing. He crept toward the children's room and peeked in.

Ella stood by the crib, rocking Addie back and forth. Her voice tapered off as she lowered the baby onto the mattress. She tucked a blanket around the girl, then softly ran a finger down her cheek. Ella then went to the bed, leaning down to kiss both boys on the forehead. She lingered by Isaiah, holding a hand over his forehead. The little boy murmured in his sleep. With one more light, maternal caress, Ella turned for the door.

She stopped cold when she saw him watching.

Cody held up a hand. "Sorry," he whispered. "I didn't mean to startle you."

Ella studied him for a moment, then resumed her walk to the door. "It's all right." She gestured toward the children. "They're asleep."

"Good." Cody beckoned for her to follow him. "I'll show you our room."

He said it as casually as he could, but even so, Ella released a sharp gasp. He dared not glance back lest he catch a horrified expression on her face. He should turn and give some kind of reassurance, but he couldn't muster the courage. Instead, he increased his pace until he reached the room, where he plunked the carpetbag on the bed.

The only bed.

Ella's footsteps sounded behind him. Well, if she hadn't run screaming for the hills, maybe that was a good sign.

Cody faced her. "I'm sorry. I didn't think about the room arrangements..."

She stepped forward, shaking her head. "It's not your fault. That's not something I thought of either." She looked at the bed, and her throat contracted. "I suppose we will be sharing that?" Her voice sounded small and nervous.

He shook his head before realizing what he did. "I can bunk on the floor."

Ella's teeth sank into her bottom lip. She stared at the planks beneath her boots. "I don't want to be the reason you can't sleep in your own bed."

"I'll be fine." Cody squared his shoulders. It would be freezing on the floor, but she didn't need to know that. "I'll just grab an extra blanket while you get ready for bed."

He slipped from the room before she could reply. The only extra blankets he had were old horse blankets in the barn, so he'd need to make another trip outside. Frigid air surrounded him as he dashed to the outbuilding and retrieved the blankets.

His nose wrinkled at the smell, but it was better than spending the night cold.

Well...less cold, at least.

He trudged back up the stairs and walked through the open door to his—their—room.. Ella squeaked. Something clattered to the floor. Cody was rendered mute, transfixed by the sight before him. His wife stood beside the bed in a modest nightdress. Auburn waves cascaded over her shoulders and fell to her waist. Her beauty smacked him like a physical force. The strangest urge to reach out and feel whether her hair was as soft as it looked overwhelmed him.

He cleared his throat, cheeks warming. "I...uh...sorry. Didn't mean to startle you."

Ella twisted her fingers together. She looked anywhere but at him. "It's fine."

Cody dumped the blankets on the floor at the foot of the bed. He reached for the hairbrush that had fallen from her hands when he barged in. "Here."

"Thanks." She all but whispered the word.

They stood in awkward silence for a few moments. When Cody couldn't take the tension any longer, he rubbed a hand over his jaw. "You should sleep."

Ella fidgeted with the brush. Her mouth opened, then closed. She put the brush on the small nightstand before crawling under the bedcovers. Cody arranged the blankets on the floor. Without bothering to change his clothes, he lay down on the hard wood. Cold nipped against him. He bit back a sigh and closed his eyes.

It was going to be a long night.

*E*lla chewed on her lip. Cody grunted and moved yet again. Would he be able to fall asleep at all? It felt like hours had passed since they went to bed, and he still hadn't settled.

Guilt smothered her. He would be exhausted come morning. She drew in a breath. *Can I invite a stranger into my...his bed?* Her heart thumped hard. Fear clutched her, and in that moment, she wasn't sure if it was stronger than the guilt.

She wrestled with herself for a few minutes. The house only had two bedrooms. Was she selfish enough to confine Cody to the floor indefinitely? It didn't seem fair. But when she thought of sharing the bed, her palms turned clammy.

A light snore interrupted her thoughts. Deep, even breathing came from the foot of the bed. He must have fallen asleep.

Ella relaxed. No decision had to be made tonight. She could ponder it more later. Maybe now she could fall asleep too.

But sleep wouldn't come. She sighed, letting her thoughts wander. After the wedding, her panic hit strong and hard. Knowing that she now belonged to another scared her. But in her heart, she knew she made the right decision—not only for herself, but for her new family. She'd seen the way Cody's tension melted after the preacher pronounced them husband and wife. He carried a heavy load on his own. If she could help lift it, she'd do so happily. And she already felt an attachment to her new children.

A little alarm in her head warned against letting down her guard, but she tried to ignore it. If this marriage was going to work, she needed to attempt trusting her husband, and she had to gain his trust in return.

Ella stifled a sigh. That wouldn't be easy, not for her. Trust had to be earned. Though Cody showed signs of being a good man, and though he had Travis and Cassie's approval, Ella's fear of men ran deep. Howard had ensured that.

A tear escaped. *Why did I allow myself to stay in such a horrible situation?* Tori often told her she needed to grow a backbone, but Ella hadn't been able to. Her one act of defiance had been leaving home and traveling to Harmony Springs. And that only happened because she feared for her life. Shoving the memories away, Ella turned her focus elsewhere.

This house had been a sweet surprise. She wasn't sure what she'd been expecting, but it wasn't this. Cassie had mentioned her brother built the house for her, and Ella could see the feminine touches that had to have come from her sister-in-law. While the structure of the home itself was solid and pleasing to the eye, the details inside revealed a woman had lived there. Lacy curtains hung at the windows, nicely upholstered furniture decorated the rooms, and pretty carpets accented the hardwood floors.

Most likely, the barn was just as well built. She'd have to explore it tomorrow.

An odd noise sounded over Cody's breathing. She sat up, straining her ears. A whimper. From the children's room? Ella pushed the blankets aside and set her feet on the floor. She nearly gasped at the cold. Back in Boston, servants kept the fires stoked to ward off the winter's chill. Here, things were different. Though she didn't remember it being so chilly at Travis and Cassie's home. But she'd also never gotten out of bed in the middle of the night.

Shivering, she headed out the door to the next room. Addie sat in her crib, sniffling. When she saw Ella, she reached up her arms.

Ella lifted the child. "What's the matter, sweetie?" she whispered.

Addie gnawed on her fingers. Another whimper passed her

little lips. The child's gums must still bother her. She wrapped the baby in a warm blanket before making her way to the stairs.

The dark discombobulated her. Ella had no idea where matches might be to light a lamp. She moved slowly, one hand in front of her to make sure she didn't crash into anything. It didn't take long to find the kitchen. By then, her eyes had adjusted to the dark. She found a pitcher of water and a rag. Dipping a finger into the liquid, she found it to be cold. Ella soaked the rag, wrung it out, then offered it to Addie. The child chomped on the cloth.

Exhaustion filtered through Ella's limbs. She made her way back upstairs. Cody's gentle breathing remained deep and even. Ella crawled under the warmth of the covers and tucked Addie in beside her.

Tomorrow, her life as a rancher's wife began.

CHAPTER 7

*I*cy cold woke Cody. He groaned, his body wracked with shivers and his neck stiff. Why was he so numb?

Slowly, events from the night before flashed through his mind. Dinner at Cassie and Travis's. Telling Travis he intended to take a wife. Ella offering herself for the role. Their wedding.

And his new sleeping arrangement on the floor. Cody glanced at the grate. Stone cold. No wonder he couldn't feel his legs. He struggled to his feet, hopping in place to get his blood pumping.

His new wife roused. She looked around, confusion shadowing her face. Then her gaze landed on him, and she sucked in a breath. "Oh. I guess it wasn't a dream."

One side of Cody's lips twitched. "No, ma'am."

She eyed him, pulling the blankets up to her shoulders. "You're cold."

There was no denying her simple observation. Cody nodded once, reaching for his warm flannel overshirt. "It'll be better once I start the fires."

Ella ran a hand through her tangled hair. "Will you show me how?"

He paused, one arm halfway through the sleeve of his shirt. "You?"

She slid from the bed, wincing when her feet touched the icy hardwood, though she tried to hide her shock. "Yes. It's something I have to learn, isn't it? You'll be out on the range during the day. The fires won't keep themselves going." She turned back, tucking the covers around something. A tiny baby sigh escaped the blankets. Addie?

Ella turned toward him. "She was uncomfortable during the night. Her gums hurt. I decided to keep her with me."

Why did she sound defensive? He held up his hands. "Fine by me."

She stared at him a moment. A little smile soon tugged at her lips. "You're different."

The way she said it, different must be good. He'd take it.

Her body convulsed with shivers. Cody took two long steps toward her, intent on giving her the piece of clothing in his hands. Ella shrank back at his abrupt movement. Too late, he realized advancing on her like that wasn't the smartest idea. He retreated a step before holding out his shirt. "Put this on."

As her teeth began to chatter, she shook her head. "I'll be fine once the fires are going."

Stubborn woman. Muttering under his breath, he opened the shirt and wrapped it securely around her shoulders despite her protest. "This is the coldest winter we've had. I'd rather you not freeze to death. Wouldn't want to try finding another wife so soon."

She stared at him for a moment. Cody tried not to cringe. Had his attempt at humor been that bad? He was about to apologize—again—when Ella's lips turned upward. She slipped her arms into the sleeves and buttoned his shirt with nimble fingers. It nearly swallowed her, but at least it would keep her warm.

"Thank you."

A man could get used to the light of gratitude in his wife's eyes. It sure made her look pretty too. Halting the direction of his thoughts, Cody nodded. "It's nothing." He headed for the bureau and grabbed another shirt. Shrugging into it, he gestured at the door. "Let's get this house warmed up."

Her hand came to rest against his arm, stopping him in his tracks. He glanced her way. The moisture in her eyes slackened his jaw. Ella dropped her hand, crossing her arms over her waist. "I'm not used to kindness from men. Travis was the only male I trusted for a long time, and it took a while for him to earn it. So you offering me your shirt, marrying me to protect me from my father and ex-fiancé, being kind..." Her chin wobbled, but she raised it in determination. "It's not 'nothing' to me."

Judging by the uncertainty in her eyes, it took a lot for her to admit that. Cody processed that information, his gaze never wavering from hers. "I'm glad you're open to trusting me."

A tiny smile lifted her lips. "I don't have much choice." She regarded him with those fathomless green eyes before looking away. "If Travis trusts you, I trust you. He has good instincts about people."

"Did he like Howard?" He almost groaned as soon as the words left his lips. *Why in the world did I ask that?*

Her body stiffened. "No." She stalked past him, heading for the stairs. "Should we start with the kitchen stove?"

Message received. Cody shoved his curiosity to the back of his mind and joined his wife. When they reached the kitchen, he pointed to a stack of wood near the door. "First, we gather some materials. There's kindling in boxes by each fireplace. That goes in first." He reached for a handful of the kindling and put it in the center of the stove. "Then we arrange some wood.

Start with a couple smaller pieces, then add the larger ones like so." When everything was adjusted to his liking, he motioned toward a matchbox. "Then we light it." Moments later, a roaring fire warmed the kitchen.

Ella scrutinized the stove. Cody hid a smile. Did she have any idea how adorable she looked with a wrinkled nose and focused gaze? Blinking, he banished the thought. "You ready to try the fireplace in the parlor?"

"Yes."

Cody let Ella lead. He offered direction when she asked but allowed her to make the fire on her own. It took much longer than it had in the kitchen. Her brow furrowed in frustration with each failed attempt to light the wood. Even so, Cody remained where he was. Experience had taught him that failing was part of the learning process. Ella would get it.

And she did. After nearly ten minutes of her trying, a fire crackled in the hearth. He had to give it to her—she was a determined woman. Not once had she uttered a word of complaint. Her failures only seemed to increase her desire to get it right.

That would serve her well in the wilds of the West.

The front door banged open. "Cody?"

The voice belonged to Hank, his foreman. Cody straightened. "In the parlor."

"Sorry to bother you so early, Boss." Hank's voice came closer. "But the wind blew over part of our fence, and some of the cattle got out..." He stopped abruptly as he came into the parlor and caught sight of Ella. His gaze darted between the two of them. "Uh—I didn't realize you were...entertaining a lady friend."

Cody flushed hot, annoyed at the insinuation. He rubbed his sore neck. "This is my *wife*, you greenhorn."

Hank ignored the insult and looked at Ella with curiosity. "Married, you say? Must've happened yesterday."

Cody crossed his arms, taking a step back to stand beside her. "It did." He looked at Ella, jerking his chin at the ranch hand. "Ella, this is Hank. He helps me run Brooks Ranch along with two other men. You'll meet them all before long."

Hank swept off his hat. His sandy hair shone almost blond in the firelight, and his brown eyes hinted at curiosity. "Nice to meet you, ma'am. I didn't mean no disrespect. Sorry if I gave offense."

Ella moved closer to Cody. It shouldn't have given him such satisfaction, but the simple motion proved she trusted him at least a little. Either that or she was using his body to shield herself from view. Her cultured voice betrayed no hint of her feelings. "It's a pleasure to meet you, Hank."

Hank slapped his hat back on his head. "Boss, we really need you in the west field. It's going to take all four of us to get that cattle back and repair the fence." His face tightened. "We don't need to lose any more livestock."

Heaviness settled in Cody's stomach. No, they didn't. If he lost any more head of cattle, he would be in deep financial trouble.

Ella's hand settled on his arm. He turned his head, looking at her over his shoulder. She nodded toward Hank. "Go on. The kids and I will be fine."

He hesitated. "Are you sure? I haven't had time to show you the basics for the kids…"

Her hand tightened briefly before relaxing and dropping to her side. "I'll figure it out. You take care of your cattle."

Urgency pulled at him, but still he couldn't seem to make himself move. Ella gave him a little push toward the stairs. "Go change. I'll brew some coffee for you to take along."

"How'd you know I like coffee?"

A faint smile touched her lips. "Cassie told me."

Hank cleared his throat. The man shifted from foot to foot. "Boss, please hurry."

That propelled him into motion. Within minutes, he'd dressed in all the necessary gear and made his way back downstairs. Ella met him with a canteen in hand and a wrapped bundle. He accepted them. "Thanks. What's this?"

"Bread, cheese, and dried meat. I found them in the pantry while the coffee brewed. You need to eat if it's going to be a long day."

Her thoughtfulness touched something deep inside him, something he hadn't felt before. There was no time to analyze it, though. He needed to get to the west field. Glancing around, he realized Hank was gone. "Where'd Hank go?"

Ella pointed at the door. "He said something about riding to a neighbor to ask them about caring for the barn animals today."

Cody groaned. "I forgot about that."

"Then it's a good thing he remembered. Now go. We'll be fine."

This woman possessed a strength inside that astounded him. What else might be hidden under that cultured demeanor? As he said goodbye and hurried out the door, he was surprised to find he genuinely wanted to know more about the woman he'd married.

≈

*E*lla's shoulders ached with tension as Cody rode away at a gallop. She wasn't sure how she managed to hold herself together when she encouraged him to get to the pasture. As she looked around the kitchen, a knot formed in her gut. The last thing she'd wanted was for her new husband to leave. She was all alone in a strange house, responsible for the welfare of three children. One of whom might still be sick.

She drew in a deep breath. One thing at a time. That was how she'd get through the day. But first, coffee.

A steaming cup sat on the table, one she'd poured for herself after filling Cody's canteen. She found a bit of sugar in the pantry and a small jug of milk on the counter, both of which she utilized to create a comforting brew. Ella took her drink to the parlor. She sank into the sofa and slowly sipped the hot liquid. Closing her eyes, she tried not to think about anything but the present moment and the flavor of coffee on her tongue.

The familiarity of the morning ritual calmed her. She finished the drink and washed her cup, then trudged upstairs to change into some warm clothes. Since she had no money of her own, Cassie had lent her several outfits. Ella would have to ask her new husband for funds to build a proper wardrobe for the harsh Montana winter. A part of her shrank at the thought. Even if Cody hadn't admitted to some financial trouble, asking for money never felt right to her. Over the years, she'd had no choice but to seek funds from her parents. There was precious little she was allowed to do to earn income for herself.

She had just finished slipping on some warm shoes when a cry came from the children's room. Ella hurried there, pushing open the door. Addie slept in her crib, and Jonah had his thumb in his mouth, eyes closed. Her gaze landed on Isaiah. The little boy moaned, his head moving from side to side. She sat on the side of the bed and held a hand to his forehead. It felt a little too warm. Ella touched his arm, rubbing up and down. His eyes opened. They appeared glassy and dull. Her heart went out to him.

"Hello, Isaiah. Remember me? Your Uncle Cody and I got married yesterday. That makes me your Aunt Ella."

The boy's breaths came in little pants. "You...held Addie...at church."

Her brows rose. That was what he remembered? "That's right. How do you feel?"

His eyelids fluttered shut. "My head hurts."

She brushed some of his hair back. He flinched and opened his eyes again. Ella removed her hand. "Why don't you come downstairs with me? I'll make you something to help you feel better."

Isaiah eyed her, suspicion burning in his gaze, but he allowed her to pick him up and carry him to the kitchen. The room felt pleasantly warm with a fire blazing in the stove, the one Cody had lit to make the coffee. Hopefully, that meant Isaiah's bare feet were also warm.

She placed him in a chair, then set about making some of Cassie's recommended willow bark tea. While the tea steeped, she sliced a piece of cheese from a wheel in the icebox, then tore a hunk of bread from a loaf. She put both on a plate and set it before Isaiah. "Here. Eat. You need to regain your strength."

Isaiah's gaze remained on her as he nibbled the simple fare. How could such a small child radiate such mistrust? Ella reined in a bark of laughter. She, of all people, knew what it was not to trust. Maybe little Isaiah was a kindred spirit.

She went back to the tea. After discarding the leaves, she scooped a generous portion of sugar into the cup and brought it to the table. Ella kept it by her at first, waiting for the tea to cool a bit before offering it to Isaiah.

He finished his bread and cheese. Silence pulsed heavy in the room. Ella searched her brain for something to say, landing on what she hoped was a safe topic. "Do you like living here?"

The boy's brown eyes hardened. "No. I want my house back."

Oh. Wrong question. Isaiah crossed his arms over his chest, defiance flitting over his face. Ella scrambled for something to say. "Do you like horses?"

The anger in his eyes intensified. "I hate horses! They killed my mommy and daddy!"

Pain radiated behind Isaiah's anger. She wanted to reach out and comfort him, but that would likely be the wrong move. Instead, she tested the tea with the tip of her finger. It had cooled enough for him to drink. She set it in front of him. "I'm sorry about your parents. You must have been very sad to lose them."

He blinked at her. Tears welled in his eyes as his lips trembled. "I miss them."

Nothing in the world could have stopped Ella from pulling him into her lap. She embraced the child, heartened when he buried his face in her shoulder and clung to her. Maybe she'd be able to gain his trust after all. When he pulled back, she offered the cup of tea. "Drink this. It will help your head feel better."

Isaiah took the cup and lifted it to his lips. He took a big gulp. All at once, his eyes bugged out, and the liquid spewed from his mouth. Ella gasped as the lukewarm tea seeped into her dress. Isaiah stared at the cup as though it was a snake. "It's yucky!"

Apparently, the sugar hadn't helped. "It might not taste great, but you need to drink it so you feel better. It will help."

"No!" Isaiah shrieked and shoved the cup away. It fell into Ella's lap, soaking the material of her dress. A tiny bit of liquid also splashed onto the boy. He proceeded to wail at the top of his lungs. If his head hurt before, it must be splitting by now. Ella felt a headache of her own coming on.

Isaiah's cries were soon joined by others from upstairs. Ella bit her lip, trying to keep a groan from escaping. She could barely hold onto Isaiah as his little body thrashed in a tantrum. Afraid of dropping him, she looked helplessly toward the stairs, Addie's and Jonah's cries tearing at her heart.

What had she been thinking, marrying Cody and agreeing to mother these children? She clearly couldn't care for them the way she thought she could.

Over Isaiah's screams, Ella heard the front door open.

Terror shot through her. She stood abruptly and whirled to face the kitchen entry.

An older woman stood there, hands splayed on the hips of her green dress. Her white hair was tucked into a neat bun. She tutted, blue eyes taking Ella's measure. "Well, dearie, it looks as though I've arrived just in time."

Ella backed up until she butted against the table. "Wh-who are you?" The woman didn't look sinister, but why was she in their house?

Isaiah stilled and sniffed, his chest heaving with heavy breaths. Ella held him closer, her eyes never leaving the stranger.

The woman chuckled. "There's no need for such worry, young lady. I'm Hattie O'Dell, but you can call me Miss Hattie. Everyone does. My family lives on the ranch several miles down the road. Young Hank came a'calling, saying you needed some help with the animals." She nodded at Isaiah. "When I heard the set of lungs on this young'un, I figured you might need some help in here too."

At the mention of Hank, Ella sagged against the table in relief. "That...would be nice."

Miss Hattie sized her up. "You aren't from around here, are you?"

"No, ma'am."

"Hmm." The woman bustled into the room and took Isaiah from Ella. "You skedaddle upstairs and see to those other young'uns. I'll take care of this one." She eyed Ella's dress. "And you might want to change. You're bound to get a chill if you don't."

This woman might be older, but she appeared to be a bundle of energy and wasn't afraid to take charge. After such a strange morning, Ella was in no frame of mind to argue. She simply nodded. "Yes, ma'am."

Thank You, Lord, for sending help. I need it.

CHAPTER 8

*H*attie O'Dell was a godsend. Ella was convinced of that within an hour of the woman's arrival. Not only did she take care of milking the cows and feeding the barn animals, she insisted on staying with Ella for the day to help teach her the ropes. Hattie got Isaiah and Jonah settled in the parlor with a set of blocks, and she sat at the table giving Addie a bottle while Ella worked on the breakfast dishes.

"You're gonna feel in over your head, missy, make no mistake. That's why you gotta lean on those around you. There ain't no shame in asking for help, of your neighbors and especially of your new husband." Hattie shook her head. "I wish I'd known that in the early days of my marriage. It's a wee bit overwhelmin', isn't it?"

Ella blinked. "Were you...?" She bit her lip, not wanting to seem rude by prying into this woman's life.

Hattie chuckled. She volunteered the answer to Ella's unspoken question. "I've been in your shoes, a long time ago. My first husband left me a widow with two young'uns to care for on my own. I couldn't do it by myself, so I answered an ad as a mail-order bride."

Ella's mouth dropped open. "You did?"

"Yes, ma'am. Mr. O'Dell lost his wife to scarlet fever, and he had two littles to care for and a ranch that needed daily tendin'. We struck up a bargain to help each other. Love wasn't part of the deal." Her face softened. "'Til it was."

Something twinged inside Ella's heart. "You fell in love with him?"

"That I did. I'm mighty glad I let myself too. I can be a stubborn woman and was all set to live out my days without love. My Billy eventually got through, just by bein' himself. I can't tell you when my heart knew it was his, but I was completely smitten before I even realized it." She chuckled. "We had two more children together, bringin' the grand total to six. It was a large, chaotic household, but one I wouldn't trade for anythin'."

Tears sprang to Ella's eyes. She swiped them away, confusion pulsing through her. When she felt Hattie's touch on her shoulder, she nearly dropped the plate in her hands. With a hard swallow, Ella turned to meet her eyes.

Hattie's shone with compassion. "You'll be all right, Miss Ella. Cody's a rare gem, despite appearances. He'll treat you right."

Did anyone not like the man? A reluctant smile tugged at Ella's lips. "So I'm told."

Hattie bounced the baby in her arms. "Keep your heart open, young lady. You just might fall in love with that handsome cowboy of yours. It would be good for both of you. He'd never admit it, but I think Cody's starved for love. He's carried a chip on his shoulder from the moment he left that orphanage, always lookin' out for others and makin' sure his sister and now these children are cared for. I think havin' someone to care for him for a change is the key to unlockin' that gruff exterior he hides under."

That unfamiliar sensation went off again in Ella's chest. It felt as though someone squeezed her lungs together, making it difficult to breathe, combined with a strange lightness that left her feeling dizzy.

"I...I don't...think...I'm c–capable..."

Hattie patted her arm sympathetically. "Somethin' tells me that heart of yours also needs unlockin', dearie."

Ella wasn't sure she wanted her heart unlocked. It was safe as it was, hidden behind walls that would rival any fortress. Loving someone meant opening herself to pain. Did she even want to let Cody in, giving him the power to hurt her?

A moan sounded from the direction of the parlor. Desperate for a distraction, Ella placed the plate on the drying rack and ran her hands over a towel. "I'll see to the boys." Even if Isaiah had been actively avoiding her since the tea-spilling incident.

Hattie's knowing gaze followed her out of the kitchen. A chill slid down Ella's spine. Just how much could Hattie see? She shook off the notion and made her way to the parlor.

Isaiah lay on the floor. He pressed one hand against his eyes. Jonah sat beside him, prodding his shoulder.

Alarm crept through her. She sank to her knees beside the boys. "Isaiah?"

He moaned in response. "My head."

A quick touch proved the fever had not returned, though Ella knew from experience that didn't mean a person would feel better—and children seemed more susceptible to pain. An ache an adult could handle without complaint could be devastating for a child.

"Would you like a cold cloth?"

Isaiah nodded.

Jonah looked at Ella, a plea in his eyes, as if he begged her to help his brother.

She stood. "I'll be right back." She hurried back to the kitchen.

Hattie glanced at her from where she rinsed Addie's bottle with one hand. "Everythin' okay?"

"Isaiah said his head hurts. I'm here for a bowl of water and a soft cloth."

Hattie nodded at a drawer. "Cloths are in there."

"Thank you." Ella fetched a bowl. She poured some water, placed a cloth inside, then headed back to the parlor to tend to the sick child. Her own worries paled in comparison to Isaiah's illness. Would he get better soon, or would she have to send for a doctor?

~

Cody secured a final length of rope along two posts. That should be enough to keep the cattle in until he could properly repair the fence. He let out a sigh of relief, his breath puffing white in the frigid air as he looked around the west pasture. It was the smallest of the four, his animals generally preferring the flatter east or south pastures. At least they'd found the missing livestock without much trouble.

Hank came alongside him, wiping sweat from his brow despite the cold. "It's a good thing there's four of us. Joey and Eddie did great roundin' up those missing cattle."

Cody nodded his appreciation to the two young ranch hands standing nearby. "You boys saved the herd. I owe you my thanks."

The twins alternated between grins of pride and modest looks at the ground. "Just doing our job, Boss," Eddie said.

Cody clapped a hand first on Eddie's shoulder, then on Joey's. "You boys have turned out well. Don't you forget that. You've come a long way from your orphan days."

Joey glanced up. "Thanks to you. Without this job, who knows where we'd be now."

At twenty, the twins were finally leaving behind the stigma

of their past. Raised at the same orphanage as Cody but ten years his junior, they'd always been interested in cowboys, dreaming of one day having their own ranch. He'd hired them two years ago when they aged out, knowing it would bolster their confidence and strengthen their dream. He might have a reputation as a bear, but with orphans, his heart was for helping. That was why he hired them. It was why he'd helped Cassie start her café. It was why he accepted his three young charges, even though he knew nothing about being a father.

It seemed that soft spot extended to hurting young women.

And yet he'd left his wife on her own all day. Darkness had started to fall, and though winter had earlier sunsets, it was still getting late. He adjusted the hat on his head and turned to his workers.

"Thanks for everything today, boys. Let's turn in for the night. Tomorrow will be another early start. We've got to properly fix that fence."

"Yessir." Eddie rubbed a hand over his neck. "Boss...Hank said something earlier. Is it true you got hitched?"

Cody shot Hank a glare.

The man looked back with a wide grin. "Lucky for you, I didn't tell them what I thought when I walked into your house this morning."

The twins leaned forward, eyes wide.

Heat crept up Cody's neck. He had no intention of rehashing that little misunderstanding. "Yeah, boys, I got married. Did it for my kids. They needed a mama."

Joey whistled low. "Never thought I'd see the day you married. Especially after what Miss Liza did to you."

Something revolted in the vicinity of Cody's heart. Not a subject he cared to dwell on. "Yeah, well, it is what it is. I'm a married man, and I need to get home to my wife and kids."

How was it possible for a statement to feel so strange and so right at the same time? Cody thought on it as he rode home and rubbed down his horse in the barn. That he no longer had to live in the house by himself was less lonely. But he wasn't so sure he'd be good at the whole husband and father thing. Giving Preston a final pat along with a sugar cube, Cody squared his shoulders and headed for the house.

The aroma of savory meat and stewed vegetables tickled his nose as soon as he opened the door. His mouth watered. A moment later, he detected a hint of something acrid. Someone yelped in pain. Cody bolted toward the sound, his hat dropping to the floor.

A muffled whimper came from the kitchen. He burst inside, then drew to an abrupt halt. Ella stood by the oven with her right hand cradled to her chest. She had her left hand pressed over her mouth, though it couldn't hide another strangled cry. It took him three seconds to assess the situation. The oven door stood open, a tray of biscuits hanging almost halfway out. No towel lay on the floor by Ella's feet.

She'd burned herself trying to take the tray out with her bare hands.

He was at her side in five long strides. Ella jumped when she saw him. Tears made her green eyes appear even bigger than they were. Cody rescued the biscuits and shut the oven door. He put a firm arm around Ella's shoulders and steered her toward a pitcher of water. With one hand, he grabbed the handle. His other reached for the arm she cradled close to her chest.

"Give me your hand."

She did so without argument. Cody guided it into the pitcher, making sure her hand was submerged. He chanced a glance at his wife. Her throat worked, and she sniffed several times in a row. She looked at the floor. "I could smell the biscuits burning. My only thought was to get them out fast. I forgot to use something to protect my hand."

Her voice was quiet. Tight. Cody hated that she sounded so

small, as though she expected a reprimand. Words poured out of him. "When I brought Cassie home from the orphanage, I wanted to make her a special welcome dinner. Never mind the fact that I knew nothing about cooking. I tried making biscuits that evening." He chuckled under his breath. "It didn't go well. I also forgot to use something to protect my hands, and I burned them so badly, Cassie had to take me to the infirmary in town. Not exactly the best welcome for my little sister."

Ella stood stock still beside him, though her gaze traveled up to his as he spoke.

He leaned closer as he put the pitcher back on the table. "Things like that happen, Ella. And it's okay. We live and we learn." When had his voice turned so gravelly?

She drew in an unsteady breath. "You're not...upset with me?"

He shook his head, trying to control the anger that sprang up at whoever had scarred her. "As I said, these things happen." He guided her to the table. "Sit."

Hang it all. He'd gone from gravelly to gruff. To his surprise, Ella didn't flinch. She simply sat in the chair, water dripping from her hand onto her skirt. He fetched a towel and pressed it against her wound. "Dry your hand. Gently."

She did, her gaze following him as he opened a cabinet and brought out a small basket. He walked back and took the seat next to her, then selected a jar from the basket. "Let me see your hand again."

Ella held it out, the tiniest bit of hesitation in the motion. Cody took it gently in his. Her smooth, soft skin brushed against his callused hand. Dipping the fingers of his other hand in the jar, he began smoothing the ointment over her burned fingers.

She studied his movements. "Is that honey?"

He nodded. "My ma always said honey could cure a burn better than anything a doctor had. She kept a jar full at all times. I picked up the tradition when I had a home of my own." Cody gave her fingers a final swipe, then rummaged through the basket for the small white bandages inside. "It looks like only three of your fingers are burnt, along with a bit of your upper palm. I'll wrap the fingers individually so you have use of them."

Ella watched him. He had finished wrapping her fingers and turned his attention to her palm when she finally spoke. "You have memories of your parents?"

He stilled. "I do. They died when I was ten, so my memories are well formed. Cassie was only five. She barely remembers them at all."

"May I ask what happened to them?" Ella's voice was barely a whisper.

Cody swallowed hard. He didn't like remembering the accident, but if he wanted his wife to trust him, he needed to share things with her. "We were in a wagon, riding west to claim land. My pa wanted a ranch of his own, and the government was giving out land almost for free, so long as a family could care for the land and make it profitable."

"The Homestead Act."

Surprised, he nodded. "You know about that?"

"I've heard of it. Never knew anyone who took advantage of it, though."

"Pa did. We were coming from Missouri. My parents had their eyes on the Montana Territory. I couldn't understand why they wanted to leave the United States, but I was excited about the adventure. We'd almost made it here to Harmony Springs when..." His throat closed. Even now, twenty years later, the memory sparked intense pain. "We were traveling along a deep ravine. The wagon hit a rock and tipped. My pa fell first. There was no saving him." Cody's throat felt thick, as though a heap of molasses had gotten stuck inside. "Ma knew the wagon was going to go over the edge. She told me to get out as fast as I could while she grabbed Cassie. My feet hit the ground, and I hurried around the wagon. Ma must have realized she couldn't get both herself and Cassie out in time, so she chose to save my sister. She looked at me...and it was as though time froze. She knew she was going to die. Her face was sad but determined. She threw Cassie to me just as the wagon plummeted down the ravine." His stomach turned. "I didn't have time to process what happened. Cassie screamed in my arms, crying hysterically. I had to be strong for her."

Ella's soft gasp puffed against his neck. She reached up with her free hand and laid it against his cheek. "I'm so sorry."

Tears blurred his vision. "It was a long time ago."

Her fingers trailed down his jaw before leaving his face. "That doesn't make it hurt any less. You watched your parents die, Cody. That's something that will scar a person for life." She covered his hand with hers. "I see why caring for your little ones was so important to you. They experienced a similar loss, and you saw yourself in them."

He looked down. "Something like that."

"You're a good man, Cody Brooks."

That brought his gaze back up to hers.

Ella's lips turned up in a gentle smile. "Everyone keeps telling me that, and I know soon enough, I'll believe it myself. You have a selfless spirit."

Her gentle praise thawed something long frozen in his heart. A touch of heat entered his cheeks. "I'm just trying to do the right thing."

One side of Ella's mouth lifted higher than the other. "Exactly."

Cody's face went hot. He brought his attention back to her hand, wrapping her palm in a few deft movements. "There you go. It might sting for a bit, but you'll be good as new in no time." He stood, taking the basket back to its cabinet. "Supper smells good."

Ella stood, running her uninjured hand down her skirt. Her smile became self-deprecating. "Miss Hattie made the stew, so I imagine it's delicious."

He paused, glancing back. "Miss Hattie was here?"

"She came this morning and was a lifesaver. I don't know what I would have done without her help today. She's with the children now."

As if on cue, Hattie came bustling into the kitchen. "I don't know how long it takes to pull biscuits from the oven, but...oh!" Her eyes landed on Ella's bandaged hand. "Did you burn yourself, dearie?"

Ella nodded.

Hattie's gaze moved to Cody. "There you are! I was wondering when you'd be home." She clucked her tongue. "It's nigh suppertime, you know."

He chuckled. "Hello, Miss Hattie."

She wrapped him in a warm embrace. "Now that you're here, I'll be taking myself off to my family."

"Won't you stay for dinner?" Ella asked.

Hattie smiled. "Thanks for the offer, but I need to get back. My grandkids ain't used to me being gone for so long. I'll come back for a bit tomorrow. I can teach you to do laundry." She headed for the door. "The young'uns are in the parlor with their toys. I'll be seein' you both soon." With a wave, she left the house.

Cody took some bowls from another cabinet. "Why don't I serve the stew with you?"

Ella's eyes widened. "But...isn't that my job?"

"I'm thinking you could use some help." He motioned to her hand.

She stared at him as though he was some foreign creature. Slowly, she shook her head. "You want to...help?"

The incredulity in her tone spoke volumes. Cody rested a

hand on her shoulder. "I take it you're not used to a man offering assistance."

She ducked her head. "Not like this."

A smile pulled at his lips. "You might as well get used to the idea, Mrs. Brooks. This marriage of ours is a partnership. I intend to pull my weight and hope you do the same."

Ella blinked rapidly, her mouth dropping open. He'd shocked her.

His smile broke free. "So...you want to ladle while I hold the bowl?"

Snapping her mouth shut, she nodded. "Yes. That will be fine." Her words sounded breathless, as if she couldn't quite figure him out.

It broke his heart that being treated with kindness and respect warranted confusion for Ella. He vowed to do whatever it took to make her feel at home on the ranch. It would be good for her. It would be good for the children.

And it would be good for him.

CHAPTER 9

The next morning, Ella woke to muffled grunts. She slitted her eyes open. Cody sat on the floor, rubbing his neck. Guilt sliced through her as he craned his neck this way and that. The man shouldn't be sleeping on a pile of blankets in the middle of winter. In his own home. Because of her.

She stifled a sigh. How could she continue to put him through such misery? She'd seen the way he stretched his neck when he thought she wasn't looking. He deserved the comfort of his own bed. But was she brave enough to invite him there?

Cody got to his feet. She let her eyes fall shut, contemplating her dilemma. Minutes later, Cody had a fire blazing. Ella welcomed the warmth. She stretched and opened her eyes.

And promptly shut them again, trying and failing to erase the image of her shirtless husband from her mind. Her cheeks flamed. It looked as though ranch life kept him physically fit.

His footsteps neared the bed. "Darlin', I know you're awake. You're redder than a sunburnt cowboy."

Being a redhead had its drawbacks. She peeked up at him through her eyelashes, relieved to see that he now wore a shirt. "Sorry," she squeaked. "I didn't know you were dressing."

His hands rested on his hips. "No harm done. How's your hand?"

She blinked, trying to keep up with the abrupt change in subject. "It stings a little but is fine otherwise."

"Good." He looped his suspenders over his shoulders. "I thought I'd come back early today. Take you and the kids shopping in town."

Ella pushed herself up. "What?"

"You need practical clothing. The kids are outgrowing what they have. We'll visit the seamstress to get that taken care of."

"But...aren't you strapped for money?"

"Not so badly I can't provide for my family."

The matter-of-fact way he said the words told her this wasn't a snap decision. She scooted back against the headboard. "All right."

Cody shifted from foot to foot. "Well, then...I'll get some breakfast going."

"I can do that." She pushed back the covers.

He put a restraining hand on her shoulder. "I've got it, Ella."

Something sparked in her chest. She stared up at him, caught in the brilliance of his eyes.

Cody blinked, then blinked again. He took a step back, letting his hand drop from her shoulder. "See you downstairs."

Ella chewed her bottom lip. The warmth from his hand lingered on her skin long after he walked out the door. She slipped out of bed and readied herself for the day. As soon as she finished tying her hair back, Addie babbled from the other room. Ella headed there.

In her crib, the little girl sat playing with her toes. When she saw Ella, she clambered to her feet and held up her arms. Ella's heart surged with love for her new daughter. She lifted Addie and cooed. "Oh, sweetie, you need a clean diaper, don't you?" Ella kept her voice low so she wouldn't wake the boys while she chatted and changed the baby's diaper. Isaiah and Jonah slept through it all. With Addie on her hip, Ella eased over to Isaiah and touched his forehead for fever, relieved to find it cool. She ran a hand over his hair, then did the same for Jonah. Tapping Addie's nose, she headed for the door. "Should we go see Uncle Cody?"

By the time she made it downstairs, the fires Cody had built had warmed the house. He turned when she entered the kitchen. His gaze landed on Addie. A smile touched his lip, his eyes softening before he turned them toward Ella. "The boys still asleep?"

"Peacefully."

"Good." He pointed to a bowl on the table. "Eat up. It's not much, but it's warming. I'll get a bottle ready for Addie."

Ella lowered herself into a chair. The steaming bowl of oatmeal smelled of brown sugar and cinnamon. She settled Addie on her lap before taking a bite. The oats had a pleasant, chewy texture, and it tasted good. By the time Cody brought the bottle over, Ella had nearly finished the bowl.

Her husband chuckled. "You have quite an appetite."

She ducked her head and accepted the bottle, distracting herself by feeding the baby. No one in Boston dared comment on a woman's eating habits. To hear Cody mention it in a nonchalant way confused her.

His hand came to rest on her shoulder. "That's a good thing out here, Ella. I didn't mean any disrespect."

She glanced up. Compassion radiated from his eyes. "I believe you. It might take me a little time to adjust to the forthright manner of speech in the west."

"You'll get there." He cleared his throat, gruffness finding his voice again. "I've got to be going. See you later." Snatching his hat, he disappeared out the door.

Ella stared after him. How could he be soft one moment and rough the next? Perhaps the gruffness was a front, a way to protect himself from further hurt. Though she had to admit that he didn't frighten her. For that, she was thankful. Howard had always frightened her. Cody exuded a sense of safety. A bear he might be, but Cassie was right—he was more softy than grizzly.

She looked down at Addie. "I suppose if he took the three of you in, he must have a good heart. He does, doesn't he?"

The baby gazed up at her as she drank the bottle. No sooner had she finished than Ella heard the boys moving around upstairs. She stood and placed Addie's bottle in the sink. The pot of oatmeal sat warm on the stove, ready for the boys. Had Cody even taken the time to eat? If he had, he must have eaten even faster than her. A glance in the sink showed that he had indeed eaten his own portion of oatmeal.

Footsteps pattered down the stairs. Ella turned as Isaiah and Jonah entered the kitchen, rubbing their eyes. Isaiah stopped cold when he saw her. "What're you still doin' here?"

That tone didn't sound promising. But much like Cody's gruffness, Isaiah's probably hid a world of hurt. Shifting Addie to her hip, Ella replied in an even tone. "I live here." She moved to the pot. "Your Uncle Cody made oatmeal for breakfast. Sit at the table and I'll fix you a bowl."

Jonah moved readily to his chair.

Isaiah stood dumbstruck before an apprehensive look entered his eyes. "It ain't yucky like the tea, is it?"

Ella spooned some oatmeal into the bowls. She sprinkled extra sugar over the top for good measure. "Not at all." She set the bowls in front of the boys, then poured a bit of cream in each one. Her hand stung from the activity, but she tried to ignore the pain.

Jonah tucked into his meal. Isaiah stared at the bowl. He poked at the oatmeal with his spoon. Ella turned her attention to Addie. Her time educating girls in Boston had taught her that sometimes ignoring rather than engaging a child led to the desired result. She glanced over her shoulder to see Isaiah eating his food.

A smile tugged at her lips. Thank God for small victories.

$\sim$

Cutting work short felt strange, but Cody knew his ranch hands could carry on in his temporary absence. Now, as he stood in Mrs. Greyson's seamstress shop, he sent up a prayer of gratitude for workers he could trust.

Ella walked quietly between rows of fabric with the children in tow. She touched various kinds of material. Cody trailed behind them, watching her curiously. How would she determine which cut of cloth to use?

Ella pointed to several bolts. Each looked practical and comfortable. She focused on him. "You need new clothes too."

"I'm fine."

She eyed his pants. "That fabric is nearly worn through. It won't keep you warm when it snows."

Mrs. Greyson nodded her approval, lopsided bun swinging with the motion. "Excellent observation, Mrs. Brooks."

Cody shot the woman an annoyed look, which she ignored.

Ella placed a hand on his arm. "You can let others take care of you, too, Cody. This is a partnership, remember?"

The quiet words, for his ears only, softened the fight inside him. He covered her fingers with his own. "I'll try to keep that in mind."

Her smile warmed his stomach. When her hand dropped back to her side, he missed the touch. Cody's brow furrowed. What kind of reaction was that?

Ella voice dropped to a whisper. "Can you afford it?"

He'd saved money for clothes over the years. It was a fund he didn't touch often. "Yeah."

She smiled, turning to the seamstress. "This one for my

husband." Ella pointed to a thick brown material. Cody peered over her shoulder, impressed. As Mrs. Greyson bundled up the fabric, he looked at his wife. "You made your decisions quickly. How'd you do that?"

A half smile formed on her lips. "I lived in Boston. Fashion is something I know well."

Isaiah tugged at Cody's jacket. "Can we go?" The whine in his voice, coupled with the child rubbing his eyes, told Cody the boy was tired.

"Almost. We just need to tell Mrs. Greyson what outfits to make." He turned to Ella. "Are you satisfied with your choices?"

"Yes. Thank you."

He eyed the fabric Mrs. Greyson gathered for Ella. His wife had chosen practical—and inexpensive—material in solid colors—navy blue, dark green, and brown. While they would look pretty on her, a sudden impulse came over him. With Ella's attention distracted by the children, he stopped beside Mrs. Greyson. "Please add the green and flowered light blue fabrics for my wife."

"Of course." She leaned forward, a wide grin on her face. "It seems you're a quick study in the secret to being a good husband."

Cody suppressed a snort. Doubtful. He just had a feeling Ella would appreciate the prettier colors, much as Cassie did.

Their business was soon finished, and the remainder of the day at home passed without incident. Once the children were in bed for the night, Ella yawned. "May I turn in early?"

Cody looked up from stoking the parlor fire. "You don't need to ask permission. If you're tired, go to bed. I want you to feel at home here."

A blush stained her cheeks, and her gaze fell to the floor. "I'm sorry."

He groaned. Clearly, the words hadn't come out right. Straightening, he went to her. "Don't apologize. What I meant is that I want you to feel safe. I'm not your master. You can make your own choices."

Her throat worked. When she finally looked up at him, tears swam in her eyes. "You don't know how much that means to me."

To his shock, she leaned forward and hugged him. His arms remained at his sides as bolts of lightning raced up and down his spine.

Ella quickly pulled back. Her cheeks went bright red. "Thank you." Turning abruptly, she hurried up the stairs.

Cody watched her go. Something unfamiliar curled in his chest. He suddenly wanted nothing more than to hold her in his arms and soothe away any lingering fear or doubt she might possess.

And that was exactly what he couldn't do. Not without risking his heart.

~

Despite her exhaustion, Ella tossed and turned, unable to fall asleep. Without Cody's solid presence in the room, fear clutched her in its cruel talons. How she could be so dependent on him sleeping near her after only two nights was a mystery. Most men gave her reason to distrust them. With Cody, she felt safest when he was close. It made no sense, but it was true.

After an hour, she pushed back the covers. Sleep wouldn't come so long as she was alone. Ella shivered in the cold room. The fire had long since died down. She donned a warm shawl that Cassie had lent her along with slippers for her feet. Keeping her steps quiet, she padded downstairs. Dim light flickered in Cody's office. What was he up to at this hour? She crept to the door.

Her husband sat in a chair with something on his lap.

When she knocked on the door, the thump soft and quiet, he looked up. Surprise lit his eyes. "Ella. I thought you'd be asleep."

She shrugged. "Sleep was elusive." As she came closer, she saw the item in his lap was a book. "What are you reading?"

A hint of pink touched his cheeks. He snapped the book shut. "Nothing."

His gruff tone heightened her curiosity. "Nothing looks a lot like something." The playfulness in her voice surprised her. She halted. What was she thinking? If he didn't want to tell, he wouldn't appreciate her prying. Howard hated it when she questioned him. A knot settled in her stomach. She lowered her eyes. "I didn't mean to intrude. Goodnight." Spinning around, she made for the door.

A hand on her arm halted her progress. Cody's grip held her in place. "Ella. Look at me."

She dragged her gaze upward until it met his. No annoyance rested in his blue eyes. The look of compassion there nearly did her in. He gentled his tone. "Come sit with me. Please."

She allowed him to lead her to the smaller sofa in the parlor. When he sat beside her, his large body took up a majority of the space. Ella sucked in a soft breath as their shoulders brushed. Cody didn't seem to notice. He extended the book he'd been reading toward her.

Ella pressed her lips together. "You don't have to show me this if you don't want to."

"I want to." He pushed the book into her hands.

For a moment, she didn't move. The book sat in her grasp, lighter than she expected. The cover looked worn and faded. Carefully, Ella opened it to the first page. Neat, flowing script met her gaze. It only took a few moments to decipher the contents. Blinking, she looked up at Cody. "Poetry?"

The pink in his cheeks deepened.

Understanding rushed over her. "You were embarrassed to be caught reading this?"

"Maybe a little." Cody's half smile appeared. "Reading poetry isn't considered a manly pastime."

"It just means you have a sensitive, romantic side."

Her husband chuckled. "Those are two traits no one has ever accused me of."

Was that a teasing note in his voice? Ella found a smile of her own. "Maybe they should. There are worse things."

"Perhaps." Cody flipped to the first page. "This one is my favorite."

Ella read the title. Her jaw dropped. "Elizabeth Barrett Browning's *Sonnet 43*?" Her gaze found his. "I love that poem."

Matching surprise flashed over his face before a smile replaced it. "Does that mean you're a romantic at heart?"

Her throat clenched painfully. Ella closed her eyes, fighting for control. When she opened them, her words came out in a whisper. "I used to be."

Cody's piercing gaze seemed to expose her. No doubt he saw more than she cared to reveal.

With a quick intake of breath, she held the book out to him. "Will you read it to me?"

Too late, she realized how that must sound. Mortification filled her while heat gorged her cheeks. Cody didn't blink. He accepted the book and slowly began to read in his gruff, deep voice.

> How do I love thee? Let me count the ways.
> I love thee to the depth and breadth and height
> My soul can reach, when feeling out of sight
> For the ends of being and ideal grace.
> I love thee to the level of every day's
> Most quiet need, by sun and candle-light.

Ella's breath hitched. Cody's eyes remained trained on the page, but every word felt as intimate as a caress. She let her own eyes drift closed as he continued.

> I love thee freely, as men strive for right.
> I love thee purely, as they turn from praise.
> I love thee with the passion put to use
> In my old griefs, and with my childhood's faith.
> I love thee with a love I seemed to lose
> With my lost saints. I love thee with the breath,
> Smiles, tears, of all my life; and, if God choose,
> I shall but love thee better after death.

When he stopped reading, Ella opened her eyes. Her husband had his gaze fixed on her. There was raw vulnerability in his expression. A swarm of butterflies took possession of her stomach, beating their wings and rendering her mute.

Cody broke their connection first. Clearing his throat, he looked down at the page. "My mother made this book. She filled it with her favorite poems."

It took Ella a moment to understand what he told her. "She wrote all this by hand?"

"Yeah. Ma was a classic romantic. One of my earliest memories is of her and my father sitting together like this, reading poems to each other." His throat worked. "It's now one of my most cherished possessions."

His lingering grief wrapped around her. Without thinking, Ella threaded her fingers through his. "I'm sure she'd be glad to know you treasure a poem she loved."

Cody glanced at their joined hands. "Do you know which part of *Sonnet 43* she liked best?"

Ella felt self-conscious holding his hand so boldly, but she focused on providing what little comfort she could. "Tell me."

"'I love thee to the level of every day's most quiet need, by sun and candle-light.'" He fell silent for a moment. "She used to say the proof of real love lay not in big gestures and grand hopes, but in the little joys and trials of everyday life. That it had to be built on a foundation of trust, respect, and faith."

Some unrecognizable, deep emotion welled up inside Ella. She attempted to compose herself before speaking. "I think I would have liked your mother. She sounds like a wise woman."

Cody's hand tightened over hers. "She was."

They sat without speaking for a minute before Cody set the precious book aside and tugged Ella to her feet. He kept hold of her hand and gave it a squeeze. "It's late. We should probably turn in."

She raised her free hand to his chest. "Thank you, Cody."

"For what?"

"For trusting me with that story. I feel as though I know you a little better now." In an attempt to insert some levity, she smiled. "Cassie is right. You're a big softy."

Cody's jaw slackened, and he stared at her for a moment. He shook his head. "I'm going to have words with my sister over that comment."

Ella laughed softly as he extinguished the light. "It won't change the fact that she's right."

"Humph." Cody began walking, guarding her from bumping into furniture in the dark room. "Just make sure that stays between us."

A smile curved her lips. "Your secret is safe with me."

"Good."

Hand in hand, they climbed the stairs to their room. Ella took a deep breath as Cody spread his blankets over the floor. She gathered her courage and touched his shoulder. "You shouldn't be sleeping on the floor."

He stilled.

Ella soldiered on. "We can share the bed. It'll be much warmer."

Cody's eyes searched hers. "You're really okay with that?"

"Yes."

"All right." Neither of them moved. Cody gestured to the bed. "Ladies first."

Ella took a deep breath and slipped under the covers. She chewed on her lip when Cody got in beside her. The bed suddenly felt much too small. Their bodies touched no matter how close to the edge she lay.

Long minutes passed. Old fears welled up. Cody's breathing evened out, but his hip remained firmly pressed against hers. Despite their earlier connection, Ella stifled a groan. All she could think of was the last man she'd trusted...and how terribly it had all turned out. Maybe she should turn onto her side. Then perhaps their bodies wouldn't touch so intimately.

Before she could, Cody moved in his sleep, flipping to face her. His arm flung over her, his hand coming to rest against her waist. Ella forgot how to breathe. Her husband's face rested inches from hers, his warm breath puffing against her cheek. She waited for the inevitable panic to set in.

It never came. Instead, a soothing warmth crept through the entirety of her body.

But that was impossible. Whenever Howard so much as looked at her, she'd felt anxious. His touch had been even worse. He possessed none of the gruff, rough exterior that Cody did. Quite the opposite. Howard could charm anyone with his charisma and flowery words. Cody was more likely to growl. But when it came to who she would trust more, the answer was easy—as proven by the fact that she'd married one to escape the other.

Her confusion grew. She should be terrified right now, yet all she felt was relief. Cody might be sleeping, but his arm curled around her spoke of a protectiveness that she was coming to realize was essential to who he was. Hadn't he been protecting her since the moment they met?

Ella forced her body to relax. She was in Harmony Springs. She was safe. No one could harm her now...

Howard's angry face appeared in her mind, his handsome features twisted in the malevolent scowl he'd worn the last time she saw him. She could still feel his hand biting into her arm while his other delivered a blow to her face. Her body convulsed, as if the knowledge of what came next was about to happen again.

Cody murmured something in his sleep. He nestled closer, his body flush against hers. Ella gasped. His warmth seeped into her cold memories as much as her cold bones. Instinctively, she turned into his unconscious protection, letting her forehead rest against his solid chest. Why he didn't terrify her, she couldn't say. His strength should be enough to send her running. Yet all she knew was that his simple act of moving toward her calmed the storm inside. He banished memories of Howard's cruelty just by holding her.

The final ropes of tension faded away. Ella let herself forget everything except the safety she felt in this man's arms. As she lay ensconced in his embrace, her eyes drifted shut, and her mind quieted enough for her to sleep.

CHAPTER 10

On Saturday morning, Cody slipped out of the house before dawn and headed for the barn. Yet again, he'd woken with Ella in his arms, a common occurrence since they'd bonded over his mother's poetry. The first time it happened, he panicked. He'd felt happy and warm, surrounded by a cloud of lavender, when he realized something wasn't right. When his eyes opened and he found his wife nestled against him, cradled in his arms, he'd almost leapt out of the bed. His body jerked and woke Ella. To his surprise, she hadn't seemed bothered by his embrace.

Things between him and his wife alternated between comfortable and stilted in the days that followed. Despite that, she was clearly growing more at ease in his home, taking to her role of mother as if she'd been born to be one. Isaiah gave her a hard time, but Addie and Jonah took to her as naturally as she did to them.

His own feelings were clear as mud. Cody wanted to keep his distance, to keep his heart locked away where it couldn't get hurt. But his protective instincts proved stronger than his fear.

He couldn't bear the anxiety on Ella's face when she thought she'd made some perceived mistake. Whatever her former fiancé had done to her, it left deep marks.

With a grunt, Cody grabbed a pitchfork. Maybe some manual labor would ease the confusion in his chest. He mucked the stalls with more vigor than usual. By the time the sun climbed toward the horizon, sweat covered his body and he'd long since shucked his jacket.

The two milk cows clamored for his attention. Cody paused to catch his breath before placing the pitchfork against a wall. "Sorry, gals. I lost track of time."

"Can I help?"

An involuntary yelp escaped him as he whirled around to face the owner of the unexpected voice. Ella stood a few feet away, wrapped in a thick shawl. She wore an apologetic expression. Cody inhaled long and slow to calm the rapid beating of his heart. "Mornin'."

"Good morning. You're up earlier than usual."

How could he tell her it was both thrilling and disconcerting to wake up with her in his arms every day? Cody couldn't figure out how that happened. He went to sleep with his back to her in an attempt to prevent that outcome, but when morning came, she lay nestled against him and his traitorous arms held her close. At least she didn't usually wake before him.

Now she stood, head tilted and green eyes trained on him. He searched his mind to remember her comment. "I guess I didn't sleep well."

Ella fiddled with the fringes of her shawl. "Is that my fault?" Before he could deny it, she hurried on. "You're not used to sharing a bed. That must feel strange."

It did. He'd never shared sleeping space with anyone before getting married. "A little. I'd wager it's the same for you."

She nodded. A soft expression flitted over her face. "I find I don't mind it like I thought I would."

Her words knit together a wound deep inside, one he hadn't realized stood in need of healing. "That so?"

"I mean...well...I feel..." She cleared her throat and spoke in a rush. "I feel safe with you."

With his prickly nature? "We've known each other for two weeks."

Pink dotted her cheeks. "It doesn't make sense to me either." She looked at the ground. "Travis's assurance of your character seems to have worked its magic."

That said more about her trust in Travis than her feelings for him, but Cody appreciated the sentiment. "I'm glad you're not afraid of me."

Her lips quirked. "Not usually, anyway."

"I'll take it."

One of the cows released a loud grunt. Ella jumped.

Cody hid a smile, reaching for a pail near the wall. "Were you serious about wanting to help?"

"Yes."

"All right. Let's teach you how to milk the cows."

Ella eyed the animals as she moved closer to him. "They're so big."

Cody smothered a smile. Big? Wait 'til she saw the cattle on the range. "They're Jerseys, one of the smallest breeds of milk cow." He pointed to the one in the first stall. "That's Sadie. The other is Becky."

"Hmm." Ella turned her gaze on him. "Those are very feminine names."

"I can't take credit. Cassie named them."

"That I can believe."

Cody opened Sadie's stall and nudged a stool near her as he reached for a pail. "Have a seat."

Ella positioned herself on the stool. Her eyes never left Sadie's. "Nice cow."

Sadie grunted and swished her tail, flicking Ella in the face. His wife squealed. She tottered backward, nearly falling off the stool.

Cody caught her. "Easy. Sadie's harmless."

"Harmless?" Ella rubbed her cheek. "Since when do cows have such strong tails?"

Cody bit his lip hard. Even so, he coughed to cover a chuckle, then eased Ella back onto her seat. "Maybe she wants to test your mettle, darlin'."

She glanced up at him over her shoulder. Her green eyes bore into his. "Is that a term people use out here?"

He floundered for words. The endearment slipped out so naturally, he didn't even think about it. "Uh...no." Would his reason placate her or make her run? He swallowed. "It's what my pa called Ma. I guess since you're my wife, it felt like the right thing to say." He tugged at his collar. "If it makes you uncomfortable, I won't use it."

Ella held his gaze. "I don't mind. Especially if it has happy memories connected with your parents."

Warmth shot through his gut, which rendered breathing difficult. Cody dropped his eyes, wondering at his reaction as well as his unconscious choice to call Ella *darlin'*. The fact that she remained open to it surprised him—but he couldn't help being pleased.

His gaze fell to her hands. The right one still bore bandages from her burn. "How's your hand?"

"It's better, though it feels a bit tender. At least I can touch things without any sting."

"Good." He motioned to Sadie. "Squeezing the teats might aggravate it. If that happens, we can try this another time."

Ella flexed her fingers. "I should be fine."

"All right." He squatted beside her. "Now, the trick to

milking is to pull the teats with the right pressure. Too light won't produce any milk, and too hard will make the cow angry."

"Angry?" Ella's voice pitched high.

Cody smiled and patted her arm. "It'll be fine. Watch me." He took hold of two teats and began to milk. The stream of white liquid pinged as it landed in the pail. After a minute, he paused. "Your turn."

With a look of intense concentration, Ella reached forward and took the same two teats in hand. She squeezed. Nothing happened. Dismay flashed over her face as she looked up at him. "It didn't work."

"You have to put your thumb and index finger at the top of the teat, against the udder. The rest of your fingers go below them." He positioned her hands. "Squeeze the top of the teat with your index finger. Use your other fingers to squeeze from top to bottom, and make sure you use a slight downward pull."

She gave it another attempt. Still nothing. Her teeth sank into her lower lip as she tried a third time, drawing Cody's gaze. He forced his eyes back to the cow even as a foreign desire tripped through him, a desire to take her in his arms and...

Nope. He blocked the mental image. Being attracted to his wife was *not* a part of their arrangement. The last thing he needed was to daydream about kissing her. Never mind the fact that her lips looked soft and welcoming. Sharing a kiss with her would be no hardship. He'd probably enjoy it.

A growl sounded low in his throat. *Get a hold of yourself, Brooks!*

Ella flinched, dropping her hands from Sadie. "I'm making more work for you. I should head back to the house."

Cody's arms shot forward without his permission, locking her in place. "That wasn't aimed at you."

She stilled in his arms. Her brow furrowed. "You sounded frustrated, and there's no one here but me."

Angry at himself for frightening her, Cody inhaled deeply

before responding. "It's nothing you did. Something came to mind that felt...unwelcome. I'm sorry."

Ella looked down. "You don't have to apologize."

Yet again, anger at the men in her past rose inside of him. A man's strength lay in protecting the women in his life, not using it to terrorize. Pushing down the reaction so as not to frighten her again, Cody gentled his voice. "Want to try again with Sadie?"

Ella kept her hands in her lap. "I don't know what I'm doing wrong."

"Nothing. It just takes some practice." When she still didn't move, Cody squatted behind her and put his hands over hers.

Ella gasped, encircled in his arms. "What are you doing?"

"Helping." He guided their hands to Sadie's teats. "Take hold."

When she complied, Cody wrapped his hands around hers. "Now, let's take this slowly, okay? One squirt at a time." He increased the pressure of his hands, helping Ella to squeeze and tug correctly. Milk began to stream into the pail.

She let out a delighted giggle. "It's working."

The scent of lavender assailed his senses. Cody leaned closer, his nose almost buried in Ella's silky hair. He closed his eyes and breathed her in. He hadn't been allured by a woman in so long, he'd forgotten what it felt like to be swept up in a moment. For a few blissful seconds, he let himself get washed away like a wave leaving the shore.

"Cody?"

Too late, he realized their hands had stilled. When he met her eyes, they were only inches apart. Ella's were wide, her breath escaping in shallow gasps through parted lips. The desire to kiss her returned. The slightest of movements would make that a reality. Would Ella welcome his advances, or would he shatter the trust that had been building between them?

Deep down, he knew the answer. With every ounce of self-control he possessed, Cody lurched backward, rising to his feet. "I think you've got it. Give it a go on your own."

Confusion wrinkled Ella's forehead. She stared at him unblinking before breaking eye contact. "Of course." He barely caught her mumbled words. She began to milk again, proving that she had indeed gotten the concept down.

Cody backed out of Sadie's stall. "I'll work on Becky."

Ella nodded without a word. The silence between them hung heavy. Cody chastised himself for his stupidity. His wife clearly needed to heal from whatever happened in her past, and he'd nearly messed up.

That could not happen again.

~

*E*lla strolled down the street toward the seamstress's shop on Saturday afternoon. Cassie had volunteered to watch the children so Ella and Cody could get some things done in town. Thankful for the reprieve, they'd decided to split up so they could finish faster. Cassie promised them a hearty lunch once they got back to her house. Cody gave Ella the choice of whether to visit the mercantile for some groceries or the seamstress shop to check on the clothes they'd ordered. Awed at the fact that he gave her a choice, she picked the seamstress shop.

Mrs. Greyson grinned when Ella came through the door. "Mrs. Brooks, how lovely to see you. Are you here to pick up the outfits?"

"Yes, ma'am."

"I'm not finished with all your dresses, but some are complete. The children's and Mr. Brooks's clothes are done and wrapped. Would you like to see the dresses before I wrap them?"

While she didn't mind one way or another, Ella sensed Mrs.

Greyson would gain some happiness by showing off her work. "I'd love to."

The older woman beamed. "Excellent. Let me get those for you." She bustled to a rack. "Here's the first one."

Ella smiled in approval, taking in the navy dress. Simple and practical. "It's perfect."

"I'm glad you like it." Mrs. Greyson replaced it and pulled another dress out. "This one will be stunning on you."

Ella blinked. The light-blue fabric boasted tiny white flowers throughout, bringing to mind a meadow on a summer's day. It was lovely, but not a fabric she chose. "That's not my dress."

"Of course it is, dearie. Mr. Brooks selected it himself. Along with this one." She took another dress from the rack. The color matched that of a holly leaf, with lace trimming the collar and long sleeves. Ella pressed a hand to her lips, disbelief coursing through her. "My husband chose those?"

"That he did. He's got a good eye."

Slowly, as if in a trance, Ella reached out and touched the green fabric. It felt smooth as butter under her touch, but it also possessed a solid durability. Beautiful and practical. Not something she would have expected from Cody, but his thoughtful gesture chipped away another section of the wall surrounding her fragile heart.

"I didn't know."

Mrs. Greyson grinned. "That's the best part. He let it be a surprise." She sighed, a hand over her heart. "Love is a beautiful thing, isn't it?"

Ella wouldn't know, but she forced a smile and didn't correct the woman's assumption.

Mrs. Greyson must have taken that as agreement. She gathered up the three dresses. "I'll just wrap these and get the other packages. Is your wagon outside?"

"It will be shortly. Cody said he'd meet me here once he's finished at the mercantile."

"Perfect. Give me five minutes." The woman hurried to the back of the shop, dresses in hand. Ella wandered the aisles, but she didn't see the fabric. Her mind turned to her husband and the way he gifted her two dresses. What struck her most was that she'd noticed both fabrics when choosing dresses but thought them too pretty for ranch life. Yet they were the ones he picked for her.

What had been his motivation? A little shiver went through her. Howard had sent her gifts of clothing on occasion, usually when there was a big event they were expected to attend together. Never once had he chosen something she liked, but she'd worn it anyway to appease him. Cody, after knowing her such a short time, picked something she would have chosen for herself. She didn't know what to make of that.

She couldn't deny the kindness he possessed. He might hide it from the world behind a stoic exterior, but living with him proved his heart was true. She already knew him to be a good, protective man. Travis and Cassie trusted him. And there was their interaction in the barn yesterday, a memory that still took her breath away.

Sparks had churned between them when she noticed how close their faces were. For a moment, she'd been sure he was about to kiss her. Equal parts panic and anticipation filled her, and Ella still couldn't say which had been stronger. When he backed away as if struck, disappointment and relief flooded her. Never before had she felt both emotions at the same time. Her reaction confused her.

A little sigh left her lips. For so long, she'd been a romantic, hoping for a love that stood the test of time. Howard broke her of that dream. She'd thought she had no choice but to marry him. Then that fateful night happened when she took her future into her own hands. Running away might have been foolish, but it led her here. And Harmony Springs was taking hold of her heart as surely as…

Ella jolted from her thoughts as a rough hand grasped her arm. Someone spun her around with a grunt. "I ought to have known you'd be flittering away your time in a dress shop."

Her heart plummeted to her stomach. She knew that voice. When she raised her eyes, fear clawed her insides. "Father. What are you doing here?"

"That's all you have to say for yourself?" Giving her a shake, his hand dug harder into her upper arm. "How could you, Ariella? Do you have any idea the scandal you've caused by disappearing without a word?"

Some of her fear diminished as her spirit rose to the surface. "Scandal? *Scandal*? You don't care about what happens to me in private, but you're concerned when it impacts *your* image?" She jerked away, tearing herself from his grip. "If you're so worried about scandal, you should never have engaged me to Howard!"

A resounding slap sent her reeling backward. Ella's hand went to her stinging cheek.

Her father advanced, his eyes hard. "That connection is best for our families. Howard was heartbroken by your disappearance. You're coming back with me and making things right."

The unladylike snort that escaped her made Father frown. Ella backed away farther, putting a table of cloth between them. "I'm not going anywhere. Harmony Springs is my home."

Father sneered. "I say what you are going to do, and you're coming with me." He rounded the table with alarming speed, once more grabbing her arm. Ella's fear flared up again. She struggled against his strong grip. "No! Let me go!"

A new voice broke into the fray, gruff and familiar. "Get your hands off of *my wife*."

All at once, Father stumbled away. Ella's hand went to her arm. Already, she could feel a bruise forming. Her eyes found her father again. His face was red with anger as he tried to wiggle away from Cody, who held him in a vice grip. Her husband wore a thunderous expression. Gone was the soft-hearted bear. With her father, he was all grizzly.

Father recovered his composure. "I beg your pardon, sir." His voice took on the cordial quality that fooled many a member of society. "You must have the wrong young lady. This is my daughter, Ariella Mountbatten. I've come to bring her home."

"I know who you are, and I know my wife. She's Ella Brooks now."

His voice held a note of possessiveness that screamed *mine!* Under any other circumstances, it would've raised Ella's hackles. Right now, it felt downright protective. She wanted to scurry into the shelter of his arms and never let go.

Her father laughed, a note of scorn in the sound. He glanced at Ella. "You mean to tell me you've been here a couple weeks and married this..." His eyes turned to Cody, scanning him up and down. Disdain marred his face. "Farmer?"

"Rancher." Cody released her father and stepped to her side. He held out his arm.

Ella scooted beneath it, gratified when he looped it around her and pulled her close. She burrowed into him. His strength calmed her. He would keep her safe, of that she was sure.

Father's eyes narrowed. "I don't believe you. My daughter would never marry someone so beneath her. And in so short a time!"

Cody growled, the sound dangerous. "Believe it."

Mrs. Greyson appeared from the back room, her arms full of parcels. "Here we are," she chirped. "I'm sorry you'll have to come back for the remainder of the dresses, Mrs. Brooks. I hope it won't be too much of an inconvenience." She stopped when she saw Ella's father. "Good afternoon, sir. I'll be with you as soon as I finish with Mr. and Mrs. Brooks."

For once, Father was struck dumb. He stared at the seamstress, then at Cody, then at Ella. And his anger erupted. "This is a conspiracy!"

Mrs. Greyson frowned. "Whatever do you mean?"

"This man"—he jabbed a finger in Cody's direction—"is *not* married to my daughter. Not when she is engaged to someone else."

Ella bristled. "Cody is my husband. You might not like the fact, but a fact it remains."

Her father took a step forward.

Cody matched it, standing in front of Ella to shield her. "You will not touch her again. She is no longer under your thumb."

The bell above the door jingled. Ella peeked around Cody's broad back to see Travis enter the shop. She took her place against her husband once more as Travis crossed his arms over his chest. "Trouble here, folks?"

Father turned. His face reddened. "You!"

"Mr. Mountbatten." Though Travis wore an even expression, his eyes sparked fire. "I'd say it's a pleasure, but I don't care for lying."

"You had something to do with this, didn't you?" Father poked Travis in the chest. "*Didn't you?*"

"Careful, sir." Travis's eyes became pools of steel. "Assaulting a law enforcement officer earns jail time in these parts." He took a step forward, every inch of his expression threatening. "And your people can't help you here."

For the first time, something resembling fear crossed her father's face. He looked around the room again, his gaze landing on Ella. "This isn't finished, Ariella." With that, he burst through the door of the shop and thundered down the street.

Ella's legs gave out. She slid toward the floor, but Cody

caught her up in his arms. "Easy, darlin'," he murmured. "I've got you."

She clung to him, not caring that Travis and Mrs. Greyson witnessed her trembling. "If you hadn't come in…"

He rubbed her back. "But I did. We'll get through this."

Ella closed her eyes, drawing strength from his certainty and praying hard that he was right.

CHAPTER 11

*D*inner at the Doyle house felt solemn. Cody appreciated the fact that Travis and Cassie tried to keep the conversation going, but Ella retreated into herself. They said their goodbyes earlier than usual. When his wife stared blankly at the wagon floor the entire trip, Cody began to worry. For the sake of the children, he kept quiet. He didn't want to scare them. But after they were in bed, he invited Ella to the kitchen.

She followed, hands folded and eyes downcast. Cody helped her sit before making two strong cups of chamomile tea. He watched Ella as he dolloped honey into her cup. Was this how she lived life in Boston? Constantly submissive and frightened? His heart hurt for her.

When the tea was ready, he brought it to the table. As he sat, he slid a cup her way. "Drink this."

Ella lifted the cup to her lips. The movement looked stilted, as if she did it only to appease him.

Cody reached out, grasping her hand. "Darlin'…"

Her gaze met his, her eyes looking straight through him. The bleakness in her expression sent ice galloping through his veins. He put a hand on her cheek. "Hey. It's going to be all right."

A tear slid down her cheek. "You don't know that." Her whisper came out full of anguish.

Cody tightened his grip on her hand. "You're my wife, Ella. It's my job to protect you. That's exactly what I intend to do."

More tears escaped her eyes. "You're more than I deserve. I'm broken, Cody. You should have a wife who can give her heart to you without painful baggage."

"I come with baggage too. Yours doesn't frighten me. We'll get through this together."

She sighed softly. "How do you do that?"

"Do what?"

"Switch from grizzly to softy without batting an eye."

Cody let out a startled laugh. "What?"

A tiny smile lifted Ella's lips. "With me, you sometimes display gruff tendencies, but I think that's just who you are. More often than not, you show tenderness and kindness. With my father, you were menacing. Terrifying, almost. I would have been afraid if that had been directed at me. But since you were protecting me, I felt safe." She covered their joined hands with her other one. "It doesn't make sense, but I feel more protected with you than with anyone else."

A jolt of electricity passed through him. "Surely, Travis deserves that honor."

Her gaze remained on his. "A few hours ago, I would have agreed. But the way you handled my father showed me you can stand up for others. I think I knew deep down that you would. Now I have proof."

Her praise warmed him. He squeezed her hand. "I can't promise to always be soft with you, Ella. It's not in my nature. But I do promise to be good to you. I will stand up for you, for the kids, for my sister and Travis. That's what family does."

She blinked rapidly. "The only member of my family who cared before was my sister."

Cody watched her for a moment, debating within himself. Finally, he asked the question that had been burning inside since the confrontation in the store. "What happened, Ella? Why did you leave Boston?"

She inhaled sharply. Her hands tensed on his. Cody released them, and she wrapped her fingers around her mug of tea. He waited while she took a few sips. Hoping his question hadn't been too forward, he sipped on his own drink while his wife regained her composure. An eternal minute later, she spoke.

"My parents were always determined that I should marry well. They set strict guidelines on who I could see, with a list of how potential suitors would benefit the Mountbatten name. Every man who sought a courtship had to go through my father." She took a long breath and another sip of tea before continuing. "The first man to court me was Miles Stranham. In my naïveté, I thought he harbored tender feelings for me. It turned out he only wanted my money. My parents wanted the prestige that came with his family name. Miles used me as surely as my parents used him."

Cody's hands itched to take Ella's again, but he sensed the timing wasn't right. Her eyes looked glassy while her memories flowed.

"I refused several suitors after that, nursing a bruised heart. Howard was the first man to catch my interest again. We'd known each other for several years, both of our families coming from old money. He didn't seem like the kind of man who needed my wealth. Howard said all the sweet things and took me on romantic dates. I was blinded by his charm. When he asked me to marry him a couple months into our courtship, I had no reservations." A shuddering breath shook her. "After we got engaged, things changed. He wouldn't commit to a wedding date, pushing it off time and again. Then he got annoyed at the smallest things. At first, I attributed it to him feeling pressure at taking over the Archambeau holdings from his father. Then he began to criticize everything I said or did. Nothing was ever good enough for him. And then..." She swallowed hard, looking down at the table.

Maybe now was the time. Cody reached out, laying his hand palm up on the table, giving Ella the choice whether to take it or not. She stared at his hand for a minute before slowly sliding her palm into his. Cody curled his fingers around hers. "Take your time, darlin'. There's no rush."

She gave him a grateful look. Two sips of tea later, she started again. "He became abusive. At first it was his words, but eventually, he hit me whenever I disagreed with him. That's when I got frightened. I told my parents, but they dismissed my fears. They said I had a duty to the family, a duty to bring in more wealth and power. Howard had both. I showed them the bruises, thinking that might sway them."

Anger swept through Cody. "It didn't?"

"My mother told me I would marry Howard no matter what. My father said he'd add to the bruises if I broke the engagement as I said I would."

Cody's blood boiled. "He what?"

Ella sighed. Cody resisted the urge to saddle Preston, gallop into town, and show Mr. Mountbatten the kind of treatment a man who threatened his own daughter deserved.

"I suppose I'd always hoped that despite their cold demeanor, my parents loved me." Ella laughed, the sound harsh. "Apparently, I was wrong. In the three years I was engaged to Howard, only Tori took my side as he became more and more abusive. Sometimes I had bruises that lasted for weeks."

He had to restrain himself from reacting. Cody drew in a

long breath through his nose. "Men like that should be locked up."

Ella pursed her lips. "And that's not the worst of it."

Dread crept over him. "There's more?"

Her fingers tightened around his. "For all his abuse, Howard never tried to...press for favors better left for marriage." Her cheeks flushed a deep pink. "The extent of his physical affection—when things were good—was kissing my hand at the end of an evening. About a week before I left Boston, he tried to kiss my lips. I was shocked and turned away before he could. He got angry, calling me horrible names. He thought with the wedding only a month away, he was entitled to certain liberties. I disagreed."

If he'd been angry before, it was nothing compared to what he felt now. Cody clenched his teeth. "Did he press you?"

"Not that night." Ella closed her eyes. "But the night I ran away? Yes. He'd been drinking at a party we attended. I left early, thinking he'd stay and mingle with other members of society. Instead, he followed me home." When she opened her eyes, her mind seemed far away. "He barged into my room. I got mad and insisted he leave. He laughed. Laughed!" Indignation flashed over her face. "As if my request was ludicrous. When I told him again to leave, he trapped me against the wall. I screamed, but no one came."

Cold fear swept through Cody's heart. "Did he...?" He couldn't finish the question, but Ella shook her head.

"He tried, but no. There were a couple hat pins within reach. I managed to grab one and stabbed him with it."

"That was brave."

Ella sighed. "Or stupid. That's when he gave me the worst beating yet. It's why I had those bruises when I came to Harmony Springs. I'd never seen him so angry. Tori came home then and found us. She brought one of the footmen with her, a burly man who threw Howard out. When my parents got home, we told them what happened. Tori made a passionate case for why the engagement should be over. My mother and father didn't let her finish. They repeated my duty was to the family and that I would marry Howard at the end of the month. That's when I knew I had to leave."

Silence filled the space between them. Cody ached for his wife. She'd known such sorrow and pain. He slipped an arm around her shoulder. "You did the right thing, Ella. It was the smart option."

She looked at him with clear eyes. "I'm glad I came."

Her words curled around him, layers of meaning unspoken. Cody's heart hitched, then galloped. The trust shining in Ella's eyes meant more to him than anything had in a long time. They sat quietly for a moment, hands linked as he processed what she'd told him. Something still didn't make sense. "Why was your father so insistent on Howard in particular? Surely, there were other men who would have been suitable."

Ella's brow furrowed. "I'm not sure. He let me break up with Miles. My father is a stubborn man, so his demand that I marry Howard felt in line with his character. But now that you ask..." Her voice trailed off and her frown deepened. "That is odd."

"Maybe the morning will bring something to light." Cody stood, gathering the teacups. "It's getting late. We should turn in. You've had a hard day."

She chuckled, no humor in the sound. "It was going well enough until *he* showed up." Ella wrapped her arms around herself. "Cody, what if he tries again? What if he shows up when you're at work?"

Cody plunked the cups in the sink before turning to her. "Have you ever shot a gun?"

Her face blanched. "No."

He reached out, cupping her arms gently. "I'm not suggesting you'll have to use it. But if your father comes here and tries to make you leave, it would give you and the children a measure of defense."

"Is that really necessary?"

Cody felt her shiver. "This is the West, Ella. There are all kinds of dangers here, wild animals and snakes chief among them. Knowing how to shoot is a skill most people have in these parts. I'd feel better if you could defend yourself if the need came up." He slid a hand to her shoulder. "Though I hope I'll be here if you ever need protecting."

Her cheeks turned pink. "So do I." Biting her lip, Ella glanced at the floor, then met his eyes again. "But if it gives you peace of mind, I don't mind learning."

"Good. We'll start first thing in the morning."

Ella's eyes widened. "So soon?"

"Darlin', your father is here now. The sooner the better."

She chewed her lower lip. Cody's glance landed there without thinking. He jerked his eyes back up in time to see Ella look at him.

"All right."

Relief flooded him. "Thanks." He let her go, stuffing his hands in his pockets. "You're probably wondering what kind of man you married, huh?"

He meant it as a joke, a way of lightening the mood, but Ella studied him with a serious air.

"You're the kind of man who buys pretty dresses for his wife because he thinks she'll like them."

Cody cleared his throat, heat crawling up his neck. "Mrs. Greyson told you?"

She smiled. "I was bound to find out, wasn't I?"

"I suppose so." He rubbed at the stubble on his cheek.

She tilted her head, gaze steady on his. "You had no ulterior motive, did you? You did it because you thought I'd like them."

The temperature of his skin increased. "Something like that."

Moisture welled in her eyes. "I thought so." Leaning forward, she slid her arms around his waist. "Thank you. The dresses are lovely."

As he had on the night they'd talked about poetry, Cody froze in place. This time, though, he recovered quickly enough to wrap his arms around her before she pulled away. They stood for a few long seconds, close enough for him to feel her heartbeat against his chest.

Pure, strong affection rose inside of him. Ella was becoming a very important part of his life. They might not have known each other long, but for better or worse, she was his wife, and he'd do anything to keep her safe.

Ella huddled in her coat near the barn, eying the shotgun in Cody's hands. Morning sunlight glinted off the shiny metal. The weapon looked menacing. She'd never liked guns, and the thought of shooting one didn't sit well with her. But if it allowed her to protect her family and gave her husband less to worry about, it would be worth pushing through her discomfort.

Cody glanced her way. His half smile pulled at his lips. "It's not gonna bite you, darlin'. You can come closer."

She preferred the safe distance between her and the gun for as long as possible. "Just let me know when you're ready for the lesson."

"I'm ready. C'mon."

Ella took halting steps in his direction. When she reached his side, Cody nodded toward a tree ten yards away. "That's your target. We're going to practice shooting at something large before moving to a smaller target."

"Smaller?" When did her voice get so squeaky?

Cody slipped an arm around her shoulders, giving her a single squeeze before letting go. "It'll be fine, Ella. I promise."

She inhaled through her nose. "All right. Let's get to it."

"To start, lift the butt of the gun to your right shoulder." He demonstrated, then held the gun out to her. "You try."

The weight of the weapon hung heavy in her hands. Ella hoisted it up and attempted to copy the position Cody showed her. "Like this?"

"Not exactly." He put a hand on her shoulder. "May I?"

She nodded. Cody moved behind her, his arms encircling her as he reached both hands for the gun. "You nestle the back right here in the hollow of your shoulder." He pulled the gun to the correct location, pushing it snugly against Ella's shoulder. "Feel how that holds it in place?"

All she could feel was Cody's strong chest resting against her back, pushing all thoughts of the hunk of metal in her hands far from her mind. "Mm-hmm."

"Then you hold it firmly with both hands." He cupped her hands in his, moving them to the right spot on the gun. Ella closed her eyes and inhaled his woodsy scent. When had pine and cedar wood become such a comforting smell?

"Now all you have to do is aim and pull the trigger...and brace for the kickback. Your jacket should absorb some of the shock."

That brought her back to reality. "Does it hurt a lot?"

"It might sting at first, but you'll get used to it. The tighter you hold the gun against your shoulder, the less it will hurt. Now, close your left eye and locate the tree."

Ella did as instructed.

Cody released her but didn't step away. "Fire when ready."

She let out her breath and squeezed the trigger. The gunshot exploded in her ear. She staggered backward into Cody, her shoulder buzzing as she dropped the weapon.

His hands landed on her upper arms. "The hardest part is over."

Rubbing the sting away, Ella peeked up at him. "It is?"

"Yep. Though we'll have to see about your aim." He winked and scooped up the gun, then started for the tree. Ella gaped after him, amazed that a simple wink could send her heart fluttering. This man, this husband of hers, was breaking through her defenses all too easily, gruff exterior and all, chipping away at her walls one block at a time.

"Not bad!" he called, breaking into her thoughts. "You grazed the tree. That's a good start. Try again."

They spent the next half hour working on her new skill. By the end of it, she could hit the middle of the tree without much problem. Cody grinned like a proud parent. "I'd say this was a success. Next time, we'll work on a smaller target."

"Thanks for teaching me." They walked toward the house. Ella massaged her shoulder. The pressure gave slight release to her aches. "It does give me a bit more peace of mind."

"Good. I'll keep the gun loaded, but far out of reach of the children. There's a rack above the front door that will hold it. You should be able to get to it easily if needed." He exhaled slowly. "Though I pray you never need to."

When they got to the house, Cody hung the weapon above the door. Ella reached up to test the height. To her relief, she could retrieve it without a problem.

He touched her shoulder. "How does it feel?"

"Not great, but nothing I can't handle."

Little footsteps sounded upstairs. They both looked up, then at each other. Ella braced herself for Cody's departure. "I'll get the kids ready. You probably need to get out to the fields."

"I'm not going."

Ella blinked. "You're not?"

"No. I found Hank early this morning and asked him to keep things running today. The boys will be fine on their own."

Suspicion raced through her. "Is it because of me?"

"It's because of your father. I don't feel right leaving you here on your own, not until we have a handle on what he's up to."

"But...are you sure? I know Hank is capable, but you're the boss. What if they need you?"

"Then they know where to find me." Cody shrugged out of his winter coat, hanging it on the rack before helping Ella out of hers. "We haven't really gotten to spend time together as a family, at least not for a full day. Consider this a bonding experience for us all."

Ella couldn't help staring at the man she'd married. He gave her another half smile, then turned toward the kitchen. "If you get the kids ready, I'll make breakfast."

CHAPTER 12

*H*e should take days off more often.

Cody looked around at his unconventional family. They sat on the parlor floor, a blanket spread out beneath them with a picnic basket in the middle. Ella had suggested the indoor picnic. The children were intrigued by her idea. Isaiah even grew excited, making suggestions about the kind of food they should have on their "picnic."

A fire roared in the grate nearby, keeping them cozy. Addie sat contentedly in Cody's lap. Jonah glued himself to Ella. Isaiah kept a bit of distance, throwing Ella guarded looks on occasion, but he seemed to be enjoying himself overall.

His wife wore the flowered blue dress Cody chose for her. As she doled out food, he admired her. Yes, she possessed a rare and natural beauty, but she also had a strength of character that made her stunning. Might real love eventually find them? Though his heart seized at the thought of being that vulnerable again, another part of him deeply desired the connection that came from loving a woman.

He also knew it was too soon to contemplate that. Ella

might trust him, but their arrangement was a practical one, and his own heart stood in need of healing. He'd be content with friendship for now.

Ella handed him a plate. The scent of savory roast beef, spicy mustard, and tangy pickles filled his nostrils. Mouth watering, he took a big bite.

"Mmm." He raised the sandwich in Ella's direction. "Very good."

She took her own bite. A look of pleasant surprise crossed her face. "It is."

"You thought it wouldn't be?"

Isaiah piped in before Ella could. "She makes yucky tea, but her food is good."

A smile took over the surprise on Ella's face. "Thank you, Isaiah. That was a sweet compliment."

"Don't get used to it."

Cody ruffled Isaiah's hair. "Is that any way to talk to your mama?"

Isaiah froze. Defiance filled his eyes. "She's not my mama."

Whoops. Cody tried to smooth things over. "I didn't mean any disrespect to your first mama, Isaiah. She loved you very much, and I think she'd be happy to know that your Aunt Ella is taking care of you now that she can't."

Tears welled in the child's eyes. "I miss her."

Cody shifted Addie, about to reach for Isaiah, but Ella spoke first. "Isaiah, I know I'll never replace your mother. I don't want to. She has a very special place in your life. You'll always love her." She held out her hand. "But if you don't mind, I'll do my best to make her proud by raising you and your brother and sister with lots of love and happiness. We can make a family together. I think your mama would like that, don't you?"

Isaiah stared at her hand. Cody held his breath, wondering if the boy would accept it or throw a tantrum. Slowly, Isaiah reached out and slipped his little hand into Ella's. "You think Mama is happy we're here?"

"I didn't know her, but I do know most mothers want what's best for their children. If your parents asked Uncle Cody to be your guardian, they must have known he'd take good care of you. So yes, I do think she's happy you're here."

With a little cry, Isaiah threw his arms around Ella's neck, burying his face in her shoulder. She blinked. The look on her face grew tender. She encircled Isaiah's body with her arms, gently rocking him.

Jonah pressed into her side, gazing up at her. She smiled at him, earning a rare, answering smile from the toddler. He got to his feet and tilted his head. One chubby hand reached out, resting on her shoulder. "Mama?"

Cody's mouth dropped open. Jonah hadn't said a word since Jake and Harriet died. Then what he'd said registered, and Cody's heart pounded.

Ella stared at the child, shock written on her face. "What did you say, sweetie?"

"Mama." He whispered the word. This time, it sounded less like a question and more like a statement.

Isaiah peered at his brother, frowning. "She's not our mama."

Jonah frowned back. "My mama."

Isaiah looked as though he wanted to argue the point.

Cody put a hand on the boy's back. "It's all right if Jonah chooses to call Aunt Ella that, Isaiah. It's up to him. You don't have to if you don't want to."

"But she's our aunt."

Ella interjected softly. "I can be both. If Jonah wants to call me Mama, that's fine. If you want to call me Aunt Ella, that's fine too. I love you both the same, no matter my title."

"Humph." Isaiah let his hands drop from Ella's neck,

though he didn't go far. He plopped down on the floor beside her. "That's weird."

Cody's lips twitched. "That's life, buddy."

A knock sounded at the door. Ella's glance darted in that direction before finding Cody's. Pure panic filled her face.

Cody stood, balancing Addie in one arm and placing his other hand on Ella's back. "It's all right. If it's him, I'll send him packing."

Her expression eased. Cody leaned down, handing the baby to his wife. "I'll be right back." He looked at the kids. "The three of you stay with Aunt Ella."

"Mama," Jonah insisted, snuggling against her side and clinging to her arm.

At least that should put a smile on her face. Cody walked for the door. He put a hand on the sidearm he wore before opening it. Relief made his body sag. "Travis. Good to see you."

His friend eyed the gun strapped to his hip. "There a reason you're wearing that in the house?"

"I'll give you one guess."

Travis nodded his approval. "You're taking care of that wife of yours. Good. She's fortunate to have you at her side."

Cody's blood heated anew at the memory of how roughly Ella's father had handled her. "I can't believe such an awful man produced a daughter as sweet and kind as Ella."

"That's part of the reason she's so skittish."

"Makes sense." Cody stepped to the side, waving Travis in. "Where's the man staying?"

"He left town this morning."

Cody's head snapped up. "He what?"

"That's why I came. I wanted to let you know."

"Ella'll want to hear that."

He led the way to the parlor. Ella looked up. The same relief Cody felt reflected on her face. "Hello, Travis."

"Good to see you, Ella. I came by to let you know your father left town on the morning train."

"Really?" She frowned, hugging Addie closer. "That's odd. He never gives up that easily. I expected him to remain in town and try convincing me to leave...or threatening me somehow."

Travis scratched his beard. "It does seem out of character. Maybe he saw the futility of it, seeing as how you're hitched to this guy." He jerked a thumb at Cody.

"Hey! 'This guy' has a name, thanks." Cody nudged his friend.

Travis nudged him right back. Cody appreciated the levity Travis brought to the moment. Ella, however, looked worried. She chewed on her lower lip, a sign Cody had come to realize showed her concern. Her mouth opened, then she looked down at the children.

Cody read her thoughts as if they were displayed on paper. She didn't want to frighten the kids. He stepped toward them. "Isaiah, Jonah, why don't you play with blocks once you finish eating? Aunt Ella and I are going to talk to Sheriff Travis for a bit."

"Okay." Isaiah reached for his plate.

Cody helped Ella to her feet, noting the way she held Addie carefully against her. Jonah joined Isaiah, leaving the adults free to talk. They moved into the hall, away from the little ears.

Travis leaned against the wall, his eyes on Ella. "Are you worried your father might try again?"

"Maybe. I just can't figure out why he left. And there's something else, something Cody and I talked about last night."

Cody slipped his arm around her shoulder. She gave him a little smile, then focused on Travis again. "My father refused to let me break my engagement to Howard. He was unreasonable about the whole thing, which makes no sense. There are any number of men I could have married if it was simply about the money. Why insist on it being Howard?"

Travis tapped a finger against his leg. "Pride, maybe? Your engagement was well-known, and the connection was highly enviable. To break it off would have raised more questions than your father wanted."

"Perhaps." Ella rested her head against Addie's. A silent sigh lifted and lowered her shoulders. She wasn't convinced.

He let his hand move from her shoulder to her lower back. "You don't think that's it?"

She raised those luminous green eyes to his. "I think it's a valid point, and likely part of the truth. I just can't help feeling there's more to it."

"Then we need to be vigilant." Travis pushed up from the wall. "I'll contact a friend of mine on the Boston force. He might be able to dig around, find out if something's off."

Ella let out a soft breath. "Thank you, Travis."

He nodded. "In the meantime, try to enjoy your freedom. If your father learned anything in his time here, it's that your husband won't let him push either of you around. I think he finally got a lesson he couldn't ignore."

Ella gazed up at Cody, a gentle smile on her lips. "Indeed."

That single look stayed with him the rest of the day. Who knew gratitude could be so warming? In Ella's eyes, he found the respect he hadn't known he wanted.

~

A full week after her father left, Ella was able to relax. There had been no word from him. They hadn't heard from Travis's friend on the force either. Nothing to corroborate her anxious thought that there might be more to the story.

Life settled back into a comfortable routine. Jonah continued to call her Mama, melting Ella's heart more with each use of the word. Isaiah appeared to be conflicted over his brother's choice, but he stopped correcting Jonah after a few days.

One afternoon, horse hooves sounded in the yard. Ella peered out the window, smiling when she recognized Cassie. She met her sister-in-law at the door with an embrace. Ella gave her a warm smile. "I'm surprised you're here. Did you shut down the café for the afternoon?"

Cassie removed her coat and hung it on a hook. "No. I have a couple ladies who work with me, and one of them took over when I said I wanted to come see you. I hope I'm not intruding."

"Not at all. Would you like some tea?"

"Yes, please."

Ella led the way to the kitchen. "Your timing is perfect. The kids got sleepy after lunch and are napping. We'll be able to have a conversation without interruption. At least until they wake up."

"I hear you've had a bit of a breakthrough with Jonah."

"We have. He's calling me Mama now. It's the only word he's said so far, but..." Her throat worked with raw emotion.

Cassie put a hand on her arm. "But you feel more like a mother now that he's given you the title?"

Ella nodded through her tears. "I'd been wondering what I could offer these children, hurting as they are. Jonah's acceptance of having me as a mother was more than I could have hoped for. Even Isaiah is resigned to my presence here, though he's struggling with the reason for it." She paused with a hand on the kettle. "He's broken, understandably so. His road to healing will be a long one. I just hope I'm patient enough to help him through it."

"You will be. There has been so much improvement already in the children. They are hurting and they will struggle, but that's life. You and Cody are hurting, too, for different reasons.

Family is a place where those hurts and struggles can be shared and eased in a healthy way, through love and grace."

Though a pang of sadness pierced her heart, Ella smiled. "I hope you're right. In my experience, family is a source of hurt."

Cassie waited until Ella put the kettle on the stove, then wrapped her in a hug.

Ella sighed, leaning against her friend for a few moments. When they pulled back, she wiped at a tear. "You and your brother didn't have an easy time of it either."

"No. But we knew our parents loved us. That makes a difference." Cassie took one of Ella's hands, giving it a squeeze. "Which is why Isaiah, Jonah, and Addie are blessed to have you. My brother wasn't sure what to do with the kids on his own. He was all thumbs when it came to their care. Since you've come along, he's more at ease with them. It's as if the pressure of being a single parent paralyzed him. Now that you're here, he's risen to the challenge because he knows he's not alone anymore." She wiped a tear of her own. "Thank you for being here for him. He needed you as much as you needed him."

A flush heated her cheeks. "I don't know if I'd go that far. Cody would have worked with another woman if necessary for the sake of the children."

"Oh, I'm sure he would have. But I don't think it'd have yielded the same result. You're good for each other." A twinkle filled Cassie's eyes. She leaned forward and lowered her voice to a whisper. "I'm calling it now. You two will be in love by summer's end."

Love? Heat zinged through her stomach, making it lurch. Ella sputtered. "Th-that's a bit of a leap. Cody and I are just finding our way to friendship. Love is a whole different feeling."

Cassie snorted. "Not really. In an ideal world, you would be married to your best friend. If you and my brother are getting to friendship already, especially considering your rocky start, the chances of you finding love are excellent." She tilted her head. "Don't tell me you never dreamed of love."

"Of course I did." The kettle whistled. Ella busied herself preparing the tea. "What girl doesn't hope for love?"

That hope had been smashed by life.

Cassie leaned against the counter. "And now that you're a woman?"

Ella poured steaming water into mugs. "By default, if I fall in love, it must be with my husband. I don't know if I hope for that. It feels..." She struggled to find the right word. "Strange." Her eyes widened, and she turned to Cassie. "What I meant was..."

Laughter danced in Cassie's eyes. "You don't have to explain. I understand. You do still hope for love, but you're married to Cody and have no other option for finding it. Thinking about falling in love with someone you haven't known long but are permanently connected to seems strange."

Ella let out a breath. "Precisely." She carried the mugs to the table and motioned for Cassie to sit. "Your brother is a good man. You were right—he's all soft under that gruff facade. I like him."

Cassie took up her mug. Her blue eyes, so like Cody's, considered Ella with grave intensity. "But you're afraid to be vulnerable enough with a man to lose your heart?"

Tears pricked her eyes. She stared down at the table. "Yes."

"I could tell you it'll all turn out all right, but none of us knows the future." Cassie reached out, covering Ella's left hand. "You don't have to force anything, Ella. Sometimes the best things in life happen naturally." She leaned back again, peering at Ella over the rim of her mug. "But please, don't close yourself off if you start falling. Don't shut Cody out because you're afraid. He deserves happiness too. I want that for you both."

Throat working, Ella nodded. "I'll try."

"Good. Now, I have some news to share with you." A wide grin filled Cassie's face.

The abrupt change in subject threw her, but Ella recovered, setting her cup down. "What's that?"

Cassie glowed as she rested a hand on her stomach. "Well—I had a visit with Doc today. Want to guess what he told me?"

Ella gasped, hands flying to her mouth. "Are you having a baby?"

"Yes!" Her friend squealed, eyes lit up with excitement. "Isn't that wonderful?"

"Amazing. How did Travis react?"

"He's over the moon. I think he's about to go into overprotective mode." Cassie rolled her eyes. "He actually said I should take the buggy to see you rather than riding my horse. Silly man." Her tone belied her words, warmth visible in her eyes. "Travis will be a great father."

"I can't wait to see that. What about Cody? Did you tell him?"

"Not yet." Cassie grinned. "I want to surprise him when he gets home this evening, if that's all right with you."

"Of course. Would you like to stay for supper?"

"Thank you—that sounds great."

Ella clasped Cassie's hand, giving it a light squeeze before letting go. "I'm happy for you. You must be so excited."

"I can't wait to meet this little one." Cassie lifted the cup to her lips, shooting Ella an innocent look. "When can I expect a niece or nephew?"

Choking on a sip of tea, Ella slapped a napkin to her mouth. "Cassie!"

"What?" Her friend looked like a perfect little imp, head tilted and eyes batting. "It's a legitimate question."

Never had Ella been asked something so forward. Her cheeks burned, and she scrambled for something to say. "That's not something Cody and I have talked about."

"Whyever not?"

Oh gracious, she wasn't going to get out of this. Ella cleared her throat. "Our marriage is different. This entire arrangement was one of necessity."

Cassie's eyes widened. "Is this a marriage of convenience? You don't plan on ever having kids?"

Ella shifted in her seat. "We never specified that."

"So there's a chance I'll get to see those nieces and nephews? You two would have such cute children."

How much more could her cheeks possibly heat? Ella picked up a napkin and fanned her face.

Cassie put a hand over her mouth, a little laugh escaping. "Oh dear. I've embarrassed you. I'm sorry. Sometimes I just say whatever comes to mind, and because I'm pregnant, I have babies on my brain."

Shaking her head, Ella managed a smile. "I know you mean well. To be honest, this is something Cody and I should have talked about before we got married. The only thing we agreed on was that we couldn't promise the other love." She lifted one shoulder. "Going into this marriage, I just assumed that it would be one of practicality. I didn't consider the idea of having children with him."

Cassie rested her arms on the table. "Did you want them before you married my brother?"

"I did. One of my dreams was to have a big family." She swallowed down the pain that arose at the thought of never nurturing a little life within. "Now I have three. That might have to be enough."

"Ella, you need to talk to Cody."

Heat rushed through her entire body. Just the thought of having such a conversation mortified her. "No. I can't bring that up."

Cassie grasped her hand, looking Ella straight in the eyes. "You can. Communication is essential to a healthy marriage, no matter how it came about. This is a topic that needs approaching. Especially if you always dreamed of having children."

The thought terrified her, but Cassie had a point. Ella gulped in a breath. "Awkward conversations are not my strong point."

Gifting her a gentle smile, Cassie released her hand. "You're stronger than you think, Ella. You can do this. The hardest part is starting the conversation."

Certain she was the color of a tomato, Ella drained the rest of her tea. "I'll think about it."

CHAPTER 13

Cody leaned against the porch railing, inhaling the frigid night air. Early March was upon them. Spring would soon arrive, but for now, the cold of winter remained. He crossed his arms over his chest and surveyed the darkened landscape. All looked peaceful.

His lips curved in a smile. Cassie's news at dinner surprised him, but he was happy for his sister and Travis. They'd take to parenting like a duck to water.

The door creaked open behind him. Cody glanced over his shoulder to see Ella emerge from the house. He turned to face her. "I thought you went to bed."

"Not yet." She had a thick blanket wrapped around her body, shielding her from winter's chill. "There's something I want to discuss with you."

Noting the hesitation in her voice, Cody motioned toward the porch swing. "Let's sit."

They settled on the swing. Silence fell between them for several long minutes. Ella exhaled, her breath puffing white in the air. "It's beautiful here at night. The stars look bigger than they did in Boston."

Cody gazed upwards. The heavens practically shone with the white dots. He rarely noticed, having seen it every day since coming to Montana. But now, seeing the stars through Ella's eyes, he once more appreciated the beauty and peace. He let another minute pass before looking her way. "What is it you wanted to talk about?"

She sucked in a breath, avoiding his gaze. "It's not that I *want* to talk about it, exactly. Something came up today while Cassie was here, and...it's something we should...uh..."

His curiosity heightened. "Something we should talk about?"

Ella nodded rapidly. Her breath came in quick gasps.

Cody grew alarmed. "Hey." He looped his arm around her shoulder, pulling her close. The movement was jerkier than he intended. Ella let out a small squeak. He gentled his hold. "Sorry."

She finally met his eyes. "I'm sorry. I knew this wasn't going to be easy, but I didn't anticipate such a case of nerves."

What in the world did she want to tell him? He squinted, thinking of anything Cassie might have brought up. "Did my sister talk about anything other than babies today?"

He meant it as a joke, but Ella stiffened. "That's it."

"What's it?"

"That's what she thought we needed to talk about."

His brows shot up. "*She* thought we had to discuss... babies?"

Ella nodded, her eyes finding the stars once more. Based on her reaction and the tenseness in her body, Cody could imagine what Cassie said. "Oh no." He scrubbed a hand over his face, his voice gruff. "Please tell me she didn't."

"She's just trying to help." Ella avoided his gaze. She wrung her hands together. Was the movement unconscious? He placed his one large hand over both of hers. Ella slumped forward a bit, then turned to face him. "I might have admitted to her that I always wanted children of my own. She asked if that was still the case."

His heart stuttered. "And?"

She chewed on her lip, her breathing once more picking up speed. "And...well, yes. That's still my heart's desire." Was it his imagination, or did her face turn darker?

Ella plunged on. "But our relationship...it's not that kind of marriage. Or rather, we never really defined what it would be. And we don't love each other, so...it just seems...it seems like our marriage is one of convenience."

Cody sat still as a stone, processing her words. She wanted children. He'd never stopped to think about starting a family, considering he'd inherited a ready-made one. It hadn't occurred to him that his wife might want babies. In hindsight, he should have thought about it. Most women wanted that.

The full implication of what that meant for their relationship smacked him in the face. Cody tugged at his collar, suddenly warm. He got to his feet and rubbed his neck. Ella wasn't the only one sporting a blush. He paced the length of the porch a couple times before stopping in front of her. His wife watched him, the blanket surrounding her like a shield.

How to approach such a topic? Cody leaned against one of the porch rails and faced Ella. "I admit this isn't something that ever crossed my mind. Are you wanting a baby...soon?"

"No!" Her tone held a note of panic. "Of course not. I'm still getting used to mothering the three we have now."

"Ahh...good. That's good."

He sounded like a stammering schoolboy. Cody rammed a hand through his hair.

Ella rose. "Did you hope for a family? Before...all this?"

Memories assailed him. Cody clenched his teeth, wanting to push them away, but that wouldn't help the situation. "A long time ago, yes."

Ella stepped closer. "What happened?"

She'd opened up to him about her past. Maybe it was time for him to do the same. Cody drew in a deep breath. "When I was nineteen, I thought myself in love. Liza and I met at a barn raising for a neighboring family. She'd come West in hopes of adventure and romance. The fact that she showed interest in me, an orphan with nothing, bolstered my pride. I was sure I didn't deserve her, but she insisted she loved me. We were together for a year before I asked her to be my wife. She said yes."

He closed his eyes with a shake of his head. How foolish he'd been. And so, so young. "She always talked about wanting to continue on to California. I thought when she agreed to marry me that she'd put that behind her. Looking back, the warning signs were there. I ignored them, thinking our love would be enough for her." He sighed. "I was dead wrong."

Ella put a hand on his arm. "What happened?"

"Our wedding day arrived. It was a small affair, just Cassie and a few of our friends. When the church doors opened, I expected to see her walk down the aisle in a white dress. Instead, she wore a yellow traveling outfit and announced she was heading to California."

"Oh, Cody." The sadness in Ella's voice wrapped around him as she laid her head on his shoulder. "I'm so sorry."

He laughed without mirth. "That's not even the worst part."

She looked up, shock on her face. "It's not?"

"No." He closed his eyes, pressing his lips together. "She wasn't alone. The banker walked into the church with her. They were holding hands. Liza told me she fell for him and that they were in search of a new adventure. Together." He clenched his fists. "I was so busy starting up my ranch, I didn't realize she'd been spending time in town. A lot of time. With him."

Ella's mouth fell open. For a full minute, she said nothing.

Then, something akin to anger burned in her eyes. "Liza sounds like a fool."

"Maybe it's for the best. If she hadn't left then, she would have left me after our wedding. It might have been months or years, but she wasn't happy in Harmony Springs." He sighed. "She wasn't happy with me."

"And that's exactly why she didn't deserve you. You're a keeper, Cody Brooks. She clearly didn't know what she had in you. Though I can't say I'm sorry she left." She gave him a shy smile. "Her loss was my gain."

His heart leapt. He had to grip the rail behind him to keep from reaching for his tender-hearted wife. "Ella…"

She gazed up at him, her eyes reflecting the stars. "So that's why you haven't fallen in love again? You didn't want to get hurt?"

"Something like that. It broke me, shattered my confidence. I can see now that what I felt for her wasn't real love, but it still wounded me enough to avoid women at all costs." His lips quirked. "Until you."

Ella laughed, though it sounded nervous. "Not that you had much choice. It was me or an unknown mail-order bride." She pulled the blanket closer. "At least your heart will remain safe."

Would it? Cody wasn't so sure. Ella was steadily chipping away at his resistance. It was her heart he wondered about.

"My heart belongs to you." He said it without thinking.

Ella stared at him, mouth hanging open.

If only he could stuff the words back in his mouth. That had come out wrong, and he knew how it sounded. "I mean, as my wife, you're the only one with any kind of claim to it. Love or not. We're becoming friends, right?"

She nodded, her eyes glued to his.

Cody chuckled, a nervous tick in his chest. "That's all I meant."

"Hmm." Ella tilted her head. She bit her lip again, then

moved toward him. "I'm thankful for your friendship, and I'm thankful you married me. I can't imagine being tied to anyone else." She shuddered. "Especially not Howard. We would have been married by now if I stayed in Boston."

Cody put an arm around her shoulders as a shiver ran through her. "We should get back inside. You're cold."

She smiled at him. "I'm fine. Just trying to process this entire conversation."

And he'd never answered her question. As they walked inside, he took a long breath to fortify himself. "Ella, I don't want to be the reason you don't get your heart's desire."

She looked at him, unwrapping the blanket from her body. "What?"

"Children. I think...I think I'd be open to that. With you. Eventually."

"Oh." Her cheeks turned pink yet again. "I guess...that's..."

Ella's face turned redder by the second. Out of nowhere, she burst into laughter. Cody jumped. Ella bent over, hands on her knees, almost howling with amusement. It was contagious. Before he knew it, Cody was laughing too. Their mirth lasted several minutes. Only after they reined it in did he speak again.

"I suppose laughter is good medicine?"

She wiped a tear from her cheek, still smiling as she nodded. "That was the most awkward conversation I've ever had. But Cassie was right. We needed to have it."

"Why is she always right?"

Ella laughed again. "A sister's prerogative?"

A new lightness filled the air as they looked at each other. Cody put out his hand, and Ella took it. "Thanks for being willing to have hard conversations, Ella. It was tough, but it means a lot that you broached the subject."

That took trust, and he prized her trust in him. He knew it wasn't easily earned.

She smiled. "Thanks for telling me about Liza." Her nose

wrinkled. "Even if she doesn't have the good sense God gave a duck."

Cody grinned, not bothering to hide his amusement. "A duck, huh?"

"I stand by that statement."

"I like it." But not nearly as much as he liked the new Mrs. Brooks.

~

On Saturday evening, Miss Hattie surprised Ella and Cody with an invitation to watch the children so they could have supper in town. She bustled into the house, making Ella jump, and waved her and Cody out. "Off now, you two. It's high time you had a date. Just because you're married, it doesn't mean there's no need for romance."

Ella's cheeks heated. She pressed her hands there. Cody chuckled, holding an arm out to her. "I guess we're going to town."

"Have fun!" Hattie called after them, Addie on her hip.

Cody led Ella to the barn. "Horses or wagon?"

"Riding sounds nice."

"Riding it is."

When they got to the barn, Cody halted. "I don't have a side saddle." He scanned her long skirts. "Maybe the wagon would be more prudent. I'm sorry, Ella."

She chuckled. Moving closer to him, she tilted her head back to meet his gaze. "It's fine. The wagon is nice too. I don't mind."

Breathing a sigh of relief, he smiled. "Good. I'll have to see about getting a side saddle for you soon."

"Only if we can afford it." Ella's brows rose. "Now, can you teach me how to hitch the horses to the wagon?"

"My pleasure, darlin'."

To her own delight, Ella proved to be a quick study. Within five minutes, they were ready to go. When they reached Cassie's restaurant, Cody tied the horses to a hitching post and offered Ella his arm. She slid her hand into the crook of his elbow. "Chivalrous."

"According to Miss Hattie, this is a date. I have to be chivalrous."

She smiled. "It's nice seeing a new side of you."

"My mother made sure to teach me good manners. The orphanage might have taken some of it out of me, but then Miss Hattie took over once I started ranching." He smirked. "She made sure I knew how to treat a lady."

"And now she's making you use those skills."

Cody chuckled. "So it seems."

They made their way into the café. Cody pulled out a chair for Ella, seating her as properly as any man in Boston had. She raised a brow. "You do know what you're doing."

He settled into his own chair. "I'm rusty. It's been ten years since I've had a date. At least I know you won't leave me."

The words sounded teasing, but his eyes held a hint of vulnerability. Ella laid her napkin on her lap without releasing his gaze. "I'll hold to our vows."

He nodded slowly. "As will I."

Cassie appeared at their table, breaking the connection between them. "Howdy. I'm happy to see you two. And a little confused. What are you doing in town?"

"Miss Hattie decided we needed an evening together." Ella smiled at her friend. "So here we are."

"That woman knows what she's doing. Playing matchmaker, she is." Cassie grinned.

Cody rolled his eyes. "Not much point in that. It's not as though we can be unmatched after marrying."

Cassie pushed his shoulder. "Not matchmaking for

marriage. Matchmaking for love." She waggled her eyebrows. "By summer's end, I'm telling you."

Ella blushed.

Cody looked between her and Cassie, brow furrowed. "Huh?"

"You'll see, brother. Now, what can I get you two?"

Cody looked at Ella. "Are you ready to order?"

She nodded. "Coffee with cream and shepherd's pie sounds wonderful."

"I'll have the same, minus the cream."

Cassie smiled. "See, you're already acting like most married couples, ordering the same food."

Ella tipped her head. "Is that a thing?"

"I think she made it up." Cody raised his brows. "Didn't you, Cass?"

She shrugged. "All I know is, Travis and I do the same. Therefore, it must be a married people trait."

Cody laughed. "I don't think that's how it works."

"I'm gonna believe it until proven wrong. I'll go get that coffee now." With a toss of her curls, Cassie sauntered off.

Ella leaned an elbow on the table, resting her chin in her hand. "Has she always been so perky?"

"Yeah. She's been my sunshine in an otherwise dreary couple of decades."

"You two have a strong relationship, don't you?"

"For so long, we only had each other. That created a bond most siblings don't have. When Travis came along, I had a hard time letting Cassie go. I was a thorn in his side until we finally became friends."

Ella hid a smile behind her hand. "You played the protective older brother?"

"I might have earned my reputation for being a bear during that time."

Cassie returned with a carafe of coffee. "That he did. Drove me crazy, until I realized why he was doing it." She ruffled Cody's hair. "It was his way of showing he wanted what was best for me."

He ducked. Running a hand through his blond waves, he tried to push them back into place.

Ella smiled as a stray lock curled over his forehead. "You've got one more." Without thought, she reached out and set it into place. Cody went still at her touch. Their eyes locked. For a few beats of her heart, the two of them were the only ones in the room.

When Cassie cleared her throat, they both jerked. She looked between them, an amused smile on her face. "Don't mind me. I'll just head back to the kitchen and let you enjoy your alone time."

Cody's face looked a little flushed. "It seems Miss Hattie isn't the only one playing matchmaker."

Maybe it was the setting or the fact that they were on a date, but Ella felt a surge of courage. "Does that bother you?"

He blinked. "No. Why?"

She lifted one shoulder. "Just curious. Some people get annoyed when others meddle in their personal business."

"Ah." He regarded her for a moment. "Like Howard?"

Ella nodded. "Howard, my parents...most people I've known, to be honest."

"Normally, I probably would be annoyed. But I know my sister and Miss Hattie want to see me happy. They've told me that often enough. This is their way of helping that along." He leaned forward. "They want you to be happy too."

"It's nice to have people on our side." Ella let out a small breath. "I'm all too used to backstabbing and silly politics. Besides my sister, there's been no one who really cared for me. It's all about image. Nothing else matters. That's part of the reason my father was so angry when he came. He hated that my disappearance caused a scandal for the family."

Cody frowned. "Scandal? Why is that scandalous?"

"Wealthy heiress runs away in the middle of the night, leaving her fiancé and family without a word." She shook her head. "The society papers probably had a heyday with that."

"Don't they realize it's people's lives they're reporting on? Sounds like gossip to me."

"It's all gossip. Some members of society thrive on the perceived fame. I hated it."

A little smile spread over his face. "That doesn't surprise me. You don't strike me as an attention seeker."

She shuddered. "I'll happily stay out of it."

Cassie arrived with plates of steaming food. She set it before them with a flourish. "Enjoy! If you need anything, let me know. And make sure you come say goodbye before leaving."

"We will." Cody gave her a one-armed hug. "Thanks, Cass."

"Anytime."

After she left, Cody reached out his hands to Ella. She took them and closed her eyes while he blessed the food. They enjoyed their first few bites without talking, the tangy flavors of beef, gravy, and potatoes bursting on Ella's tongue. "Cassie's food is amazing."

Cody nodded his agreement. He studied her for a few moments, then suddenly put down his spoon. "Ella..."

The door opened. Her gaze flitted up. Her own spoon clattered to the table, a horrified gasp on her lips.

Cody looked at her in concern before glancing over his shoulder. He turned back to her. "What is it?"

"That man. I know him."

The well-dressed Bostonian spotted her. He moved around tables in fluid, practiced motions until stopping at their table. "Miss Mountbatten."

She gritted her teeth. "Mr. Blackwell. What are you doing here?"

Cody reached across the table, gripping her hand in his.

Mr. Blackwell held up a folder. "I'm here on behalf of your father. He's asked me to find a reason to dissolve this marriage."

CHAPTER 14

Cody eyed the lawyer sitting in their parlor. He didn't feel comfortable with the man in their home, but it was better than creating a scene at the café. Had it only been an hour since they first saw Blackwell? Thankfully, Hattie had taken the boys out for a picnic when Cody and Ella returned home and said a lawyer was on his way. Addie was upstairs napping. The children shouldn't have to witness...whatever was about to happen.

Mountbatten's hireling reminded him of a snake—smooth, sneaky, and poised to strike. Ella sat beside Cody, holding fast to his hand. Hers was slick with moisture. He slipped his other hand over their joined ones, running his thumb over her wrist to bring her comfort.

Blackwell sniffed and pointed at their hands. "You don't need to pretend for my sake."

Glaring at the man, Cody stiffened. "There is no pretending here."

His tone must have conveyed his emotion. Blackwell blinked, looking taken aback. He recovered quickly. "Miss

Mountbatten, I've been hired by your parents and Mr. Archambeau..."

"It's Mrs. Brooks." Ella's voice sounded small, but it didn't waver.

Blackwell frowned. "I beg your pardon?"

"My name is Mrs. Brooks, not Miss Mountbatten."

The lawyer's lips thinned. "Your family and Mr. Archambeau are convinced the marriage can be annulled. You aren't cut out for a life of menial labor in this backwoods town. Don't you miss being a wealthy heiress to the Mountbatten fortune?"

Her grip on Cody's hand tightened. "No."

"Are you sure? Living in this podunk town can't be easy." Blackwell's brow rose in a condescending manner.

Cody bristled at the insult. Ella remained calm. "I love Harmony Springs. It's the first place I've been truly happy."

The man sneered. "You'd rather live in this ranching town than Boston?"

"Yes."

She hadn't hesitated at all. Gratification washed over Cody. He slid one hand from hers and slipped it around her waist. Ella leaned into him in response.

"Mr. Archambeau asked me to convey that he misses you and wishes you'd return home. He still wants to marry you, Miss Mountbatten."

Ella went still. "I'm already married. Cody and I joined ourselves together until death do us part. I'm not about to break those vows."

Blackwell turned to Cody. "And what about you? What price would make you dissolve this marriage?"

Cody bit his tongue to keep from retorting in anger. He drew in a long breath before speaking. "Like my wife, I believe marriage is forever. When I make a vow, I keep it. End of discussion."

"Maybe you misunderstood, Mr. Brooks. The Mountbatten

family is prepared to reimburse you handsomely to end your marriage and return their beloved daughter home." Blackwell held up an envelope. "You'd never want for money again."

Did the man know about his financial troubles? And did he really think that was enough to tear Cody from Ella? He snorted, not bothering to look at the envelope. "Beloved daughter? They don't care about Ella, and you know it. She's staying here."

The lawyer sighed. "I wish you'd take the easy way. It's a substantial amount of money, Mr. Brooks."

"I don't want your money," Cody practically growled. "I want my wife."

It surprised him how much he meant those words. The thought of losing Ella sent chills down his spine.

Blackwell removed his spectacles. "Is this a marriage of convenience?"

Ella froze beside him. Cody steeled his voice. "That's none of your business."

"It is my business if it means the marriage can be annulled."

Cody didn't like the man's tone—much less, his suggestion. "A marriage cannot be annulled unless the man or woman wishes it to be. Considering neither one of us wants to dissolve this union, your argument is invalid."

Annoyance flashed over the man's hawk-like face. He tapped his briefcase with his fingers. "But are you truly married? If there's no plan to have children, then this"—he motioned between Cody and Ella—"isn't valid."

Maybe having a grizzly side had its benefits. "Not that it's any of your concern, but we do intend to have children. So again, your point holds no water." Thank God he and Ella had that conversation.

Blackwell didn't seem inclined to give up. He leaned forward, sharp gaze biting into Cody's. "Why did you marry so quickly?"

"My children needed a mother. I planned to send for a mail-order bride, but Ella volunteered to marry me instead."

The lawyer frowned, looking at Ella. "This was your idea?"

She nodded. The man's frown deepened. He glanced at his notes. "We could still cite coercion since you may have felt as though there was no other choice…"

"Coercion!" Ella's voice came out shrill. "If you want to know what coercion looks like, try asking Mr. Archambeau what he attempted the night I left Boston! Ask him about the bruises he left on my body. Or how he manipulated me for years. Or said he would force me to marry him. Ask my parents how they ignored my pleas to break the engagement and insisted I marry Howard despite his abuse. *That* is coercion."

She pointed a finger at Blackwell. Her voice went quiet and steely. "When I met Cody, I quickly found out he was different. I offered to marry him to give the children a mother. He tried to talk me out of it. This was my choice. I'd do it again if given the chance. My husband is an excellent man, and we are raising three orphaned children together. Life here might be hard, but it is good. I regret nothing."

Pride straightened Cody's spine. Ella might be terrified, but she wasn't backing down. He couldn't help but admire the fire in her eyes.

Blackwell looked at Cody again. "Consider carefully, Mr. Brooks. Miss Mountbatten belongs with people of her class. If you don't let her go, there are those who might be inclined to use other methods of persuasion to gain their objective."

"This conversation is over." Cody pinned the lawyer with a fierce look. "I suggest you leave the property before you find yourself in an unfortunate accident."

Rearing back, Blackwell widened his eyes. "There's no need to sound hostile."

"No need to sound hostile?" Heat rushed through Cody's veins. He stood, towering over the lawyer. "You come to my town claiming you plan to take my wife from me. You come into my home and ask rude questions. You try to bribe me to end my marriage, and you use veiled threats as a fear tactic." Each word grew in volume as he tried—and failed—to control his anger. "So you'll excuse me if I sound *hostile*." He stepped closer, hands on his hips. "And if you don't get out of our home in ten seconds, you'll see exactly how hostile I can be."

Blackwell hopped to his feet. "No need to threaten. I'm going." He shot a glare over his shoulder when he reached the door. "But this isn't over."

The door slammed behind the man. Cody turned to Ella. He barely registered how close she was before she burrowed against him, trembling.

Her hands gripped the front of his shirt. "I should have known my father leaving wasn't the end of it."

Rapid, unsteady puffs of breath penetrated the cloth and warmed his skin. Cody wrapped his arms around her, pulling her close. She buried her face in his chest. Her body shook so hard, he had to brace his feet to keep her from pulling them both down. "He can't do anything, Ella."

"He'll try. And did you hear what he said? He's not just working for my father. Howard is his client too."

Cody's brow furrowed. "Is that significant?"

"It means Howard might show up here to try to get me back."

"Then he'll have me to deal with." Who knew his tone could be so menacing?

Ella pulled back, studying him. "How do you do that?"

"Do what?"

Her smile, fragile and gentle, pulled at his heart. "Make me feel better without trying."

Apparently, she didn't require an answer. She leaned into him again, but this time, her trembling stopped. A soft sigh escaped as she fully relaxed. Cody held her, lending the strength he knew she needed and trying not to notice how perfectly she fit in his arms.

A cry from upstairs broke them apart. Ella smoothed back her hair and met his gaze. "Addie's up. I'll go get her and check on the boys."

Cody could only nod, his gaze following her as she headed to the children's room. Her bravery in the face of fear astounded him. She stood her ground and refused to give in to Blackwell's bullying. It was another thing Cody could add to the list of traits he admired about his wife.

He held back a snort. Admired? Things had gone well past admiration.

And that terrified him.

❧

Ella paced in the parlor. No lights glowed at such an unearthly hour, but she'd been restless and unable to sleep. Not wanting to disturb Cody, she'd made her way downstairs, releasing her nervous energy with constant movement.

So far, it hadn't helped.

The visit with her father's lawyer impacted her more than she cared to admit. Mr. Blackwell had been to their Boston home a number of times. Ella always avoided him. Maybe it was his roaming eyes or his condescending tone. Whatever the reason, she didn't like him. When he came through the café door, she'd known they were in for a fight.

Ella shivered in the chilly room. Spring might be coming, but for now, a bitter chill hung on through the nights. She turned once more and made her way across the dark room. Moments later, pain exploded in her leg as it hit the corner of a chair.

"Ouch!"

She hopped backward, only to trip over the carpet. A little

shriek escaped as she fell to the floor. Her grunt coincided with a light entering the room.

"Ella? Darlin', where are you?" Cody called.

Mortification joined her pain. Though tempted not to answer and save herself the embarrassment, Ella forced herself to speak. "Behind the chair."

Within seconds, her husband appeared beside her, his face illuminated by the light of a single candle. He placed it on a table, brows furrowed. "What happened?"

She accepted the hand he offered her. "I had a run-in with the carpet."

"Why are you here? In the dark?" Cody pulled her up in one fluid motion.

Ella dropped her gaze, staring at the offending carpet. "I couldn't sleep."

"Sit."

The order sounded gruff, but she knew him well enough by now to know it was sleep-roughened. His voice was always deeper and raspier in the mornings. For some reason, it made a tingling shiver dance down her spine. She obeyed his one-word command, lowering herself onto the settee.

He sat beside her and reached toward her head. "Are you hurt?"

His fingers connected with the back of her skull. Ella jumped, not from pain, but from the electric jolt that coursed through her at the touch.

Cody froze. "Did I make the pain worse?"

"No. It's just sore. Nothing major." Nothing other than her heart beating as fast as Preston at a full gallop.

His fingers prodded her head. Ella closed her eyes. She shouldn't be enjoying it so much, but in the dim light and with the turmoil of the past day, she didn't want to think. She simply wanted to feel.

"No bumps." Cody lowered his hand. Ella almost protested

before biting her tongue. He took her hand. "What about your back?"

She shook her head. "It's fine. The only other place I felt any pain was my leg. I hit it on a chair before you came in."

Cody reached for the hem of her nightdress before jerking himself upright. "Sorry. I meant to see if it was bleeding. Probably should have asked before trying to look."

Ella stretched her leg out, lifting her nightgown enough to expose her shin. Her cheeks flushed hot at such an intimate gesture. She focused on her leg, trying to see it in the dim light. "I don't think there's blood."

Her husband leaned forward, taking her calf in hand before lifting it to rest across his lap. Ella sucked in a breath. His fingers moved tenderly over the sore spot. The calluses on his hands, evidence of how hard he worked, left behind goosebumps.

"A bruise is already forming." Cody frowned. "It looks like it's going to be a nasty one."

Ella slid her leg from his lap, letting her nightdress fall back into place. "I've always bruised easily. It's probably not as bad as it looks."

"Hmm." Cody stood, extending his hand again. "Why don't you walk for a minute to see how it feels?"

Ella let him pull her up. She paced the room after releasing his hand. Her shin stung, but she could walk fine. "See?" She came to a stop in front of him. "It'll heal soon enough."

Cody's eyes flickered in the candlelight. "Why couldn't you sleep?"

She sighed. "It was impossible to stop thinking about Mr. Blackwell and my father. Something still doesn't feel right. They're much too determined. And why does Howard want me back? He could play the part of a jilted fiancé and gain the sympathy of society. Why insist on me?"

Cody's gaze searched hers. "Did he need your family's money?"

"He's one of the wealthiest men in Boston, so unless he's greedier than I thought, no."

Silence. Then, "Is he a dangerous man, Ella?"

Fear sliced through her. "You know he is."

"That's not what I meant." His hand slid to her back, pulling her a little closer. "Some men are abusive toward women but cowards around other men. Some are dangerous to both. Which is Howard?"

"I...I don't know." Her breath came rapidly. "He put on a persona in public. Charming, charismatic, collected. It was only in private that he became a monster."

Cody's gaze intensified. "And your father?"

Ella let out a bitter laugh. "He was much the same. A character in public, insufferable at home. He charmed many important people out of their money, all while making them think they'd invested wisely. I wouldn't be surprised if he'd ended up with some enemies once they discovered what he'd done."

"Maybe his insistence that you marry Howard is connected to that."

She frowned. "But why would Howard still agree to it? If my disappearance caused a scandal, shouldn't he want nothing to do with my family?"

Cody exhaled long and slow. "Probably."

"So we're back to the original dilemma. None of this makes sense." Ella crossed her arms, a sudden chill making her shiver.

"You're cold." Cody grabbed a blanket from the settee. He threw it around her shoulders. The motion brought them closer together, so close she could feel his breath on her cheek.

They both stilled. Something crackled between them, strong and undeniable. Afraid to even breathe, Ella stared up into Cody's eyes, the blue barely visible in the flicker of candlelight.

His hands moved to her arms. "Howard is a fool."

The rough edge to his words conveyed an emotion she hadn't expected. It almost seemed like...but no, that was impossible...wasn't it?

He pulled her toward him. His eyes searched hers for a few moments as the air sparked around them. "You're safe here, darlin'. I won't let anything happen to you."

Ella pulled in a shaky breath, butterflies beating hard in her stomach. "You can't promise that."

"Maybe not." He stepped closer. "But I can promise to guard you with my very life." His hand found her cheek. "That's what a husband is meant to do."

When his eyes fell to her lips, she knew what was coming. Maybe it was the intimacy of the moment, or maybe it was the candlelight barely lighting the room. Whatever it was, no fear clutched her heart. All she felt was the promise of something new, something they could have if they both let go of their misgivings and trusted each other fully. Taking a leap of faith, Ella slid her arms around Cody's waist.

His lips found hers gently, carefully, as if he feared she might bolt at anything more. Her eyes drifted shut, unable to remain open with the cacophony of emotion blazing within. His kiss remained soft. Warmth wrapped itself around her. She'd never felt safer than she did now in this man's arms. Something else rose in her heart, a tenderness aimed solely at him. When the pressure from his lips decreased, she almost cried out in protest.

Cody leaned his forehead against hers. "We should get some rest. Morning's not far off."

She managed to find her voice. "All right."

He led her up to their room. After extinguishing the candle, they crawled into bed. As always, the small space had their hips pressed together. Cody shifted onto his side, his back to her. At least for now. She knew what would happen by morning. Ella summoned her courage and put a hand on his arm. "Cody?"

The bed creaked as he rolled to his back. "Yeah?"

The words almost died on her lips, but she plunged ahead. "Every time we wake, you're holding me."

He swallowed so hard, she heard it in the dark. "I'm sorry. It's not deliberate. It just...happens."

Was that guilt in his tone? She smiled, even knowing he couldn't see her. "Don't apologize. It's another thing you do that makes me feel safe."

A long pause ensued. When he finally spoke, his voice sounded raspy. "Then I'm glad for it."

"This might sound strange..." Oh dear. How to ask the question on her heart?

Cody's hand found hers. "What is it, darlin'?"

The endearment gave her the fortitude to finish. "Can you hold me now? On purpose?"

His sharp intake of breath made her pause. Had she just ruined the tenuous bond between them? Cheeks burning, she buried herself under the covers. "Never mind. It was silly to ask. I'll just..."

"Ella." He slipped his arms around her, pulling her into his strong embrace. "I'm happy to oblige. But only if you're sure."

She snuggled against his chest. "I'm sure." The words came out in a whisper, but she meant them with all her heart.

Cody pressed a kiss to the top of her head before settling against his pillow. "'Night, darlin'."

"Goodnight."

Nestled in his arms, Ella finally fell into a deep, peaceful sleep.

CHAPTER 15

Funny how a kiss could change things.

Cody hadn't planned on kissing his wife. Far from it. He thought Ella still needed time and space. But in that parlor, with a soft glow cast over her face from the candle and the clear invitation she'd given him, he couldn't resist.

And he didn't regret it one bit. In fact, he'd love to repeat the experience. Perhaps with a bit of passion.

His cheeks heated as he galloped alongside Hank to check the eastern pasture. When he woke this morning, Ella ensconced in his arms, he pinched his stomach to make sure he wasn't dreaming. And he had to remind himself that falling in love with his wife hadn't been part of the plan.

Yet he was already tumbling headlong with no way to stop. That kiss last night sealed it. Cody couldn't deny that he wanted love, and he wanted it with Ella.

And maybe, just maybe, she was opening herself to the possibility like he was. That morning, holding her as she slept, he'd wanted so much more. He wanted the simple, everyday, meaningful love his mother's favorite poem so eloquently stated. *By sun and candle-light.*

He wanted to talk. They *needed* to talk. But she looked so peaceful, he couldn't bear to bring her out of slumber. Instead, he'd carefully unwrapped his arms and hauled himself off to work.

"You all right, Boss?"

Torn from his ruminations, Cody glanced at Hank. "Fine. Why?"

Hank cocked his head, eyes narrowing. "You're quieter than usual. And that's saying somethin'."

"I'm fine."

"Uh-huh."

Cody grunted. "Has anyone been to the east pasture today?"

"Not yet. The boys're headin' to the north pasture to secure the fence. That old thing's been givin' us more trouble than not."

Rubbing his forehead, Cody sighed. "We need to fix that. Let's fell some trees and make new posts today."

"Sounds like a plan. Let's check the east pasture and then grab the boys to cut some trees."

Surveying the herd in the first pasture didn't take long. Most of the cows were thin, but with spring around the corner, they would soon fatten up. A few of the female cows were expecting young'uns, which would expand the herd and begin to make up for his losses over the harsh winter.

As they turned their horses for the north pasture, someone yelled Cody's name. He looked up. Eddie galloped toward them. Cody gave Preston a command. His horse took off over the field, Hank not far behind. When they reached Eddie, the younger man's eyes held a wild look.

"The north fence is down! All the cattle there are gone!"

Icy dread enveloped Cody. Without another word, all three men spurred their horses toward the pasture in question. They arrived at the fence. A wide gap yawned, one that several cows could pass through at a time.

Cody glanced around. "Where's Joey?"

"He's chasing after the herd. The ground's soft enough that their tracks were obvious." Eddie wiped his brow. "Unfortunately, it seems they went in three directions. It's gonna be tough roundin' 'em up before dark."

Scrubbing a hand over his face, Cody stifled a groan. "All right, boys. Let's find Joey and get a plan together."

It took half an hour before they located their fellow ranch hand. Joey had about thirty cows together, but deep furrows ran across his forehead. "Sorry, Boss. I thought I followed the path with the most tracks, but they split up here, there, and everywhere. I don't know where the rest of the herd is."

Two hundred and forty-two cattle missing. Cody's heart sank. Of their eight hundred total, they lost three hundred over the course of the harsh winter. He couldn't afford to lose any more. Pushing down his disappointment, Cody let out a long breath. "We can't waste any time. Let's split up and find as many cattle as possible. Report back at the north pasture in three hours."

Hank swiped his hat from his head, raking back his sandy hair. "We gotta get that fence repaired, too, Boss. Getting the cattle back will do nothin' if they just get out again." His eyes shadowed. "Not to mention if any cattle from other pastures find their way out of that blasted hole."

Cody bit back a groan. "Joey and Eddie, you rustle up the cattle. Hank and I'll get to work on that fence."

"Yessir."

The twins galloped off, leaving Cody and Hank to drive the thirty rescued cows back to the ranch. Once all of them were safely inside the north pasture, the two men went to work on a makeshift fence. It took several hours to get the wood to an appropriate length to repair several feet of fencing. As they prepared to cut away the old bits of fence still standing, Cody's boot came down on a length of rope half hidden in mud. He frowned, crouching. "Hank, c'mere."

"Yeah, Boss?"

"Do you see what I see?" Cody pointed to tracks in the soft ground. "These horse hooves aren't ours. And the fence looks like it was dragged." He picked up the rope. "See this?"

Hank sucked in a breath. "You sayin' someone pulled the fence down on purpose? Who would do somethin' like that?" He smacked his leg. "Cattle rustlers?"

Cody's stomach clenched. "Maybe." Or maybe it had something to do with Blackwell's threat.

He prayed he was wrong.

They worked for several more hours, fitting the new wood to the older fence. By the time the sun sank low in the sky, Cody felt as though he'd been hit by a train. He was covered in sweat, tired, and hungry. As he hammered the last nail in place, a whistle caught his attention. When he looked up, Eddie and Joey rumbled toward them, driving a significant portion of the herd. Relief sluiced through Cody's body. He hurried to the gate and flung it open. As the cows made their way in, he called to Eddie. "How many?"

"One hundred and eighty-three. Add that to the thirty from earlier, and we've got most of them accounted for."

But not all. Cody tried to summon gratitude for the ones that were found, but his gut churned with concern. If they couldn't find the other twenty-nine, it would be a significant loss.

Hank clapped a hand on his shoulder. "We'll find the rest, Boss. This can't be the work of rustlers. That means those cows are out there."

"I hope you're right."

"I usually am."

Hank grinned. Cody tried to take courage from his levity, but bone-deep exhaustion radiated through him. And if it wasn't rustlers… "Thanks for your help today, boys. I'll see you tomorrow."

He rode Preston home at a slower pace than usual. Cody considered himself an excellent horseman, but in his current state, he didn't trust himself to gallop. By the time he got to the barn, deep darkness settled over the land, with stars twinkling brightly in the sky.

The door to the house opened. Ella slipped outside, covered in a thick shawl. "You're home."

Was that fear in her eyes? Cody dropped Preston's reins and took several long steps to the porch. "Everything all right, Ella?"

Her breathing sounded labored. "When you didn't come home on time, I feared the worst. But you're here." She exhaled, running her hands over his arms. "You're safe."

The gentle touch nearly made him forget the day's stress. He caught her hands as they reached his, giving them a squeeze. "I'm sorry I worried you. Let me get the evening chores done, and I'll be in."

She followed him down the steps. "The chores are done."

Cody stopped in his tracks. "What?"

Ella tightened the shawl around her. "The children helped me feed the animals, and I milked Sadie and Becky. Everything's done."

"You…did my chores?"

Hesitancy flickered in her eyes. "Was that wrong?"

"No!" He put his hands on her shoulders. "Not at all. I'm just surprised."

She gave him a little smile. "It took my mind off the fact that you weren't here."

"I'm sorry, Ella. Someone pulled down the north fence, and all the cattle in that pasture got out. We had to repair the fence and round up the lost cows."

Her eyes grew large. "Someone broke it?"

"Yeah." He stopped walking, taking Ella's arm. "Go back inside, darlin'. I'll get Preston bedded down and be in shortly."

She nodded. "I'll get your supper." After he thanked her, Ella headed into the house.

Cody blew out a breath, all the worries from the day crashing into him again. He needed answers. Was this the work of unorganized rustlers...or someone under orders from Ella's father?

~

Ella sank into a chair after placing Cody's food on the table. Words couldn't express her relief to have her husband home. When he hadn't come back on time, she imagined the worst. But new concerns rose like sentinels in her mind. If someone had cut the fence...so soon after Mr. Blackwell's threats...

She pushed the thought away. Maybe it was just an unhappy coincidence.

The children had been quiet at supper. Isaiah had stared at Cody's empty space before looking at Ella, tears welling in his brown eyes. "Where's Uncle Cody?"

His tone and expression betrayed his deep fear. And no wonder. After losing his parents, it made sense he'd fear losing his new guardian.

She'd taken his hand and looked straight into his eyes. "Something must have come up. I'm sure he'll be back soon. Perhaps we can do his chores after supper so he can rest when he gets home. What do you think?"

That helped a bit. They'd completed the chores together, but when Ella put the boys to bed, a few tears fell from Isaiah's eyes. She'd wondered if he would ever fall asleep.

Moments later, she had her answer. Isaiah padded into the

kitchen, clutching a blanket, eyes red. "Did Uncle Cody get home?"

Ella held out her arms. Isaiah ran to her and allowed her to pull him onto her lap. "Yes, sweetie, he's home. He's just getting Preston bedded down."

Isaiah burst into sobs. He buried his face in Ella's chest. "I thought...he wasn't...coming back...like my daddy."

Throat tightening, she held the little boy close. "He's safe, Isaiah. He's home with us." The words were as much for her sake as for his.

The front door opened. As soon as Cody entered the kitchen, Isaiah vaulted from Ella's lap and launched himself at his uncle, still sobbing. Cody caught him. Confusion knit his brow, but he lifted Isaiah into his arms. "What's wrong?"

Isaiah only burrowed closer to Cody and cried harder. Ella felt like doing the same. Despite how their marriage began, Cody steadily made his way deeper into her heart. That tender kiss last night sealed it. Her reaction to his late arrival whispered that she could no longer deny her feelings. Whatever they might be.

Cody sat in the chair beside her.

She put a hand on Isaiah's back and leaned toward Cody. "You coming home late made him remember his parents' accident."

Understanding lit his eyes. He patted Isaiah's back. "It's all right, bud. I'm fine."

Cody's discomfort while holding the boy was evident. His large hands looked out of place against so small a child. But the tenderness her husband showed to Isaiah melted her heart. Being a father didn't come naturally for him, but he was a good one.

His stomach growled, which spurred Ella into action. She rose and held out her arms. "Come, Isaiah. Uncle Cody needs to eat."

Isaiah shook his head and clung all the tighter to Cody.

"I've got him." Cody stood, giving Ella a reassuring look. "I'll put him back to bed."

"Are you sure?"

He nodded. "Be back soon."

She watched as he headed out of the kitchen. Warmth stole over her along with pure admiration. Strong attraction churned inside. Ella blinked. *Am I falling for him?* She pressed a hand to her stomach, dismissing the thought. There would be time to dwell on that later.

She tested the heat of Cody's stew and wrinkled her nose. She couldn't serve him tepid stew. Ella returned it to the stove, then busied herself washing dishes. As she set the last plate on the rack to dry, Cody returned. "Sorry about that. Isaiah was right ruffled."

She set about scooping the stew into another bowl, then tore a hunk of bread off a fresh loaf. "He's scared."

Cody thanked her as she set the food in front of him. Instead of picking up his spoon, he pressed his lips together. "I get it. Loss is horrible. He'll always carry that with him."

Ella sat beside him, waiting while he said a quiet blessing over his supper. When he began to eat, she softly asked, "Are you speaking from experience?"

He chewed on some bread, a faraway look on his face. "Yeah."

Ella knew better than to say anything more. She sat back, letting him process his thoughts while he ate for a while. After a couple minutes, he put down his spoon and released an audible sigh. "I don't want Isaiah to end up like me."

What? Clamping her lips tightly to keep from speaking, Ella waited for him to continue.

Cody ran a hand through his already ruffled hair. "Losing my parents, never getting adopted...it shattered me. I never felt like I was good enough for others." He blew out a hard breath, his head dropping. "That's why I fell so easily for Liza. She wanted me for me, and that stoked my pride. Or so I thought. Being jilted...it showed me yet again I wasn't enough. So I've kept myself locked up, gruff and distant, refusing to be hurt again." He swallowed. "I don't want that to happen to our kids."

Something about the way he said *our kids* unleashed a current of flutters in Ella's stomach. She'd begun thinking of the kids as theirs too. They were becoming a true family. He might have a hard time showing his affection, but it was there. It was obvious in the way he took the children in, gave them a mother because it was best for them, worried over their future.

She reached out, covering his large hand in both of hers. "Cody, you're the best thing to have happened to the children. I think they're going to be fine, because they have two parents who love them and will do anything for them."

His face shifted. Hope glimmered in his eyes. "You think so?"

"I do." Ella pressed his hand. "And if it helps, I think you're enough just the way you are. I rather like my gruff, soft bear."

As soon as the words left her mouth, she realized how they sounded. Her eyes widened, and her breath stuttered. She might as well have made a declaration of love.

Cody's gaze caught fire. He lifted his free hand to her cheek, the motion both tentative and strong. His warm palm branded her skin. "How did you work your way so quickly into my heart?" he murmured, his gaze roaming her face.

Ella's lips parted as if of their own accord. Cody's gaze dropped. His eyes lingered on her mouth. He leaned forward.

She froze, a battle raging inside. His kiss last night felt good and safe. But now, outside of the quiet intimacy of candlelight, a kiss seemed like a bigger step. One she wasn't sure she was ready to take.

Her husband paused, his gaze flitting up to meet hers. Hurt flashed over his rugged features. He began to pull away.

Pain ripped through Ella's heart. After all he'd just confessed, her hesitation added another scalding rejection, another proof that he wasn't enough. Gathering her courage, she slipped a hand behind his neck to halt his retreat. "Don't stop."

It was impossible to miss the desire written on his face. Still, he didn't move. His eyes searched hers. "Are you sure?"

"I trust you."

Cody swallowed. A sheen of moisture filled his eyes. "That means more than you know." His attention fixed on her mouth once more. "We don't have to rush this, darlin'. As much as I want to kiss you, if you need time, we can just…"

Ella didn't let him finish. She leaned forward, brushing his lips lightly with hers. Heat stole over her as she pulled back. Never before would she have attempted such a bold move, but it had the desired effect. Cody's gaze heated. He wrapped his arms around her and pulled her closer. Ella's eyes fluttered shut. She breathed in his masculine scent, waiting for the moment their lips would meet again. Would it be another gentle kiss? Or would they share something deep and fervent? Her heart sped up in anticipation.

"Mama?"

They both froze.

Another little voice joined in the first. "Addie's sad."

Ella turned to face their two boys. Willing her heart to stop racing, she tried to speak normally. "Sad?"

Isaiah nodded while Jonah made a beeline for Cody. "She's cryin'. I think she's hungry."

Cody lifted Jonah into his arms. The little boy snuggled close.

A rush of empathy swirled through Ella. Clearly, she and Isaiah weren't the only ones who'd worried tonight. She pushed herself to her feet and held out a hand to Isaiah. "Shall we check on her together?"

He nodded, sliding his palm against hers. Ella glanced at Cody before leaving the room. No words passed between them, but the look he gave her spoke of a promise of things to come.

162

CHAPTER 16

"All the cows are accounted for?"

Ella nodded, bouncing Addie on her lap. Cassie had come to visit while Cody and Travis went to town to find Blackwell. Cody had wanted to make sure the man knew he wasn't welcome at Brooks Ranch again. Ella tried not to dwell on that while she answered her sister-in-law. "Cody said they found the final four this morning several miles from the ranch."

Cassie exhaled, leaning back against her chair. "I can't imagine the burden it would have been to lose more cattle. Cody's already struggling. This winter has been brutal."

Isaiah came skidding into the kitchen, interrupting the conversation. "Is Uncle Cody back?"

"Not yet."

The little boy pouted. "But I want to play with him and Sheriff Travis."

Ella chuckled. "They'll be back soon enough, sweetie. You have to be patient."

"Humph." Isaiah plopped onto the floor, chin in hands. "Fine."

Cassie hid a smile behind her hand. "How's motherhood?"

Addie snuggled against Ella's chest. Her little eyes drooped shut. Ella breathed in her sweet baby scent before responding. "It has its challenges, but I love being a mother."

Her friend surveyed her over a cup of tea, a smile playing on her lips. "So you're glad you married my brother?"

"I am."

Cassie shot her an impish look. "Has he kissed you yet?"

Ella's cheeks heated. The memory of Cody's gentle kiss by candlelight flashed through her mind. "That's a rather personal question."

"Ha!" Cassie pumped a fist in the air. "He did!"

Isaiah harrumphed again from the floor. "They were kissin' in the kitchen last night. It was gross."

"No, we weren't." Never mind the fact that they would have if the boys hadn't interrupted them.

Isaiah made a face. "My mama and papa used to kiss. That was gross too."

Cassie ruffled his hair. "That's just what mamas and papas do. You might as well get used to it, Isaiah. I have a feeling you'll be seeing Uncle Cody and Aunt Ella doing the same." She winked.

Isaiah gagged. Ella buried her face in Addie's soft curls.

Cassie's laughter floated to her ears. "Don't worry, Ella. Falling in love is a beautiful thing."

"Girls are gross."

The difference between the two statements made Ella laugh. "You'll change your mind someday, Isaiah."

"Ew!" Isaiah jumped to his feet and darted toward the stairs. "No way!"

Ella changed the subject before Cassie could continue her line of discussion. "How are you feeling?"

Cassie placed a hand on her stomach. "Most days I'm fine, but others I can't stand the smell of food. Which makes owning a restaurant rather difficult. Josephine had to take on some of my shifts. We might have to hire another person to help out."

A blast of cold air hit the room as the front door opened. Moments later, Travis and Cody appeared in the kitchen. Cassie pushed herself up to greet her husband. Cody slid into the chair beside Ella. His eyes looked troubled.

Her heart thundered. "What's wrong?"

"Mr. Blackwell is gone."

"What?" Ella's mouth dropped open. She looked from him to Travis and back again. "Gone where?"

"Back to Boston, apparently." Travis crossed his arms, a frown on his face. "The hotel manager said he checked out yesterday afternoon, and the station master said he caught the last train out of town."

Cody's hand clenched. "It makes no sense. He and Ella's father claimed things weren't over, and both left town soon after. Why?"

"It's a power play." The words tasted bitter on her tongue. "This leaves them holding the cards and us facing the unknown. My father thrives on this kind of manipulation. He uses it in his business deals all the time."

Travis moved to the table. "How would being away from Harmony Springs help their cause? If the idea is to separate you and Cody, they can't do much outside the territory."

"My father has contacts all over the country. He might not be here anymore, but I'd be willing to bet he has someone here in town."

Cody and Travis exchanged a look. Steely determination settled over her husband's features. "Trav, has anyone checked into the hotel recently?"

"Not that I'm aware of, but I can find out tomorrow."

"Good." Cody reached for Ella's free hand. "We'll sort this out, darlin'. If your father or Mr. Blackwell is cooking up something fishy, we'll find out."

A hint of a smile played on her lips. "Fishy?"

"You don't like fish. Seemed like a good point of comparison."

Ella stared at him. "How do you know I don't like fish?"

"Every time you see it, you wrinkle your nose."

"I do?"

He nodded.

Travis raised a brow. "You're observant, my friend. Even I didn't know that. Have you considered a career in law enforcement?"

Cassie held up her hands. "Oh, no! I don't need to be worrying about another person I love, thank you very much."

Cody snorted. "Have you forgotten the number of ranchers who've been trampled in stampedes or thrown from their horses?"

Cassie shook her head, one hand planted on her hip. "Yeah, like the time you were trampled by that wild steer?" She shuddered. "I thought we were going to lose you."

Ella blanched. Unwelcome images filled her mind. "You… you were trampled?"

"Once." Cody shot a frown at his sister, then squeezed Ella's hand. "It happens sometimes. I was fine."

Ranching life could be dangerous. Everyone knew that. But to hear that Cody had experienced such a thing…

Terrible memories sprang to mind—a coachman's lifeless body, bloodied and smashed against the pavement in Boston, the result of a horrific accident with another carriage. He'd been thrown from the carriage, trampled by his own horses before the heavy vehicle fell onto him. Ella had never been able to erase that image from mind. Now, however, she saw Cody's blank, unstaring eyes instead of the young man's. Her hand trembled.

Cody stood. He pulled a sleeping Addie from her arms and

passed the child to Cassie. "Excuse us a moment." He took Ella's hand again and tugged her toward the back porch.

The cold air hit her face and numbed her body. The tremors in her extremities intensified. "Cody...I...I can't..."

He braced his hands on her shoulders. "Look at me."

A creaky moan rose from her throat, forcing its way past her lips. She shook her head, the motion frantic, and buried her face in his chest. Her hands gripped the sides of his waist. "I can't lose you."

He stilled. For several beats of her heart, Cody said nothing. Then, in one swift motion, his arms encircled her and pressed her against him. The strength of his embrace soothed her anxiety. He rested his head on hers, his voice a murmur. "I promise you, I'll always do my best to come home to you and the kids."

Her arms went around him in return. Cody's right hand rubbed between her shoulder blades. After a few minutes, Ella pulled back just enough to meet his eyes. "I'm sorry. I don't know where that came from. Usually I have better control over my emotions." She swiped at the moisture on her cheeks.

Cody smoothed back a tendril of her hair. "Seems to me you've spent too much time keeping your feelings in check. Maybe this is good."

"Panicking over something that happened in the past is good?"

His chest rumbled with low laughter. "It's good that you're letting yourself feel. I'm sure this situation with your father and Mr. Blackwell has you on edge."

Ella sighed. "I thought I left them behind when I married you. My father finding me isn't surprising, but hiring his lawyer to break us apart?" Her head fell forward, resting against him. "He can't do anything, right?"

"Right."

The tension in her shoulders vanished, and the knot in her

stomach unraveled. She closed her eyes. "I'm glad you're in my life."

"The feeling's mutual, darlin'."

～

A couple days after Blackwell departed, Cody lumbered around the yard with Isaiah and Jonah. The afternoon sun lessened the chill of early spring. The boys giggled as they ran, a game of tag underway. The laughter gladdened him. Some of their somberness had lifted. Jonah's smiles were rare. To see them now made Cody feel as though he was doing something right.

Ella came onto the porch, Addie perched on her hip. He paused to take in the sight. His wife smiled, ducking her head after a few moments. Her sweet modesty tripped his heart. Add how motherly she looked holding their daughter, and Cody was hard pressed not to march right up to her and take her in his arms. Her recent admission about not wanting to lose him lit a hope he'd never felt before.

Little hands clasped Cody's leg. "Got you, Papa!"

His jaw slackened. He looked down at Jonah. The little boy grinned up at him, proud of his conquest. "You it!" He let go and raced off toward Isaiah.

Cody's feet stuck to the ground. Something poured through him, weakening his knees and making his body warm. *Papa.* That single word healed a crack in his heart. He felt lighter, buoyed up by a child's trust. Cody laughed and took off after his boys.

Their boundless energy kept the game going longer than he expected. As he took a break against the porch, a hand came to rest on his arm. Cody turned to see Ella standing beside him, her eyes sparkling. "You have a new title."

"I didn't expect that."

She smiled. "It speaks volumes, Cody. That boy loves you."

Tears stung his eyes. "I feel the same."

Addie babbled, patting his arm with her pudgy hand.

Cody leaned down, pressing a kiss to her soft hair. "I never thought I could love them like this." His hand found Ella's. "They truly feel like ours. Even if I don't know what I'm doing."

Ella chuckled. "You're doing better than you think." She gave him a little push. "Now, go chase those boys. I'll get some hot cocoa ready."

For another quarter hour, Cody chased Isaiah and Jonah around the yard. Jonah called him Papa again, and Isaiah—despite looking shocked—didn't contradict his brother. Cody counted that a blessing.

When the boys stopped their game of chase, breathing hard and shivering from the cold, he gathered one under each arm and hoisted them up. "Your mama has a treat inside. Want to get it?"

Jonah's head bobbed up and down. Isaiah chewed his lip. Had he picked up the nervous habit from Ella? Cody smiled at the thought. As he walked toward the house, Isaiah spoke quietly. "Do I have to think of her as my mama?"

Cody stopped just inside the house. He set the boys down and shut the door. Jonah scampered toward the kitchen as soon as his feet hit the floor, leaving Cody alone with his oldest child. He crouched in front of Isaiah. "We talked about this before, son. You can call her Aunt Ella. She doesn't mind."

Tears welled in Isaiah's eyes. "But...will Addie call her Mama? And you Papa?"

"I reckon so."

The boy's lip trembled. "That means I'll be the only one saying Uncle Cody and Aunt Ella."

Cody took Isaiah's hand. "That's all right. No matter what, we're family. That's what counts."

"But I don't want to be different."

Isaiah looked so miserable, Cody pulled him into a hug. "I understand."

"You do?"

"Yeah." He moved to a sitting position and motioned for Isaiah to sit beside him. "When I lived at the orphanage, people would come to see if they wanted to adopt a child. The other boys and girls talked easily with the adults. I didn't. Something changed in me after my parents died. I couldn't make friends. I felt alone, nothing like the other children. I was different and didn't know how to change that."

Isaiah peered up at him. "Did you ever change?"

"Not really." Cody looked the boy in the eyes. "But I'm changing now. With you and Jonah and Addie. With Aunt Ella. All of you have changed me in a good way."

"So you're not different anymore?"

Cody chuckled. "I wouldn't say that. It's still hard to talk to people. A lot of folks probably think I'm different. But I'm okay with that."

Isaiah nibbled his lip. "I guess I can be different too. For now." Uncertainty crossed his face. "What if I want to call you Papa like Jonah?"

Cody grinned. "I'd like that."

"It don't mean I will." A spark of defiance touched Isaiah's eyes, but just as quickly, it vanished. "I'll think about it."

Cody gave him a one-armed hug. "Whatever you decide, I consider you my son, and your aunt does too."

Isaiah nodded. He hopped to his feet. "Can we get that treat now?"

"Sure."

When they entered the kitchen, Ella smiled at them. "Ready for some hot cocoa?"

Isaiah clapped. "Yeah!" He found a seat beside Jonah.

Ella ladled cocoa into a mug and set it in front of the boy.

She poured more into another and offered it to Cody. "You must be cold from playing in the yard so long."

He accepted the cup. The scent of chocolate hit his senses, sweet and dark. He inhaled deeply, then took a sip, opting to remain by the stove. "This is delicious. Thanks, darlin'."

A pretty pink color bloomed in her cheeks. She busied herself pouring another cup. After taking a drink of her own, she motioned to Isaiah. "Everything all right with him?"

Cody lowered his voice to match hers. "He's feeling a little left out. Doesn't want to be the only one calling us Uncle and Aunt."

"Poor boy." Ella took another sip. Her lips pursed and her head tilted as she studied their son. "Do you think he'll ever call us Mama and Papa?"

"I'd like to think so, but of the three kids, he has the clearest memories of his parents. It hasn't been that long since they passed. He's probably processing everything. Jonah doesn't have the same inhibitions."

"Hmm." His wife set her cocoa down. "Then I suppose we'll have to love on him all the more, let him know he's just as much a part of this family as the others."

Cody let his gaze trail over her face. "You're a good woman, Ella."

She blinked. "For loving a child?"

"Yeah." He stepped closer. "And for putting up with me."

A slow smile spread over her lips. "You're not so bad." She gave him a playful push. "Now let's sit down with our children and enjoy this cocoa. Maybe we can play a game after."

Cody enveloped her hand in his, leading the way to the table. "That sounds perfect."

CHAPTER 17

Spring in Montana was different from spring in Boston. Ella preferred the western version. The days grew warmer, and the fields turned green. The Rocky Mountains retained their snowy tops, glittery and proud against the bright blue sky. The new warmth reinforced just how cold winter had been.

On a particularly quiet evening, Ella curled up on a porch chair, staring at the peaceful vista before her. In the distance, the sun made its descent toward rippling mountains. Orange rays shot high, melding into the darkening blue sky. A cool breeze tickled her face, just enough to make her shiver. Ella took a sip of her tea. The tang of lemon coated her tongue, and the warmth of the liquid evened out the spring chill.

Hummingbirds flitted in a whirl of wings around the newly blooming flowers. An occasional *moo* sounded from one of the pastures. Other than that, silence permeated the ranch. The stillness was a direct contrast to life in Boston. The city bustled at all hours in a cacophony of noise and busyness. Here in the country, Ella felt as though she could simply breathe.

She raised the tea to her mouth again. Her eyes remained

on the sky, watching as the orange softened into light pink. The breeze intensified. Ella shivered again, but she couldn't bring herself to go inside. Not yet. She would happily brave a little cold if it meant basking in such peace.

The door creaked open. Heavy footsteps crossed the porch. Before she could turn, a warm weight settled over her shoulders. She looked at the woolen blanket, then lifted her gaze to her husband. "Thank you."

He settled into the chair beside her, a mug cradled in his hands, his only response a dimpled smile.

A few minutes passed. Hummingbirds continued their evening dance, finding nectar and hurrying away afterward. One of the birds boasted colors so brilliant, it looked to be covered in jewels. It flitted around a flower, then zoomed right up to Ella. She gasped. Its wings beat cold air against her cheeks. The hummingbird darted forward, brushing against her neck before it rushed away once more.

"You made a friend."

Her mouth turned up in a smirk, responding to the amusement in Cody's voice. "He's such a pretty friend too."

Cody's lips twitched. "Is that your only requirement for friendship?"

"Not the *only* requirement." Ella tossed her hair back. "But it's a good thing you're pretty, so we can be friends."

A low rumble sounded deep in his throat. "You're calling a grown man pretty?"

"Indeed. With all that tousled hair and those sapphire eyes —you might as well resign yourself to your prettiness." Goodness, she couldn't remember the last time she'd flirted. Doing so with her husband made her spine tingle.

His mug joined hers on the rail. He stood, crossing his arms. "And would a *pretty* man toss a beautiful woman over his shoulder like a sack of potatoes?"

What?

Cody hoisted her from her seat and tossed her in the air. The blanket dropped to the ground. Ella shrieked as her stomach landed on his shoulder, her hands clutching his tapered waist for support. Not that she needed to. Cody's strong hands held her in place. Laughter shook his body. "Are you ready to give me a different label now? I'm not sure my male pride can handle 'pretty.'"

She dangled against his back, using her hands to push herself up. "If you put me down, I will."

"Promise?"

His voice held a note of teasing. Tingles shot through her heart. "I promise."

Cody gripped her waist and pulled her back over his shoulder. Her feet hit the ground, but her husband made no move to let her go. His eyes twinkled in the fading light. "All right. What's your new word?"

When had he grown a playful side? Her words escaped in a breathy whisper. "Ruggedly handsome."

His smirk turned into a smile. "That so?" He tilted his head to the side and pursed his lips before nodding. "Yeah, that's better. *Much* better"

She smacked his chest. "Silly man." Her hands paused on the solid muscles under her touch, her eyes locked on his. He truly was handsome. But his good looks were secondary to the goodness in his heart. That had attracted her to him more with each passing day. Her heart skipped a beat. Admitting that to herself felt like a major step in their relationship.

Cody stilled as their stare lengthened. His grip on her waist tightened, drawing her closer. Something crackled in the air between them. Ella's memory dug up their kiss by candlelight, a kiss that had yet to be repeated. As if reading her thoughts, Cody's eyes dropped to her lips.

Fear flickered through Ella. Howard's face filled her vision, and for a brief moment, she wanted to bolt. Cody's hands slid up her back. "I won't hurt you, darlin'," he whispered. "You have my word."

Her body released its tension. She sank into him, letting his strength hold her up. "I know. I trust you."

Cody lowered his head. He pressed his lips against hers, firm but gentle. Ella's hands curled into his shirt. His kiss made her heart pound. She was sure he could feel it against his own. She let one hand slide up to his neck, her fingers sinking into his soft hair.

Cody tilted his head, deepening their kiss. His hands spread over her back. He cradled her against him, igniting strong feelings inside while making her feel safe. She clung to her husband, matching his passion, awed at the connection they shared.

Long, sweet minutes passed. When at last they parted, Ella found herself breathless. Cody stared into her eyes, chest heaving, but still he held her close, as if reluctant to let go. A tender smile broke out on his face. He kissed her once more, then tugged her toward a chair. "Sit with me?"

She nodded, about to sit in the one beside him when he pulled her onto his lap. Ella gasped. "Cody!"

"What? I asked you to sit with me."

Ella sputtered. He laughed, reaching down for the blanket on the ground. After slinging it around both of them, he held her close. "I want to know you, Ella. Really know you. Your hopes, dreams, fears—all of it. I want to know your favorite color, your childhood memories." His face buried into her neck, his breath hot against her skin. "I want to know everything about the woman I'm falling for."

She stilled. "Falling for?"

He lifted his head slowly. Her surprise was reflected in his eyes. Cody's brow furrowed, but he nodded. "Yeah. I suppose I am."

Ella's heart swelled. She didn't respond with words. Instead, she sought his lips and showed him how she felt.

~

Cody leaned against his door, watching Ella sleep. Rays of sun flitted through the window. They landed on her hair, turning it red-gold. Hands tucked under her cheek, she wore a peaceful, relaxed look that made his heart ache.

He hadn't meant to admit his feelings last night. The words came out with no thought. But what a relief now that he'd spoken the truth. His wife had woven herself into his life seamlessly. He was close to being in love, if he wasn't already. And while she hadn't admitted any feelings to him, he knew something was there for her too. Her response to his kisses, the looks she gave him in their day-to-day life, the little things she did to show she cared—it all gave him hope that one day their marriage would be as love-filled as his parents' had been.

They certainly had chemistry. Last night's kisses had turned into more, and the only reason Mr. Blackwell might have had for an annulment—had he known—was gone.

Cody pushed up from the door and walked to the bed. Placing his hands on either side of Ella, he leaned down and nuzzled her cheek with his lips. "Time to wake up, darlin'."

She murmured something and wiggled farther under the blankets. He moved his lips to her ear. "The kids are up and ready for planting."

Her eyes flew open. "Oh!" She rolled to her back, staring up at him with a startled expression. He didn't move, keeping himself a few inches above her. Ella inhaled a soft breath. "Good morning."

"Mornin'."

Her brow wrinkled. "Did you say 'planting'?"

"Yep. We've got to get seeds in the ground for our garden.

It'll be a day-long process. I thought I'd see if you wanted to help. If not, the boys and I'll get it done."

She lifted herself onto her elbows. Cody leaned back so she could move to a sitting position. Ella pushed tangled hair out of her face. "I'd love to help. Though I know nothing about gardening."

"It's easy enough. You'll pick it up in no time."

"I'll take your word for it." She threw back the covers. "The children are already awake?"

"Yes, ma'am. Awake and having their breakfast."

Her eyes widened with alarm. "How late did I sleep?"

"About an hour later than usual."

She squeaked and jumped out of the bed.

Cody watched, amusement tickling his chest, as she raced to the wardrobe. "No rush, darlin'. The seeds aren't going anywhere."

"You just said it was a full day process." She yanked out a dress, then faced him. "I need to get ready."

He grinned, resting his shoulder against the wall. "Go right ahead."

"Cody!"

Chuckling, he pushed off the wall and walked toward her. He placed his hands on her shoulders, bending low to whisper in her ear. "You had no reservations last night."

Her face flamed as bright as her hair. "That's different. Now shoo."

"You just shooed me? What am I, a cow?"

Ella bit her lip, but a smile turned it up, anyway. She batted her eyes. "Cody, darling, would you please retire from the room so I can prepare for the day?"

Laughter welled up. "Are you flirting, Ella?"

"Is it working?" She waggled her eyebrows.

His laughter escaped. "All right, I'll leave." He winked. "But I'll be counting the moments until you're downstairs."

She tossed her head, the locks bouncing against her shoulders. "I suppose I'll hurry, then."

Oh, he liked flirty Ella. Cody hooked an arm around her waist. "Good." He pressed a quick kiss to her lips. "See you soon."

"Hmm." She flung the dress to the bed and gripped his suspenders in both hands. "Not yet." Before he could respond, she pulled him back for another, more thorough, much longer kiss.

When they parted, Cody couldn't think straight. He dropped his forehead against hers and let out a long breath. "What're you doing to me, darlin'?"

"I could ask you the same thing." Her voice sounded breathy, barely above a whisper. "I must admit, now that I know how wonderful your kisses are…"

Cody lifted his head and stared down at her, a smile playing on his lips. "Go on."

Her cheeks bloomed pink. "I just…like them…" She groaned, dropping her face into her hands. "Never mind. You can go away now and let me wallow in my mortification."

His laugh enveloped them both. He wrapped his arms around her and pulled her in for a tight embrace. "No need for mortification, Ella. I like your kisses a whole lot too."

"Mama?"

They turned as one. Jonah stood at the door. The little boy hurried toward Ella, arms extended. She swept him into her arms, placing a kiss on his cheek. "Hello, sweetie."

"Hi, Mama."

Cody's heart expanded in his chest as he watched his wife and son. They felt more like a family every day. He might be bumbling his way through, but he'd made the right choice, both in keeping the children and in marrying Ella. How dull life would be without them.

He placed a hand on Ella's back. "I'll take him back downstairs so you can get ready."

She pressed another kiss to Jonah's cheek before relinquishing him.

Cody settled the child on his hip. "You ready for a day outside, buddy?"

Jonah grinned and nodded. They made their way to the kitchen, where Isaiah sat feeding Addie little bites of oatmeal. Cody set Jonah on a chair beside his brother, then went to the stove to make a bowl for Ella. He poured in a generous amount of honey. His nose wrinkled as he stirred it together, but if his wife liked her oatmeal sweet, he'd make sure it was sweet—even if he didn't understand the appeal. Plain oatmeal suited him just fine. He added milk and set the bowl on the table, then poured a cup of coffee for her. Just as he finished, Ella came into the kitchen. Her gaze landed on the breakfast he'd prepared before lifting to meet his. The smile she sent him blazed a trail of heat down his spine.

Isaiah set Addie on the ground. "She's done. Can we plant now?"

"Almost, son. Let your ma—uh, your aunt—eat her breakfast first."

Addie babbled her agreement.

Isaiah shook his head. He grabbed Jonah's hand. "C'mon. Let's play in the yard."

The boys darted to the front door. Addie watched them go with a cry of protest. She pushed up to her hands and knees, rocking back and forth. Cody's eyes widened as she wobbled precariously. He started her way, but Ella put a hand on his arm. He glanced at his wife, confused, before looking back at the baby in time to see her face plant onto the floor. The little girl yelped.

Cody tried again to get her, but Ella's grip on his arm tightened. He froze. "What're you doing? Addie needs help!"

"No, she doesn't. Watch."

Addie rolled to her back with a pout. She gurgled, then flipped to her stomach and pushed herself into a crawling position again. When she tried to slide her knee forward, she fell again.

Ella moved a few steps closer. She picked up the baby and kissed her cheek. "There, there, love. Try again, yes?" She set Addie back on the floor.

Addie looked around a moment before getting to her hands and knees once more.

When she fell again, Cody sucked in a breath. Ella sat on the ground, repeating her short bit of comfort before encouraging the girl to keep trying. His hands clenched into fists. It killed him to watch the child fall. It chafed that his wife wouldn't let him provide the protection Addie needed. Surely, she could learn to crawl in less dangerous circumstances.

Eventually, Addie crawled a few feet before falling to the floor and staying there. She rolled onto her back and reached for her toes, gurgling and cooing.

Ella stood, a smile on her face. "Such a big girl, Addie. You're doing great."

"Great?" He looked at his wife, anger simmering. "She fell more than she crawled."

She planted a hand on her hip. "That's how she'll learn, Cody. Coddling her won't help. Sometimes, we have to fall before we can soar."

"She got hurt trying!"

"Hurt? She's fine. Look at her." Ella waved a hand at their daughter.

Cody huffed, side-eying the baby. She giggled as she finally latched onto her toes, bringing them to her mouth. Ella was right. Addie seemed fine.

His chest burned. "That's not the point. What if she fell wrong? What if she'd cracked her head so badly it bled?"

Ella's gaze softened. "You can't live in what ifs." She rested a hand on his arm. "And you can't protect everyone all the time. Hurt will happen."

His teeth clenched. "Not on my watch." The words sounded harsh to his own ears.

Ella blinked, then stepped back. She folded her arms over her chest and lowered her eyes. The submissive posture loosened his irritation. He reached for her, but Ella took another step back. "Maybe you should start planting. You said it would be a long day."

The waver in her voice hit him hard. "Ella..."

She shook her head. "Just go. Please."

Tears glistened in her eyes before she turned away. For a moment, he stood frozen in place. What was the right response? Obey her request, or ignore it to talk further? Something inside insisted he apologize for his behavior. Fear had turned him into the grizzly, and this time, it had been directed against the person he least wanted to hurt.

Cody put a tentative hand on her shoulder. It went rigid under his touch. Suppressing a sigh, he bowed his head. "I'm sorry, Ella."

She didn't respond. Sniffled.

Feeling like the worst of brutes, he wrapped his arms around her from behind. She stiffened. Cody didn't relent. They'd just endured their first fight, and he was in the wrong. It was up to him to fix the damage.

"I overreacted. Please forgive me, darlin'."

He felt her sigh. She turned. When he saw the tears on her cheeks, his heart slammed into his ribs. He reached up, wiping them away with the pad of his thumb. "I'm sorry."

A small smile appeared on her lips. "So you've said. Twice."

"I'll say it again if..."

Ella placed a hand over his mouth. "You don't need to say it again." She tilted her head, her green eyes looking intently into his. "Howard never apologized. He thought it beneath him, a sign of weakness." Her hands rested against his chest. "You might be rough around the edges, but you have humility. I admire that."

"Even if I growl?"

"Even if you growl."

She leaned forward, resting her head on his shoulder.

Cody held his breath. "Does that mean you forgive me?"

"Yes."

They held each other for another minute. When he pulled back, he stroked her cheek. "I don't deserve you."

Her brow raised high. "You're the best man I know, Cody. Don't put yourself down like that."

Pressure hit his leg. He looked down. Addie perched in a crawling position, one chubby fist gripping his pant leg. His mouth fell open. "Did she crawl all the way over here?"

Ella chuckled. "See? She just needed a chance to succeed."

Cody leaned down to pick up the baby. "Remind me to trust your judgment, darlin'. I didn't realize I could get so overprotective."

"I'll bet Cassie could tell me some stories," Ella said, a smile pulling at her lips.

He cleared his throat, moving toward the door. "I'm not confirming that. Now, enjoy your breakfast. I'll take the kids to the garden."

"I'll be out shortly."

"Take your time."

The smile she sent him proved that all was well. Cody hated that he'd hurt her, but he breathed a prayer of thanks that she forgave him so easily after all she'd been through. Disagreements were bound to happen. That was a part of marriage. But if they could work through them as they did today, he had hope that everything would be fine.

*E*lla stretched, pressing her hands against her lower back to ease the ache.

Cody knelt beside her. "I'm sorry, darlin'. I didn't think it would take more than a day to get the garden planted."

She smiled. "It has been quite rewarding. Knowing we did this together, to help sustain our family—" She shook her head, the smile turning to a grin. "I don't have words to describe it."

He responded with a smile of his own before bending down to drop seeds in a new row. Ella watched him, her heart thumping out a gentle rhythm. This man surprised her at every turn. His panic over Addie yesterday seemed strange until she remembered his protective nature. When he used his gruff tone on her, Ella hadn't known what to think. She'd been hurt. But he refused to let the matter be until they'd worked through it. In her experience, men rarely apologized. The fact that Cody did so raised her respect for him.

Her gaze wandered toward the house, where the children played under a tree heavy with blooms. Contentment washed over her. This life was better than she'd ever imagined. She had a good husband and three children to love, work that fulfilled her, and a beautiful home. What more could she want?

Turning her attention back to the task at hand, Ella planted another row of beets. Reaching for more seeds, she found the basket to be empty.

Cody stood beside her, a tired smile on his face. "We did it."

Ella looked out over the large garden patch. The freshly raked soil was dark, raised in little mounds where they'd planted their vegetables. She rose to her feet, shaking dirt from her dress. "I can't wait to harvest all this."

He chuckled. "That won't be for some time."

"I suppose the anticipation will make it even more worthwhile."

"It does for me." Cody gathered their gardening tools. "I should probably head out to the pastures. The guys are turning the soil to prepare it for alfalfa planting, and they'll be needing help."

A sliver of disappointment went through her. "And I should get lunch together for the kids."

They walked toward the barn. She glanced at the children again. Isaiah stood, hands on his hips, a frown on his face. Jonah held Addie a few paces away, his grip protective. Ella grasped Cody's arm. "Something's wrong."

Her husband's gaze went to the kids. He dropped the basket. They both ran to the tree. When they got there, Ella went down on her knees beside Jonah and Addie while Cody stopped beside Isaiah. "What is it, son?" he asked.

Isaiah pointed toward the house. "I thought I saw a man over there."

Alarms rang in Ella's mind. "A man?"

Cody scanned the area Isaiah pointed at. "I'll check it out." He looked at Ella. "Stay here with the kids."

Her heart dropped as her husband went inside their home. She gathered the children close and prayed hard.

Isaiah's little voice piped up. "It might've been Mr. Hank."

A shot of relief went through her. "Why's that?"

"He had the same hat."

Ella let out a breath.

Moments later, Cody emerged from the house. He came toward them at a jog. "House is safe. No one's there."

"Isaiah said he thought it was Hank."

Cody scratched his chin. "That's possible. Sometimes he needs something from the barn and comes to fetch it."

But wouldn't he have at least waved on arrival? Especially to the children? Ella frowned. Something still didn't feel right.

"Can we eat now? I'm hungry."

Isaiah's comment brought Ella to her feet. She lifted Addie into her arms. "Of course. How do sandwiches sound?"

A chorus of agreement came from the boys. Ella's gaze found Cody's. He wore a frown.

"I don't feel right leaving now." His voice lowered for her ears only. "Especially if it wasn't Hank."

He followed them to the house. Ella strode into the kitchen. "Boys, go wash up at the pump. Isaiah, can you help your brother?"

"Uh-huh." They took off for the kitchen door, Cody on their heels. Ella watched, knowing he wouldn't rest until he knew they were all safe. It was one of the things she loved about him.

She froze. Loved? Was that even possible after such a short time? Her mouth grew slack as she stared at her husband. He stood on the porch, leaning against a post, watching the boys, unaware of the sudden churning in her gut.

Addie squawked. Cody turned, his gaze landing on the baby. He wiggled his fingers at her, prompting a giggle that had Addie reaching out her chubby arms for him.

"Hey, what's this?" Isaiah's voice floated into the kitchen. It was followed by a scream.

Cody's gaze jerked back to the yard before he ran down the

steps. Ella followed, her heart dropping to her feet. Jonah scurried toward her, eyes round with fear.

"Isaiah, don't move!" Cody's voice held a commanding tone, but there was a waver in it.

She came to an abrupt stop when she saw the danger before them.

A basket lay on its side, the lid flipped off. Two large snakes had their beady eyes locked on Isaiah, tongues flicking and tails rattling. The boy whimpered. His little body shook.

One of the coiled snakes hissed and reared back. Ella watched in horror as Cody dove for Isaiah just before the reptile struck. Her husband tackled their son to the ground and curled his body around the boy. The snake's fangs sunk into Cody's thigh. He grunted, then let out a cry when the second snake struck his calf.

Ella grabbed Jonah's hand and rushed to the kitchen. She placed Addie on the floor beside him, her movements jerky. "Watch your sister!" She ran for the rifle hanging above the front door. Weapon in hand, she raced for the yard again.

Cody had somehow rolled away from the reptiles, but one of them poised to strike again. Her lesson with Cody came sharply into focus. Raising the rifle, she aimed for the coiled snake. The gunshot sounded loud in her ears, but she hit her target. The second snake hissed, slithering away before she could reload.

Ella dropped the gun, ran across the clearing, and fell to her knees at Cody's side.

His face was pale. A sheen of sweat covered his brow. Isaiah sobbed in his arms. Cody lifted his eyes to Ella's. "Take Isaiah."

She pulled the boy into her embrace. His tears tore at her heart. "Is...Uncle Cody...going...to be...okay?"

Cody pushed himself up until he sat on the ground. His breathing sounded labored. "I've been bitten before and survived."

Was he swaying? Fear built inside her. "We need to get you to the house."

Isaiah wiggled out of her arms. He grabbed Cody's hand. "Stand up."

"Not yet, son." Cody grunted, the sound pained. He reached into his pocket and pulled out a small, folded-up knife. His gaze settled on Ella. "Cut my pant leg so the bites are visible."

Without thinking, she accepted the knife and set to work.

Cody's breaths grew shakier. "We need something to tie around my leg."

There wasn't enough material on his pants for that. Ella jerked up the hem of her dress to reveal the bottom of her petticoat. With one slice of the knife, she cut through the fabric and tore a long strip out, then returned her gaze to Cody. "Where do I tie it?"

"Around my thigh, above the wounds. Tight."

She wrapped the material mid-thigh and pulled it taut.

Cody grimaced, but he shook his head. "Tighter, Ella. Don't be afraid of hurting me."

Isaiah whimpered. She put a hand on his shoulder. "Can you take care of Addie and Jonah for me while I take care of Uncle Cody?"

The boy's eyes were wet with tears. He nodded, casting one more look at Cody before bolting toward the house.

Ella inhaled deeply before focusing her attention on Cody's leg. She yanked the fabric together as hard as she could.

Cody winced but nodded. "Good...job." He picked up the knife and made an X-shaped cut over each wound.

"What are you doing?"

"I need to draw out the venom." Bending low, he put his mouth over the bite on his calf. He sucked hard, then spit onto the ground. He repeated the process several times. Then he tried to get to the wound in his thigh. After several attempts, his shoulders slumped. "I can't reach it."

"I'll do it." Ella got to her knees and bent over him.

"I can't ask you…"

"You're not allowed to argue with me. Your life is in danger." She put her hands on her hips. "I'm going to help you."

Over the sound of his labored breathing, she leaned toward the cut. Her stomach revolted at the sight of his blood. Determined, she put her mouth to the wound.

"Whatever you do, don't swallow."

Ella drew out what she could, spitting it out after each suction.

When she finished, Cody pointed to the pump. "Rinse out your mouth, and bring the bucket over so I can do the same."

After they'd washed, Ella put a hand on his shoulder. "Can you get up?"

Cody got one knee under him, but he stumbled when he tried to rise. Ella slid under his arm, supporting him as best she could. He trembled. "You need to go for Doc."

Panic nipped. "I can't leave you and the children!"

His blue eyes speared her. "Sucking out the poison will buy us time, but we need Doc's remedy for snakebites."

Her body betrayed her. Knees buckling, she almost went down and took him along.

Cody leaned against her, his warm breath tickling her ear. "You can do this, darlin'. I believe in you."

His assurance gave her a shot of strength. Ella helped him inside. Jonah stared as they walked slowly through the kitchen. He kept a tight hold on Addie, and Ella blessed him for listening to her command to care for the baby. Isaiah stood over both of them, silent and protective.

When they reached the parlor, Ella made sure Cody lay as comfortably as possible on the couch. A glance at his leg told her time was essential. The thigh and calf had swollen.

He squeezed her hand. "Go, Ella."

She pressed her lips to his forehead, then hurried to the

children. "I need to go to town to get Doc. Keep an eye on Papa Cody for me, okay?"

Isaiah nodded through his tears. Wishing she could reassure the children further, Ella bolted for the barn. Preston nickered a welcome when he saw her. Gathering her courage, Ella grabbed his halter and slipped it over his head. "I don't know how to saddle you, boy, and I've never ridden bareback. You're going to have to make sure we get to town in one piece, okay?"

The horse nudged her with his nose. She took that as a confirmation. It was a struggle to climb onto his back, but once she was situated, she gripped her legs around his middle. Preston took off at a gallop. Ella clung to his mane. Tears poured down her cheeks as she thought of her husband in pain and danger. Prayers shot from her heart to heaven, each one a fervent plea that he make it through the upcoming ordeal.

❧

Cody bit back a groan while Doc applied a strong-smelling poultice to his wounds. All he felt in his right leg was fiery pain. Ella sat beside him, his hand clutched in hers. Cassie and Travis were in the other room watching the children. They'd seen Ella on her way into town and insisted on coming to the ranch.

Doc tied off a bandage. Cody hissed as it pulled tight against his thigh. Twice in one day. He gritted his teeth, eying the doctor. "Was that necessary?"

The older man chuckled. "You have some fight in you. That's a good sign."

Ella's grip intensified. "Are you sure?"

The doctor placed a hand on her shoulder. "He's young and strong, Mrs. Brooks, and he survived an attack like this before."

She didn't look convinced. Cody squeezed her hand. "It'll hurt for a bit, darlin', but thanks to you, I should be fine."

Her cheeks turned pink. Cody studied her, taking in details he hadn't noticed before. Her hair had fallen from its bun, tangled from the wind. Her dress looked dusty and crumpled, and a few scrapes lined her cheeks. He frowned.

Before he could say anything, Doc turned to her. "Now, young lady, let's take a look at your injuries."

Cody pushed himself up. "Injuries?" He winced, unprepared for the wave of dizziness that struck.

With a *tsk* of disapproval, Doc pressed him back down. "No sudden movements. You need to rest."

"You just said my wife is injured, and you want me to rest?" Cody attempted to get up again.

This time, Ella pushed him down. "Listen to Doc, Cody."

He stilled under her touch, a smile threatening at her tone. "Are you bossing me around, darlin'?"

She lifted her chin. "Best get used to it for the foreseeable future."

Doc mixed something in a cup before holding it out to Cody. "Drink this."

Cody accepted the cup and peered inside. "What is it?"

"Laudanum. It'll help you rest. That's the most important thing right now."

"Ugh. This knocked me out last time."

Doc raised a brow. "That's the point. Now, drink up, and I'll be back to check on you tomorrow."

With a sigh, Cody drained the contents in one long swallow. He plunked it down and looked at Ella. "What happened to you?"

"I fell off Preston. Twice." She rubbed her arms. "I'm not used to riding bareback."

Doc chuckled. "She was riding like the wind when she came into town. Saw her tumble myself when she brought that big horse to a stop."

"What?" Cody blinked, fighting the haze settling over his vision. "Are you all right, Ella?"

"I'm fine." She placed a hand on his cheek, gently rubbing her thumb along his jaw. "Don't worry about me. You rest and heal."

He didn't have much choice, not with rattlesnake venom and laudanum making their way through his body. It sent him into such a deep sleep, he didn't wake again until well into the following morning.

When he opened his eyes, a harsh pounding in his head made him wish for the oblivion of sleep once more. Why was it so hot? He thrashed, kicking off the heavy blanket holding him down.

"Easy."

Ella's voice sounded somewhere above him. Cody searched for her. The light coming through the window increased the pain in his head. He closed his eyes with a groan. Something cool and wet pressed against his face.

"You have a fever. Doc said that might happen. Your body is fighting the venom." Ella moved the cloth over his face. "Keep fighting, Cody."

He let his eyes open into slits. His wife sat beside him. She held a cup. "Can you drink this?"

Cody's eyes fell shut again, but he parted his lips as best he could. Ella poured in water a little at a time, letting him swallow before giving him more. Voices floated in from the kitchen. "Who's that?"

"Cassie and Miss Hattie."

"Travis left?"

"Yes. He said...well, he had something to look into."

Something heavy lay in her words. Cody opened his eyes to see her expression. It was carefully schooled. Alarms rang in his mind, along with the faint thought that he should know what that something was. "What?" *Blast this brain fog.*

She shook her head. "Nothing to concern yourself with right now. When you're better, we'll talk."

He tried to push himself up. "You realize this is just going to bother me until I know what's going on, right?"

Ella quirked a brow. "Back to a bear, are we?"

Cody groaned, pressing a hand to his head. "Sorry. Feeling like this is enough to turn anyone into a grouch."

"Your head hurts?"

"Yeah."

She wet the cloth in her hands, then applied it to his forehead. "Rest. We'll talk later, when your strength is back."

"That bad, huh?"

Her lips compressed into a straight line. "Just get better. I can't lose you."

Agony laced the words. Cody reached for her hand. "Hey. I'll be fine."

She sniffed and swiped at a tear. "You don't know that."

"I have a reason to fight now, Ella. I'm not going anywhere."

His words hung in the air between them. Ella searched his eyes, her own lit with deep emotion. To his surprise, she cupped his cheeks and planted a gentle kiss on his lips. Her thumbs rubbed little circles on his jaw when she pulled back, her gaze intent on his. "You're breaking down the walls around my heart, Cody. You have been ever since you agreed to marry me." Her lips brushed against his again. "Rest."

He closed his eyes, smiling despite his pain. "Yes, ma'am."

CHAPTER 19

$\mathcal{E}$very muscle in Ella's body screamed at her, a reminder of her double fall from Preston. Even after three days, the bruises looked fresh. She pulled a dress over her head and covered the evidence of her mishaps. A glance at the bed told her Cody still slept. He'd done that a lot since his encounter with the snakes.

She walked to him and placed a hand on his forehead. His skin was cool. Relief flooded her. The fever had broken.

His eyes flitted open. "Hey."

She sat next to him. "How are you feeling?"

"Better." He pushed the covers back.

Ella took his arm to help him sit up. She brushed a lock of hair from his face. "Do you think you can make it downstairs today?"

"Maybe." Cody maneuvered his legs over the side of the bed. When his right leg took on some weight, he winced.

"Still hurts?"

"A bit." He grunted as he moved, but he walked with determination. Ella hovered beside him. They stopped at the stairs. Cody eyed her. "Seems I'm not the only one moving slow."

"You can tell?"

"You usually walk gracefully. Right now you're walking like you fell off a horse."

Ella swatted his arm. He chuckled. "Just calling it like it is, darlin'." His face sobered. "You risked your safety riding bareback. I don't know what I would've done if something bad happened while you rode to town."

She put a hand on his chest. "It was well worth it to get you help."

He pressed a kiss to her forehead. "Thanks, love."

Ella caught her breath. "Love?"

Silence reigned for several seconds. Cody's eyes locked on hers, the intensity there stealing the little air she had left.

"I hate to interrupt, but we need to talk."

Ella looked down to see Travis at the base of the stairs. An amused smile creased his face. Heat crept into Ella's cheeks. Cody took her hand and started down the steps. She wanted to protest and beg him to answer her unspoken question. Her heart beat furiously against her ribs as she wondered what he'd been about to say.

Her husband moved slowly. "I just woke up, Trav. I hope whatever it is we need to talk about is important."

"It is."

Cody turned to Ella. "Is this what you said we'd talk about when I first got bit?"

She nibbled the inside of her cheek. "Yes. Though I don't know everything. Just that those snakes weren't in our yard by accident."

"The attack was purposeful." It wasn't a question.

"Looks that way." Travis nodded toward the kitchen. "Cassie took the kids to visit with Miss Hattie, but she put coffee on before leaving."

Once situated at the table with mugs, Travis wasted no time. "As Ella said, the snakes were planted. They were apparently transported here in a basket, the one Isaiah knocked over when he saw them in it."

Ella shuddered, remembering how close her son had come to being bitten. Would one so young have been able to survive such an attack?

Travis fished a piece of paper from his pocket. "This was in the basket."

Ella frowned. "A note?"

Travis slid the paper their way.

Cody took it, scanning the words. His body jerked. "Who left this?"

"I don't know. But I aim to find out."

The hardness in Travis's voice sent shivers down Ella's spine. She reached for the note.

Cody slid it from her grasp. "No, darlin'."

She blinked. "Why?"

Something flickered in his eyes. He shook his head.

Travis speared him with a look. "She needs to know, Cody. Maybe she can help us identify who's doing this."

Another shiver went through her, this one leaving dread in its wake. Cody's struggle was evident in his eyes. He closed them, breathed out long and slow, then placed the paper in her hand. His arm looped around her shoulders. Ella smoothed the paper out and read the single sentence.

SEND ARIELLA MOUNTBATTEN BACK TO BOSTON, OR WORSE WILL HAPPEN

The paper fell from her hands. She lurched back. Cody's strong grip was the only thing that kept her upright. She stared at Travis. "Why didn't you tell me sooner?"

"You had enough going on. I wanted some time to look into who might have done this."

"Did you find anything?" Cody asked.

"Not yet. There's no out-of-towners staying at the hotel. A friend on the Boston force confirmed both Mr. Mountbatten and Mr. Blackwell are at their homes."

Another possibility whispered through Ella's mind. "And… Howard?"

"He's accounted for too. All three are in Boston."

Stormy emotion flashed over Cody's face. "That doesn't mean someone isn't here on their orders. Why else would this person demand Ella go back to Boston?"

She felt weak. "Worse will happen?"

Cody's hand closed around hers. Travis exhaled. "Ella, I will do everything I can to find who did this. Strangers stand out here. If someone is here for your father, they shouldn't be hard to find. I'll go to the shops today and ask around, see if anyone can tell us something."

Ella leaned into her husband but spoke to Travis. "Do you think this is connected to whoever broke our fence?"

Travis frowned. He scratched his cheek and shook his head. "Maybe. We'll figure that out later." He pointed at them. "You two need to rest. You're still recovering."

Ella pushed back from her chair. "I'm fine."

Cody stopped her. "Darlin', if Travis says you need to rest, I trust his judgment. I'm guessing you're pretty banged up from those falls."

"And Cassie is staying to help care for the children. Take today, rest up, and we'll regroup tomorrow," Travis said.

"'We'?" Ella asked, brows raised.

Travis chuckled. "I'll be back to report my findings. And to spend time with my wife. If she's here, I'm here."

"We won't object to that." Cody stood, holding out a hand. "Thanks, Trav."

The men shook hands, and Travis took his leave. Ella gripped her mug of coffee. It trembled as she brought it to her lips.

Cody sat beside her. "Darlin', you're going to crack that cup if you hold it any tighter."

"What?" Ella looked down. Her fingers were white. She relaxed her grip. "I'm feeling a bit anxious."

"I reckon so." Cody covered her hand with his. "Whoever did this won't get away with it."

"You can't promise that."

His brows knit into a V. "You know I'll do everything in my power to protect you."

"I know." Her throat tightened. "But look what happened to you—because of me."

Cody's voice lowered to a gravelly growl. "Not because of you. Because of someone else's choice. This isn't your fault, Ella."

"It might have been someone else's choice, but the fact remains you got hurt because of me being here. Isaiah might have been killed if you hadn't protected him from those snakes." She shivered. "And this person claims he'll strike again if I don't go back."

"You're not going back."

"Of course not. But how are we going to keep our family safe?"

"One thing at a time." He wrapped his arm around her. "We'll see what Travis finds out and go from there. Now, come."

She allowed him to lead her out of the kitchen into the parlor. Her body protested the movement. When they reached the sofa, she sank onto the cushions and closed her eyes. "What are we doing?"

The sofa squeaked as Cody sat beside her. "We follow orders. We rest."

"I guess that doesn't sound so bad." She leaned her head on his shoulder, trying to banish the fear clutching her heart. Whatever the future held, she needed to trust that God had it under control.

Whatever that might look like.

~

Despite his outward calm, waves of anger pulsed through Cody. If only he knew who to direct it at, but their assailant was a mystery.

A fact he hoped to rectify sooner than later.

When he read the words on that paper, threatening his wife, Cody saw red. He thought he'd hid it well, but the more he considered it, the angrier he became. It was a wonder steam wasn't escaping his ears as he sat beside Ella, wanting nothing more than her safety. She sat beside him, reading aloud from his mother's book of poems, and all he could think about was how to protect her.

"Cody?"

He blinked. Ella had put the book down. She stared at him, brows knit in concern. He shook himself and pasted on a smile. "Yeah?"

She put a hand to his cheek, rubbing it gently. "You're upset."

"I'm fine."

"Are you?"

He inhaled long and slow. "I will be."

"Is it the note?"

Tempted to deny it, but unwilling to shatter the hard-won trust between them, Cody nodded. "Yeah."

Quiet lingered between them for a few moments. Ella's hand fell from his cheek to his shoulder. "I'm scared."

The soft admission tore his heart. He wrapped his arms around her, pulling her close. She gasped in pain. Cody released her at once. He'd forgotten about her bruises. Berating himself, he started to apologize, but Ella spoke first.

"Don't."

"I hurt you."

"Accidentally. You wanted to comfort me. Please don't apologize for that." She settled herself against him, resting her hand against his chest. "There are no bruises on my right side."

The invitation was clear. He planted his hand on her right hip, pressing her against his body. "What're you scared of, darlin'?"

It took her almost a minute to respond. "I'm afraid of losing you. I'm afraid of losing the children." Her body trembled. "I'm afraid of being forced back to Howard."

"Over my dead body." The words came out low and fervent.

Ella stilled. She looked up at him, eyes watery. "That's what frightens me most."

How had this woman become so precious to him in such a short time? Cody lowered his lips to hers, desperate to drive away her fear. Their kiss held a passion born of the unknown. He held her as close as he dared, mindful of her injuries. She melted into him, her lips moving against his in a manner that felt nearly frenzied. That told him just how scared she was. He slowed them down, kissing her gently. His hands cupped her cheeks. They met with trails of water.

Pulling back, Cody looked her in the eyes. Her tears fell fast. His heart slammed into his ribs. He rubbed his thumbs over her cheeks.

Ella choked out a laugh. "I'm not usually this emotional."

"You have good reason to be."

She sighed and rested her head against his shoulder.

Cody tried to find words, but nothing seemed right. He settled for rubbing a hand against her back.

The next thing he knew, he woke to the warmth of a roaring fire. His sister stood nearby, Addie on her hip. He glanced down to see Ella sleeping on him. Protectiveness rose swiftly inside. He shifted his body, hoping to make her more comfortable.

Cassie tiptoed toward him. "The boys are napping. I'm going to start dinner."

"I'll take Addie."

"Are you sure?"

He nodded. Cassie settled the baby on his lap. "I'll be in the kitchen. Holler if you need anything."

Addie gazed up at him with wide, trusting eyes. A wave of unworthiness pushed its way into his heart. Could he be the father this sweet child needed?

"You're a natural with her."

Ella's sleepy words pulled him out of his thoughts.

He shook his head. "I think you meant to say 'awkward.'"

"No." She yawned and pushed herself up. "I meant what I said."

He looked at the eight-month-old. Addie grinned, showing her two front teeth. She reached for his face, planting a chubby hand on either cheek, and squealed a laugh. A responding smile tugged at his lips.

"It's obvious you love her."

"I suppose I do." He bounced the baby up and down. "Children are surprisingly easy to love."

"So are gruff cowboys."

Ella's voice was soft. His heart stilled, then pounded hard. Not daring to breathe, he turned his attention to her. She watched him steadily. "Cody, what were you going to say this morning, before Travis interrupted us?"

"Ella, once I say it, it can't be unsaid."

"I know."

It sounded as though she wanted him to speak the three words that had been begging for release. His stomach danced with dizzying speed. He drew in a deep breath and exhaled hard. "I was going to say—I love you. I don't know when it happened, but it did."

Ella's smile lit her face.

Cody fumbled on. "This wasn't how I planned on telling you. You deserve a grand gesture, something from the heart, and that…"

She stopped him with a finger over his lips. "I don't need flashy gestures, Cody. This declaration, in the middle of our everyday life, is beautiful." She paused, then softly went on. "'I love thee to the level of every day's most quiet need, by sun and candle-light.'"

The words, so familiar, rendered him speechless. He looked at the book in her lap. His mother's handwriting stared back at him. "You remembered."

Her hand found his. "Your mother knew what she was talking about. Loving another happens in the simple moments of life. By day and by night. By sun and candlelight. That's how…" She stopped, her chest rising and falling quickly. Her voice softened even more, barely audible. "That's how I fell in love with you."

Cody laughed, his heart full to bursting. He wrapped his free arm around Ella and leaned toward her.

"Well! It's about time!"

Cody's gaze shot toward his sister, who stood in the parlor entrance wearing a huge grin. "Really, Cass?"

"I can't help it if I overheard your declaration of love."

He straightened. "Just how much did you hear?"

"Enough." Cassie sauntered in, plucking Addie from his arms. "Congratulations, you two. I'm thrilled to know you found happiness together." She wiggled her brows. "Now, I'll just take this little angel to the kitchen. Ta-ta!"

Ella buried her face in his chest. He felt the heat from her cheeks through his shirt. "I'm not sure whether to feel amused or mortified."

Cody chuckled. "At least we know we have her support."

The clock chimed. He glanced at it. "Travis will be back soon."

That statement seemed to deflate his wife. He put a finger under her chin, lifting it until her eyes met his. "Whatever comes, we'll face it together. We won't do this alone."

She slipped her hand into his. "Thank God for that. I love you, Cody."

"I love you too."

And he sealed it with a kiss.

CHAPTER 20

wo weeks passed without further incident. Ella and Cody healed from their injuries, and Cody went back to the range three days after his fever broke. Ella jumped at every little sound while her husband was away. Her consolation lay in the fact that Travis rode by a few times each day. Cody had given her another shooting lesson, though he said if she could shoot a snake, her aim was excellent. They'd come up with a signal for trouble—if Ella needed him, she'd fire two shots in rapid succession. The reverberation should be enough for at least one of the ranch hands to hear and come running.

She tried not to focus on *should*.

Travis brought news that no one had seen a stranger in town beyond the usual arrivals from the train station. No out-of-towner stayed at the hotel or frequented the restaurant or mercantile. The lack of answers strengthened the perpetual knot in Ella's gut.

She tried to keep her mind on the fact that Cody loved her. That brought her joy, an airy lightness that broke through the dark surrounding the unknown. At least they had each other.

One morning in early May, as she made her way to the water pump, Addie on her hip and the boys playing nearby, she prayed for strength and peace. Positioning the watering can under the pump, she reached for the handle.

"Aunt Ella!"

She straightened and searched for Isaiah. He waved. Ella made her way to the blanket where the boys had scattered their playthings. "Yes?"

"Jonah wants you to play with us."

Ella smiled. Watering the garden could wait. "What do you want to play?"

"Dunno."

"Why don't we all lay on our backs and see what shapes the clouds are making?"

Interest gleamed in Isaiah's eyes. "Okay."

Jonah echoed the enthusiasm. Ella set Addie down beside her, then lay down. The boys quickly copied her. "All right, what do we see?"

"Twain!" Jonah exclaimed, pointing up.

"Very good, Jonah. What about you, Isaiah?"

"I see a dog."

Addie babbled and crawled onto Ella's stomach.

Isaiah bolted up with a sharp gasp. "Addie, you can't sit on Aunt Ella's tummy. You'll squish the baby."

Ella blinked. "What baby?"

"The one Uncle Cody gave you."

She put a hand on her stomach. "I don't have a baby." At least not that she knew of. It was possible. The thought sent warmth through her veins.

Isaiah huffed, planting his hands on his hips. "Aunt Cassie said Uncle Travis gave her their baby. Why hasn't Uncle Cody given you one?"

She coughed. "Isaiah, these things take time." An idea came

to mind, one she hoped would help him understand. "Do you remember when we planted seeds in this garden?"

He nodded.

"Did the vegetables start growing right away?"

"No."

"That's what it's like with a baby. A seed has to be planted in my tummy before one can start growing. It has to be the right time too. If we planted seeds in the garden during the winter, they wouldn't grow. It's the same for a baby. The right conditions have to be there before it can be planted."

He tilted his head. "Do you have to water the baby and give it lots of sun and make sure no weeds choke it?"

She laughed. "Not exactly. But I will have to drink lots of water and eat good food so the baby can grow."

Isaiah sighed, plopping onto the blanket. "Does this mean I have to be patient?"

"I'm afraid so."

The boy wrinkled his nose. "I'm not good at being patient."

Ella chuckled, running a hand through his soft hair. "You'll manage."

He fell silent. Various emotions ran across his young face. Jonah asked her about a cloud, so Ella turned her attention to her middle child. She darted occasional looks at Isaiah. He remained in deep thought. Jonah eventually started playing peek-a-boo with Addie. Ella's lips turned up in a smile as she watched, their sweet innocence a balm to her heart.

"Will a baby call you Mama?"

Isaiah's question brought Ella's eyes back to him. "Yes."

"And Uncle Cody would be its papa?"

"Yes."

Isaiah frowned. "Then I'll still be the only one not saying 'mama' and 'papa.'"

Ella reached out, tugging her son close. He allowed it,

though his little body stiffened. "We love you, Isaiah, no matter what you call us."

His lip pushed out in a pout. "But I don't want to be different from my brothers and sisters."

She took note of the fact that he would claim her children as his siblings. Ella hugged him. "What about a compromise?"

"What's a compromise?"

"It means meeting in the middle. What if you called me Mama Ella instead of Aunt Ella?"

Isaiah bit his lip and searched her eyes. When he spoke, his voice was small. "Do you think my mama would be okay with that?"

She pressed a kiss to his soft cheek. "I didn't know her, but Uncle Cody tells me she loved you very much. I think she'd be happy if you're happy."

Isaiah relaxed. He chewed on his lip. "Mama Ella. Papa Cody."

Ella held her breath.

A grin broke out on Isaiah's face. "I like it."

She hugged him again, tears welling in her eyes.

Isaiah pushed back after a moment. "Hey, why're you crying?"

"I'm happy."

"People don't cry when they're happy."

"They do sometimes." She ruffled his hair, then pushed to her feet. "Can you watch your sister while I water the garden?"

"Uh-huh."

The boys took to their game. Jonah dashed around the blanket, Isaiah giving chase. Addie chomped on her fingers in the middle of them, giggling and waving her free hand.

Ella's heart seemed to grow in size, and she praised God for bringing her into this beautiful family. Jonah caught her eye. He beamed and waved, then took off again when Isaiah drew near.

Ella laughed. The sound danced around the yard. She picked up the watering can and headed for the garden, smile still in place. Humming softly, she began her task at the end nearest the house.

A few minutes later, Isaiah tugged her skirt. "Mama Ella, Addie's fussing."

On the blanket, Addie rubbed her eyes, making little sounds of frustration. Jonah sat beside her, patting her back. Addie slumped against him. As Ella watched, her daughter fell fast asleep.

"It looks as though your brother got her to take a nap."

Isaiah didn't respond. Ella turned to see him standing with hands on his hips, brows wrinkled. "Why's the ground white?"

White? Ella's gaze fell on the moist earth. Her jaw dropped open. How had she missed the white film covering the dirt? Had she been that distracted watching the children? She plunked the watering can down. "I don't know. Have you ever seen something like this?"

"Nope." Isaiah touched the dirt. "It feels funny."

Ella stooped beside him. Her hands lifted a chunk of warm earth from the ground, and her fingers slid over the surface. They came away grainy. She frowned. Something wasn't right.

"Isaiah, let's get your siblings inside. When Papa Cody comes home, we'll show him the garden."

"Okay." Isaiah took off for the blanket, concern apparently forgotten. Ella stared another moment at the ground, as if it could give her answers.

None came.

∼

"*P*apa Cody! The ground is white!"

Cody paused in unsaddling his horse and looked down just as Isaiah ran into his legs at full speed. Grunting, Cody steadied himself against the side of the barn. Interesting welcome to coming home for the evening. "Easy there, Isaiah. What's going on?" His mind caught up with the boy's words. "What did you call me?"

"Mama Ella said I could make a compromise and use *papa* with your name. So you're Papa Cody now."

"That so?" Cody squatted down to Isaiah's level, joy rising in his chest. "And you don't mind using those names?"

"Nope. Now come with me." He grabbed Cody's hand and made for the door.

So much for processing his new title. "Whoa, buddy. I need to put Preston in his stall first."

Isaiah crossed his arms. His foot tapped against the ground as Cody set about bedding his horse down for the night. He hid a grin, knowing that would do nothing to improve the five-year-old's waning patience. His heart warmed at the fact that his son now acknowledged him in some way as his father and Ella as his mother. How had she reacted to the christening? Giving Preston a final pat, he turned to Isaiah. "All right, you can show me."

The boy latched onto Cody's hand and hauled him toward the garden. "It's white!"

"Like frost?"

"Kinda."

They made it to the garden in record time. Isaiah dropped his hand and pointed. "See?"

Cody surveyed the ground. He frowned, crouching down to touch the dirt. "Was it like this in the morning?"

"Uh-huh. Mama Ella didn't know what to do."

He rubbed some soil beneath his fingers. Curls of dread pricked his gut. Careful to keep his expression neutral, he held out a hand to Isaiah. "I'll have Mr. Hank take a look, see what he thinks. He knows soil better than me."

The sinking feeling in his chest told him he knew exactly what the white film was.

Isaiah slipped his hand into Cody's, hopping along as they went to the house. "When're you gonna see Mr. Hank?"

"As soon as I let Aunt—I mean, Mama—Ella know."

Thankfully, Hank and the twins lived in a cabin on the west side of the ranch. It would only take five minutes to get there at a gallop. He'd have to take Carter instead of Preston. His horse deserved a break after a long day.

Delicious aromas filled Cody's nose the moment he walked through the door. He detected earthy vegetables, savory gravy, and succulent chicken. Mouth watering, he followed the smell into the kitchen. Isaiah let go of Cody's hand and headed for the parlor.

Ella bent over the oven, pulling out a pan. She set it on the stove.

Cody went to her and kissed her cheek. "Hey, darlin'."

"Cody!"

She turned to him with a smile. His heart thumped hard when she slid her arms around his neck and pushed up on her toes to kiss him. He responded at once, his hands pulling her close. A man could lose himself in moments like this. When they pulled back, he smiled. "If I'd known that's the greeting of a woman in love, I'd have tried wooing you back when we first married."

Her breath tickled his lips as she laughed. He leaned forward again, catching those lips in his and kissing her thoroughly. After a while, he finally let her go. Her eyes twinkled, and she ran a hand over his cheek. "I'm glad you're home."

Reality crashed in. Cody gently gripped her upper arms. "I need to head out to get Hank."

Her lips opened as if to protest, but she paused. "Is this about the garden?"

"Yeah."

"Do you know what it is?"

"I'm afraid it's salt."

"Is that bad?"

"It depends. That's why I need to bring Hank over, before daylight disappears."

She nodded, her hands resting against his chest. "Go. I'll keep your supper warm."

He enveloped her in a brief embrace, then headed back to the barn to saddle the horse and galloped to Hank's. Minutes later, they were back at the house. Hank surveyed the ground. He scratched his head, hat held loosely in hand. "It looks like salt, Boss. But how'd it get there? Your wife wouldn't add any to the water can, would she?"

"No. Besides, the amount of salt needed for it to look like this is huge. It would take several bags' worth." Did the mercantile even sell that much?

Hank squinted. "Look." He pointed to several spots. "Boot prints. I'm guessing they ain't yours."

"Nope." Cody squatted beside the nearest one. "Whoever did this is big." He stood, then pulled off his boot and set it next to the print. "He's got a couple inches on me."

"And you're one of the tallest men in Harmony Springs."

Cody pushed his foot back into the boot. "That might make it easier to find him."

"Want me to get the sheriff?" Hank held up a hand before Cody could open his mouth. "And before ya protest, I was plannin' on going to town anyway to sup at the café."

"Then I'd appreciate that. Thanks, Hank."

Plopping his hat on his head, the foreman gave it a tip. "I'll get there lickety-split."

Cody headed into the house.

Ella met him at the door. "Is it salt?"

"Looks like it. Hank's off to get Travis."

His wife looked out the door. "It'll be nearly dark before he gets here."

"We'll light some lanterns. He'll probably come back in the morning if he needs to see things in the daytime."

Ella slipped her hand into his and pulled him toward the kitchen. "Come, eat. You should relax a bit while you can."

"Thanks, darlin'." He inhaled deeply, the savory scent lingering in the air. "Smells great."

Jonah came running into the kitchen. "Papa!" He grabbed Cody's leg, a toothy smile spread wide over his little face.

"Hey, buddy." Cody lifted the child into his arms. "Did you have a good day?"

"Uh-huh." Jonah looked at the plate Ella pulled from the oven. "I want 'tatoes."

Ella put the plate on the table. Grabbing a pitcher, she poured a cup of water and set it in front of Cody. She smiled at their son. "More potatoes?"

"Pwease!"

"He can share some of mine." Cody sat with Jonah on his lap. As he ate, he alternated taking a bite of potatoes, then offering the next to the boy. Ella joined them with a cup of tea. She got up periodically to check on Isaiah and Addie in the parlor. Cody had almost finished his meal when Jonah wiggled off his lap and headed for his siblings.

Ella watched him go, a thoughtful look on her face. "Those children share a special bond."

"They always have. Isaiah and Jonah were happy, playful boys before their parents died. Jake said they were inseparable. Both withdrew after the accident." He reached out, claiming Ella's hand. "You coming into our lives changed that."

She shook her head. "You took them in, gave them a home. They received stability because of you."

"I guess that means we make a good team."

The throaty quality in his voice surprised him. Tenderness

flashed over Ella's face. She put her free hand over their joined ones. "We do."

He started to respond, but a knock sounded at the door.

Ella gave his hand a squeeze. "That'll be Travis." She reached for his plate.

He handed it to her with a smile. "Thanks." Heading for the door, he opened it to greet his friend. "Thanks for comin', Trav."

Travis nodded. "Not a problem. I don't like the implications of a tampered garden."

"Me neither. First the snakes, now this. Someone's targeting our family. And we both know who."

"Not to mention the cattle fence being down." Travis snorted. "I'd put money on Mountbatten. He threatened you and Ella more than once. This is exactly the kind of power struggle he thrives on. He won't dirty his own hands, but he'll hire others to do it."

Cody's fists clenched at his sides.

Travis put a hand on his shoulder. "We'll figure out what's going on."

Not trusting himself to speak, Cody nodded.

He turned to see Ella in the space between the foyer and parlor. He wanted to rush to her and wrap her in his arms, protecting her from whatever scheme her father had in place. A smile stretched over her lips as she motioned to them. "You have to see this."

The men joined her. Ella put a finger to her lips, then pointed into the room. Cody peered over her shoulder.

Isaiah sat on the floor, his back against the sofa. Addie lay cradled in his lap, Jonah snuggled up to his side. The boy sang softly as he rocked his sister. She looked up at him with sleepy eyes and a contented smile. Cody recognized the tune "All Through the Night."

Ella turned. She touched his cheek with her fingers. "You

see, Cody? This is what you giving them a home did." Rising on her toes, she pressed a kiss to his cheek. "Now, you and Travis figure out the garden. I want a full report when you're done." Her fingers trailed down his cheek before she went to join the children.

Cody stood for a few moments, taking in the picture his family made. His heart swelled and his protective instincts rose once more.

He'd do whatever it took to keep them safe.

CHAPTER 21

*E*lla chewed her bottom lip, watching her husband and Travis from the kitchen window. Morning light bathed them in a golden glow. Last night had yielded limited information, which prompted Travis's return today.

Cody pointed to a tree near the garden. Travis walked to it and pulled something from the trunk. The two men huddled over it. Even from this distance, Ella saw her husband's body go rigid. His face whipped toward the house before turning back to Travis. Whatever their topic of conversation, it looked animated.

"Mama, I hungwy." A tug at her skirt accompanied the little voice.

She dragged her gaze from her husband and looked down at Jonah. "Good morning, sweetie. You want your breakfast?"

"Pancakes? Pwease?" Eagerness shone in his dark eyes.

Ella picked him up. "We can have pancakes." And it would provide her with a distraction.

Jonah laid his head on her shoulder as she walked to the kitchen. He yawned, then stuck his thumb in his mouth. Ella set him in a chair, poured him a glass of fresh milk, then began preparing breakfast. Isaiah wandered into the room when she ladled the first bits of batter into the pan. "Good morning."

"Mornin', Mama."

Ella's heart leapt. She tried not to overreact, watching as her son rubbed his eyes. Perhaps dropping her name from *mama* had been a sleepy mistake.

"Are you hungry? We're having pancakes for breakfast."

"Yeah. Can we have eggs too?"

Ella glanced at the pan. She would have to fry all the batter before she could search for eggs. "Maybe. I'll have to gather them from the coop after I finish these."

"I can get 'em." Isaiah drew himself up tall. "Papa Cody says I'm a good helper."

"Is that so?" Ella smiled at the boy before reaching for a basket beside the stove. "All right. Here you go." She handed it to him.

Jonah slipped from his chair. "I he'p too?"

"If your brother doesn't mind."

Isaiah took Jonah's hand. "C'mon, Jonah. We'll see who can get the most eggs."

They boys took off out the door. As soon as their footsteps faded, Ella returned to making pancakes. She had a sizable stack finished when noises from the children's room caught her attention. Addie must have woken. Ella laid a towel over the pancakes to keep them warm. She made her way upstairs.

Addie sat in her crib. A cherubic smile filled her little face when she saw Ella. "Ma...ma...ma."

"Hello, sweet girl." She lifted Addie from the crib, inhaling her sweet baby scent. "Did you sleep well?"

Addie babbled as Ella changed her. Her little toes danced in the air. She giggled at nothing, waving her hands and trying to catch Ella's sleeve. "Oh, no you don't." Ella scooped her up, planting kisses on her daughter's cheek. "You're getting more and more adventurous, aren't you?"

A loud squeal was Addie's reply. Ella chuckled. "Let's get you some milk."

Addie clapped. Ella sang a lullaby as they went back to the kitchen. She placed her daughter in a highchair and set about making a bottle. When it was ready, she gave it to Addie along with a torn-up pancake.

Voices alerted her to the fact that the boys were back. They burst into the kitchen, rosy-cheeked and out of breath.

"Mama Ella, the chickens didn't lay as much as usual." Isaiah handed her the basket. "They looked tired."

Disappointment slithered through her. Though his initial greeting must have been unintentional, she couldn't prevent the hope that had grown inside, the hope that he'd finally call her Mama. She suppressed a sigh.

"Sometimes that happens." She peered into the basket and counted. "Twelve eggs is perfect for today. Do you want to crack them into the pan?"

His eyes lit up. He nodded, scurrying toward a chair to push in front of the stove.

Ella washed the eggs, then brought them to her son. "Let me know if any shells fall in, okay?"

"Okay." A look of intense concentration filled his face as he cracked the first egg and let it drop into the pan.

The front door opened. Men's voices murmured from the hallway. Ella wanted to rush to her husband and find out what was going on, but she knew she needed to wait. No sense worrying the children.

Cody and Travis came into the kitchen. The boys grinned at their arrival. Isaiah finished cracking the eggs, then launched himself at Cody and peppered him with questions about the "white stuff" in the garden. Ella busied herself stirring the eggs.

Soon enough, they all sat down to eat. The boys scarfed down their breakfast, thanked Ella for the yummy food, then skipped off to play outside. Cody moved, getting into a position to see the children as they romped about the yard. Ella smiled. She loved his protectiveness.

Travis took his final bite of food. "Thanks, Ella. Breakfast was tasty."

"Your wife taught me well."

"She's good at that." His smile faded. "We've had another note."

Her stomach turned. "Another? Is that what you pulled from the tree?"

"You saw that?"

"I did." Her gaze darted to Cody. "What did it say?"

Her husband shifted and wouldn't meet her eyes.

She held out her hand. "I know you want to protect me, but I need to know."

His Adam's apple bobbed three times before he reached into his pocket and put the paper in her hand. Chills overtook her as she read the three boxy words.

Send Ariella Home

The handwriting, like the one on the previous note, was unfamiliar. She dropped it on the table and folded her arms over her chest. "My father really doesn't want me here."

A deep growl sounded in Cody's throat. "We'll get to the bottom of this, Ella."

"But these threats are getting more dangerous. You could have died after that snake bite. One of the boys could have been bitten. Now our garden is ruined from the salt, isn't it?"

"Not necessarily. If we can get the top layer of soil off before it rains, that might save the garden. I don't think you watered it enough to have an impact. Still, we'll have to plant another one just in case."

She threw up her arms. "See? They're going after our livelihood. I'm guessing whoever pulled down your cattle fence is the person responsible for this too. Yet no one has seen suspicious activity in town. How do we find someone who knows how to stay invisible?"

Several seconds of silence passed before Cody slammed his hand on the table, making Ella jump. Fury burned in his eyes. "We need to find this man, Trav. Immediately."

Travis crossed his arms. "I agree. We'll set up a watch over your house. I can find volunteers to help. Folks won't take kindly to people threatening one of our own." He stood. "I best get to that."

"Thanks." Cody clapped a hand on Travis's shoulder. "I'll take a watch tonight."

Ella bit back a protest. There was wisdom in the men's plan, but it felt wrong to inconvenience others on her account.

When Travis left, she buried her face in her hands. "This is all my fault."

"No, it's not."

"It is. You wouldn't be having these problems if it wasn't for me."

Cody took hold of her hands, firmly moving them from her face. "You listen to me, darlin'. None of this is on you. It's on whoever is trying to control you. If you let yourself believe it's your fault, they win. That's not acceptable."

His tone brooked no argument. His words almost convinced her.

Cody studied her face, and a half smile tipped up his lips. "And until you can believe it, I'll believe for both of us."

Tears stung her eyes. She slipped one hand from his to place it on his cheek. "I don't deserve you."

"Hogwash." He squeezed her knee. "It's me who doesn't deserve you."

"What!" Her mouth fell open. "Of all the ridiculous, crazy notions...!"

Cody chuckled. He tapped her chin. "Exactly."

"Oh." She leaned back in her chair. A reluctant smile formed. "You've made your point."

"Good." He kissed her forehead, then rose. "Now, I'm going to see about clearing some land for another garden. Thanks be to God, we still have plenty of seed."

"Can I help?"

"Sure. We'll make it a family affair." Cody held out his hand. "As long as we're together, that's what matters."

She slid her hand into his. Her faith in the matter might not match his, but perhaps with enough time, it would.

~

A week later, Cody sat by the barn loft window, rifle slung over his shoulder. All was dark and quiet. Somewhere near the house, Travis kept watch with Hattie's youngest son, Patrick.

It felt strange sneaking into his own barn, no lantern to light the way. The cows gave a welcoming low when he entered. He patted each one before making his way into the loft. Now he waited, eyes peeled for any strange movement. The moon provided sufficient light. From his vantage point, he could see the house and garden.

It was the third time he'd watched through the night. Travis had a steady rotation of volunteers to keep vigil at the ranch. No incidents had occurred yet. Cody was both thankful and frustrated by that. He wanted whoever threatened his family caught. Either Ella's father or former fiancé were somehow behind the incidents. Maybe Blackwell was the one hiring the miscreant. Unfortunately, unless they caught the culprit, they couldn't prove it.

He focused out the window, straining to see any movement. His eyelids drooped. He grunted, rubbing a fist over them, willing himself to stay awake. By his estimation, there were still five hours before sunrise.

Lord, please let us catch the culprit soon.

A long exhale seeped out. Cody adjusted his position, hoping to get more comfortable. Movement caught his attention. He squinted. Travis crept along the house low to the ground. Moments later, the barn door creaked. Travis still crouched ten yards away. Patrick moved from the shadows, taking cautious steps toward the barn.

Adrenaline bolted through Cody. He crawled toward the loft ladder, quiet and sure. The door creaked again, sliding open enough to let in more moonlight. A shadowy figure darted inside. The horses pawed the ground in their stalls. Preston let out a snort, one that signaled his nervousness. Even his faithful steed knew something was amiss.

The door shut behind the shadow. Cody gripped the ladder that would take him to the ground floor. His foot was on the first rung when a sloshing sound hit his ears. The scent of kerosene filled the barn. Gut clenching, Cody scurried down the ladder, no longer caring about stealth. When close to the floor, he jumped, landing with a loud thud. The shadowy figure jerked up.

"Hey!" Cody yelled. "What're you doing?"

Light flickered in front of the man. A match. His features remained obscure in the dim light, but a sickening smile curled his lips. Cody raced toward him. With a laugh, the man dropped his match. Flames sprang up in the mounds of hay.

Horror pulsed through Cody as the fire spread. The arsonist bolted toward the door just as Travis pushed it open. Shouting ensued, but Cody didn't pay attention to the words. His brother-in-law would take care of the man. Cody needed to put out the fire.

Patrick barreled in next. His sharp gasp sounded over the cackling of the flames. Cody grabbed an old blanket and beat the fire. Smoke rose in thick plumes. Preston whinnied, pawing at his stall. His other horses did the same. The cows bellowed. Panic filled the barn. For a horrible moment, Cody was paralyzed. He needed to save his animals. He needed to save the barn.

Patrick pushed him toward the stalls. "Get them out!"

Cody ran. He flung open the doors. Two horses pounded out at once. They rushed for the open barn door. Preston hung back. He butted Cody with his nose, nickering with a wild look in his normally gentle eyes. Cody slapped his horse's flank. "Go, boy!"

Another firm slap sent Preston flying for the door. Cody turned to the cows. Both let out plaintive moos. "C'mon, girls."

Sadie lumbered out of the stall, but Becky cowered back. He grabbed a rope. Looping it around her neck and nose, he tugged. Becky balked. Despite the heat in the barn, icy fear slithered through his veins. Smoke surrounded them. Cody coughed. He yanked on the halter again. This time, Becky moved. He led her through the smoke and flames to safety. Outside, he removed the rope and pushed her toward the other animals near the house.

At least the cows and horses were safe.

His gaze landed on the large man handcuffed to a porch rail. Travis had nabbed him. *Good.* Anger flooded Cody's veins. He took two steps toward the smirking culprit.

Someone grabbed his arm. Travis stood beside him, horse blankets in hand. "He's not worth it. Don't do something you'll regret." He shoved the blankets into Cody's hands. "Soak these at the pump. It'll help extinguish the fire."

The flames licked higher. If they leapt out of reach, the barn would be lost. He shot a last glare at the tied-up man, then raced to the pump. He threw the blankets to the ground. Pumping furiously, he drenched them.

"Cody!"

Ella flew down the porch steps. Her nightdress flapped around her legs as she ran to him. Her hair hung loose, her eyes wide with worry. She gripped his arm. "What happened?"

"The culprit struck. We couldn't stop him before he lit the fire." He pushed her toward the house. "Go inside, Ella."

"I can help."

"No!" Fear clutched him. "It's too dangerous. I won't risk losing you."

His wife looked as though she wanted to argue, but she bit her lip. She enveloped him in a quick, fierce embrace. "Stay safe, Cody."

When she made it to the house, he breathed easier. Grabbing the blankets, he dragged them back to the barn. Patrick and Travis each took one. They fought the fire for what felt like hours. The smoke burned his lungs as surely as the heat burned his skin. Blisters formed even as they continued their fight.

His vision grew hazy. He coughed more with each passing minute. The flames seemed to diminish, but the smoke wouldn't quit. Was the fire finally under control? Had they saved the barn?

Cody swayed. He lifted the blanket to beat more flames, but he stumbled. A deep, racking cough wrecked his lungs. Travis yelled his name. It seemed to come from far away. Then he collapsed, hitting the ground hard. Pain shot through him before everything went dark.

CHAPTER 22

The morning after the fire, Ella stared in dismay at the remains of the barn through her bedroom window. The men had gotten the fire out, but a substantial portion of the structure was destroyed, the wood blackened and unstable. Would they have to tear it down and rebuild? Or did they only need to redo the burned part?

Cody groaned from their bed. Ella flew to his side. "Cody? Are you all right?"

He coughed, the sound harsh to her ears. "I'll be fine."

His voice, raspy from smoke inhalation, never sounded so dear. Ella grasped his hand and held it to her heart. "This is my fault."

"Don't start that again, darlin'."

"How can I not?" She traced the lines of his face, red and puffy from the night's ordeal. "If I wasn't here…"

Cody pushed himself up. The abrupt movement led to a coughing fit. Ella grabbed a cup of water from the bedside table and held it to his lips. He drank several long draughts, then sank back against the headboard. "Thanks." His eyes narrowed. "Now, about your mistaken assessment…"

She fought the tears blurring her vision. "Is it? All this has happened because of my presence in Harmony Springs. Without me, your life would not be in danger."

"It'd also be a shallow existence."

Her brow furrowed. She opened her mouth, but Cody held up a hand.

"Let me finish. Before you came along, I was lost, closed off to love. Now, because of you, there's joy in my life. We've made a family. I wouldn't trade that for anything. Especially not to appease some low-life who thinks he can bully you back to Boston." He huffed. "I wish I'd been conscious to see Travis haul him away."

Ella smoothed back his soot-streaked hair. "The man probably wouldn't have liked that."

"Humph." Cody's eyes drooped.

Ella pulled the blankets up around him. "Sleep. You need your rest."

He slid down but just as quickly sat up again. "Ella, I need you to promise me something."

"Anything."

His blue eyes stared straight into hers. "Don't leave me."

There was a plea in his words. Her heart jolted at the mere thought of leaving. Leaving him. Leaving the children. It was unthinkable. Despite the danger from Boston, her place was here.

The vulnerability in his eyes pierced her heart. She leaned forward, pressing a kiss to his forehead. "I promise. You are my home, Cody. Nothing will change that."

"Good." He squeezed her hand before bringing it to his lips. As his eyes closed, his grip loosened. It took only a minute for him to fall asleep.

Ella slipped from the room and headed downstairs. Miss Hattie met her in the parlor, Addie on her hip, Jonah and Isaiah crowding her legs. The boys bolted to Ella as soon as they saw her.

She sat on the couch, a boy on either side. Isaiah looked up, his brown eyes wide. "Is Papa Cody going to be okay?"

"Yes, sweetie. The doctor came by last night while you were asleep. He said Papa Cody will cough for a while, but he'll be fine."

Isaiah's body lost its tension. Jonah climbed onto Ella's lap and curled up like a cat.

Miss Hattie sat in the seat across from them. "Thank the good Lord above. That could've been much worse."

Ella sighed. "Thank God, indeed. And Travis caught the culprit." Would that mean an end to the string of harmful events? Or was there another person who would take over? Hopefully, Travis would come by soon with information on the assailant.

Jonah looked up. "What's a cu'prit?"

Maybe this wasn't the best conversation to have in front of the children. "It's someone who does something bad. Now, I heard you two say you wanted to build a whole town with your blocks yesterday. Did you start?"

"Not yet," Isaiah replied.

"Why don't you do that now? I'm sure Papa Cody would love to see it when he wakes up."

Isaiah perked up. "Really?" He hopped to the ground. "C'mon, Jonah! Let's make it huge!"

Jonah scrambled down from Ella's lap. The brothers scurried up the stairs.

Hattie chuckled, rising from her chair to sit beside Ella. "Deftly done, my dear."

Addie reached for Ella. She took the baby and settled back against the sofa. "They worry so much. Redirection seemed a good option."

"I'm guessin' they weren't the only ones worried."

Memories from last night flashed through her mind. The harsh glow on the bedroom ceiling. The smell of smoke. "When I saw the barn in flames, my heart stopped. I can't imagine life without Cody."

Hattie reached for her hand, giving it a squeeze. "You've fallen in love with him, then?"

"Yes." A delicious glow accompanied her words, turning her stomach and arms to mush.

"I'm glad of it, child. You two complement each other. Seeing how far you've come warms my old heart."

Ella smiled. "I'm rather glad for it myself."

Addie cooed. Her chubby hands lifted to Ella's cheeks.

Ella chuckled. "How's my big girl today?" She rubbed her nose against Addie's. Her daughter laughed, clapping her hands.

"You're a natural mother, Ella. Only a few months into this, and it's as though you've been with them forever."

"Why, Miss Hattie, that might be the kindest thing you could have said. Thank you." She smiled down at Addie. "It feels like I've been their mother forever. In the best way possible." Her heart pitter-pattered. "And I feel as though I've known Cody much longer as well."

A knowing smile pulled at Hattie's lips. "If you think you're in love now, just wait. You fall more deeply as time goes on. Do you wanna know the most romantic thing my husband does? He makes me coffee each mornin', just the way I like it. He's been doin' that for the last forty years. We may be miffed at each other about any old thing, but he's never missed a day of makin' that cup of coffee." She sighed, the smile softening. "It's his way of sayin' 'I love you.' It's small and ordinary—and I wouldn't trade it for the world."

Ella caught her breath. "How beautiful." A desire to do something to show Cody her love burned in her gut. Almost immediately, a thought came to mind. "Miss Hattie, may I ask you a favor?"

"Of course, child."

"Cody's birthday is coming up. I'd like to go into town next week to pick up a gift and some grocery items. Would you mind watching the children on Thursday?"

"Happily." Hattie leaned forward, eyes bright. "What're you gonna make?"

"His favorites. Chicken pot pie and caramel cake."

"You're a sweet wife, young lady. He'll appreciate that."

Ella's lips turned up. "Don't say anything to him. I want it to be a surprise."

"My lips are sealed."

~

On the fourth day after the fire, Cody sat across from the man who'd been harassing his family. Every muscle in his body ached for him to jump across the table and wipe the smug smile off Ashton Jacobson's face. For being handcuffed to his chair, the man seemed awfully relaxed. He hadn't given Travis much information. So far, all they knew was his name. If he'd given his real one. He had an accent similar to Ella's, but it sounded rough, coarser. Clearly, he was from Boston. The only question was whether he worked for Mr. Mountbatten or Howard.

Travis sat behind his desk, hands steepled. His index fingers tapped together in a slow rhythm. He pierced Jacobson with an icy glare. "Tell us who sent you."

The man shrugged. "Don't see why I should."

"You were caught committing arson red-handed. I should think the reason clear."

Jacobson simply grinned.

"Are you working with anyone?"

"Nah. Don't want no partner gettin' a cut of the…" He snapped his mouth shut.

"A cut of the profit," Travis finished. He leaned back, crossing his arms over his chest. "So you're working for someone back in Boston and you're here alone." A slow smile formed on his lips. "Good."

Good? Cody frowned but said nothing. He didn't understand his friend's logic, yet he knew Travis had a plan.

"Looks like I can charge you with arson, cattle rustling, destruction of property…" Travis's eyes hardened. "And attempted murder."

Ah. There it is.

Fear flickered in Jacobson's eyes. "M-murder? I didn't kill no one!"

"You left a basket of snakes in the Brooks' yard. Their five-year-old son found it and almost got bitten. Mr. Brooks suffered multiple bites. You're fortunate he survived. As it stands, instead of first-degree murder, the charge can only be attempted murder."

"No one shoulda been hurt! It was meant to scare 'em." Jacobson's hands trembled. His smile was long gone.

Travis snorted. "You expect me to believe that? Those were Western rattlesnakes. Their venom can be deadly."

Sweat beaded Jacobson's forehead. "I swear…"

"And you started a barn fire with Mr. Brooks inside. You must have known he could get trapped."

"No! I thought he'd be distracted while I ran. That's all!" Jacobson swallowed. His eyes flitted to Cody. "Besides, he's fine."

Cody mirrored Travis, crossing his arms and leaning back. "I might be fine, but you've caused a lot of stress for me and my family. My wife wants no part of her Boston life, and you keep throwing it in her face." His voice rose in volume. "Whose orders are you here on? Her father's? Howard's?"

"Best think carefully, Mr. Jacobson." Travis affected a bored look. "I'd hate to see you swing on a noose."

The man blanched. "Y-you c-can't."

No, they couldn't, but the out-of-towner didn't know that. Travis shrugged. "Maybe not where you come from, but Montana's only a territory of the United States. We have our own justice system here." His eyes sparked fire. "I'm sure you've heard some tales of the Wild West."

Cody suppressed a snort. Between Buffalo Bill Cody and wildly popular dime novels, people had all kinds of assumptions about life in the American territories. Not all of them were true, but maybe the reputation for lawlessness and vigilante justice would help now.

"I'll ask again. Who are you working for?" The flint in Travis's tone would have frightened Cody if he didn't know his friend so well.

Jacobson shook from head to toe. "I dunno."

"What do you mean, you don't know?" Travis eyed him. "If you think this will buy you time..."

"Someone hired me without meetin' me. That happens a lot in my business. I was to follow Mr. Blackwell here and wait for a list of instructions by post. Whoever it is wanted check-ins wired in code after each incident."

Travis narrowed his eyes. "How many more incidents were on this list?"

"Three."

"And where is this list?"

Jacobson's fingers twitched. He reached into a pocket and pulled out a tattered piece of paper. Travis took it.

Cody leaned closer to read the contents. They all made his stomach turn. His eyes bugged on the last one. "You were going to kidnap my wife?"

His voice rose with each word. He leapt to his feet, legs bent to lunge at the prisoner, but Travis gripped his arm.

"Easy," he whispered. "I know you're angry, but you need to calm down."

Fire pulsed through Cody's veins. He stalked to a corner, pacing with his hands planted on his hips. Travis resumed questioning Jacobson. Blood whooshed in Cody's ears, his fury drowning out the interrogation. Perhaps that was for the best. The other incidents on the list burned in his mind.

Maim Brooks's horse.
Set fire to the pastures.
Kidnap Ariella and bring her home.

Cody snarled, resisting the urge to slam his hand against the wall. Taking a deep breath, he willed his anger to dissipate and focused on the interrogation again.

Travis tapped his fingers against the desk. "Why not kidnap Ella outright? Was there a reason for that?"

Jacobson shuffled his feet, head down. "I dunno. I got the feelin' the boss wanted her scared enough to come back herself."

That fit his image of Ella's father. Or ex-fiancé. Controlling. Manipulative. Power-hungry.

Cody clenched his fists, ire rising again. He couldn't remain calm in this room. Waving at Travis, he nodded toward the door to indicate his intentions, then headed outside.

The May sunshine warmed his face. Cody inhaled long and deep. He walked down the street at a brisk pace, heading for his sister's café. As it was midafternoon, her restaurant wasn't crowded. He went straight to the back where he knew she'd be working.

Cassie smiled when she saw him. "Howdy, big brother. What brings you here?"

"Your husband is questioning his prisoner."

Understanding flashed over her face. "Ah. You couldn't stay there, could you?"

"Nope. He was going to kidnap Ella, Cass. That was the final piece of his plan."

"His plan?" Her brow furrowed. "What was his motive?"

Cody sank into a chair, his shoulders slumping. "He claims he doesn't know who hired him. My guess is he's one of those shady folks who'll do anything for a price. And if Mountbatten or Howard are behind this, they probably paid good money to get Ella back."

"Drink this." Cassie put a mug of coffee in front of him. Cody thanked her and took a sip. She sat across from him. "So we still don't know who's actually behind the attacks."

"No." His stomach clenched. "What if they send someone else? This might not be over."

"Or maybe they'll give up now that Jacobson's been caught?"

The hope in Cassie's voice produced the first genuine smile Cody had since coming to town. "I pray you're right."

Half an hour later, Travis found them. He accepted a cup of coffee from his wife and sipped it as he stood. "Jacobson sang like a bird. It seems the threat of the noose worked wonders."

"Noose?" Cassie frowned. "Hanging isn't allowed here."

"He didn't know that."

Her lips curled into a smile. "Smart man."

"Thanks." Travis planted a kiss on her head. He turned to Cody. "He's agreed to wire Boston with an update to his source about the barn fire in exchange for a lighter sentence. We'll send that this afternoon."

Unease swam through Cody's gut. "It's been several days. He was supposed to send them the day after an attack. Wouldn't that raise suspicion?"

"It might, but we'll come up with an explanation for it."

"What about the other planned incidents?"

Travis took another sip of his drink. "I'm going to wire my friend on the Boston force, ask him to monitor wires to and from Harmony Springs. Maybe he'll be able to track where they end up."

Cody squeezed his mug. "Doesn't he need a warrant for that?"

"Yeah, but with the information Jacobson gave us, he might be able to get one. It's worth a try." Travis downed the contents of his cup. "You want to come with me?"

"Sure." Cody hugged Cassie goodbye and followed Travis. All the while, his instincts buzzed with fear that something was about to go terribly wrong.

CHAPTER 23

ody's unease persisted into the next week. On the
surface, everything seemed fine, but he couldn't shake
the feeling that the lapse between the fire and the wire would
tip off Ella's father. Or former fiancé. He couldn't decide who
was more likely behind Jacobson's presence in Harmony
Springs. If he had to guess, he'd say Ella's father since the man
had come to town and threatened them, sending Blackwell to
do the same. But why? Why was the man so determined to have
Ella back in Boston? Was it wounded pride...or something
more sinister?

He drummed his fingers against the parlor windowpane,
watching rain pour from the sky. The dreary weather matched
his mood.

Arms came around him from behind. Cody detected orange
blossoms. He smiled, finding one of Ella's hands where they
rested on his stomach. "Hey, darlin'. Tired this morning?"

"Mmhmm." She nestled closer and yawned. "I just couldn't
convince myself to get up on time."

"Must be the weather. The kids are still asleep too."

He turned, bringing them face to face, and enveloped her in

his arms. Cody held on tight, his face buried in her hair as he tried to get as close to her as possible.

Ella's fingers found their way into his hair. Her voice, raspy from sleep, murmured in his ear. "What's wrong, Cody?"

"I hate that we don't know what comes next. What your father might try. If anything." He pulled back, cupping one of her cheeks. "I can't protect you against the unknown."

"Oh, my love." Ella's hands curled around his suspenders. "You're not meant to protect me from everything. I won't wilt away if things happen from time to time."

"No, but..." He choked. His throat felt as though it was closing. Cody wheezed in some shallow breaths. "I can't fail you. Not like I failed..." The words died on his lips, words he couldn't seem to force from his battered heart.

Compassion radiated from Ella's face. "Your mother?"

Tears stung his eyes. The dam holding back his words broke, words he'd never spoken in the past twenty years. "It should've been me. Not her. I should've made sure Ma and Cassie were safe on the ground before I jumped out of that wagon." His voice cracked. Tears slipped down his cheeks. A cry escaped. Once he got started, he couldn't stop.

Ella held him as he sobbed. He clung to her, his tears falling onto her neck. She rubbed his back and murmured soft words of comfort.

When he regained a sense of control, he pulled back, ears burning. "Sorry."

"Don't apologize for feeling, Cody. Thank you for trusting me with your grief." She ran a tender hand over his cheeks, drying his tears. "What happened to your mother wasn't your fault."

"But..."

She covered his lips with her fingers. "You were a child. It wasn't your job to protect your mother—it was her job to protect her children. She sacrificed her life to save Cassie because she loved her. She loved you. I'd guess that if she had the choice to do it again, she would." She let her hand fall from his face to his shoulder. "Is that why you're so protective? Did it start that day?"

The thought never occurred to him before. But as he mulled it over, the truth became clear. "I reckon it did."

"That moment marked you for life. It helped turn you into the man you are now." Ella's eyes were soft as she smiled. "I love your protective side, Cody. But you have to remember it's not all you have to offer."

"Sometimes it feels like it is."

She cupped his cheeks. "You're strong and brave. You provide for your family and love us. You're a good boss. People trust you. You took on three children even though you had no idea what to do. You married a stranger to save her from her past. You have a strong faith." Her brows rose. "Should I go on?"

Cody shook his head, the right side of his mouth turning up. "You've made your point."

"Good."

She took his hand and led him to the sofa. Once they sat, she gripped both his hands. Cody held them like a lifeline.

He forced another admission from his tight throat. "With everything going on, I feel the same helplessness I did in that ravine. There was nothing I could do then, and there's nothing I can do now."

She brushed a lock of hair from his forehead. "Do what you can, and trust God with the rest."

Cody drew in a breath. "You're right. That's all we can do."

Ella's fingers trailed down his cheek. "That's another thing I love about you. You're humble enough to take suggestions."

"Darlin', that trait is mighty new."

"I don't think so. You might balk sometimes, but you're quick to apologize and admit when you're wrong." She smiled. "That's a good trait to pass down to your baby."

"We'll see. The boys are a bit stubborn, but maybe they'll mellow as they get older. Addie's too young to tell. As far as..." *Wait a minute.* His mouth dropped open. "Ella. What do you mean?"

Her smile grew. She pulled one hand from his and pressed it to her stomach. "It may be too early to know for sure, but...I think I'm pregnant."

Air whooshed from his lungs. "Pregnant? Already? Is that even possible?"

She laughed. "Yes, Cody, it's entirely possible. I missed my monthly cycle in April but thought it might be a fluke. Now I'm late for another." Her eyes sparkled. "There's usually only one reason for that."

"A baby." His gaze drifted down to her stomach. "Our baby." He touched her abdomen, awe flooding him. "How soon can Doc confirm it?"

"I'm not sure." Ella leaned back, snuggling into the cushions. "Probably not for a few months. The Irish mothers I worked with in Boston said they usually felt a quickening inside before a doctor could hear the heartbeat with his stethoscope. Those same mothers were the ones who taught me how a woman's cycle works and how it's the best early sign of pregnancy."

"Your mother didn't teach you?"

Ella snorted. "My mother would never let something so improper cross her lips." She sighed, rubbing her belly. "I'm grateful our child will grow up in the open air and sunshine of Montana."

Cody settled an arm over her shoulders. "Free and happy."

She rested her head against him. "Exactly."

*M*iss Hattie showed up half an hour after Cody left to check his cattle Thursday morning. She grinned at Ella, rubbing her hands together. "Ready to surprise that hubby of yours?"

Ella smiled back. "Oh yes. His birthday is on Saturday, and the caramel sauce for the cake tastes better if it sits for a day or two." She reached for her shawl. It might be the middle of May, but mornings in Harmony Springs had a chill to them. "Thanks for watching the kids. Addie's up, but the boys are sleeping."

Hattie cooed at Addie, who sat in a highchair eating pancakes. "Hi there, little lady." She turned her gaze to Ella. "Would you like to wake the boys to say good mornin'? They might not like it if they come downstairs to find you gone."

"Good point. I'll go up."

The boys' room was dark and quiet. Ella went to the window and opened the curtains.

Jonah sat up first. He rubbed his eyes and gave her a sleepy grin. "Mama."

"Good morning, sweet boy." She sat on the bed.

He crawled into her lap, wrapping his arms around her neck in a hug. She held him close, breathing in his little-boy scent. Isaiah soon popped up with a big yawn. "Mornin', Mama."

Mama. Ella sucked in a breath in an effort to keep her composure. "Good morning. Did you sleep well?"

"Uh-huh." He pushed the covers back and joined Jonah on her lap. "Is Papa already at work?"

If her heart raced any faster, it might burst from her chest. "Yes. He told me to give you both a hug for him."

"'Kay." Isaiah hugged her, then slid from the bed. "Is today Miss Hattie's day?"

"It is. She's downstairs with your sister."

"What about the baby?"

Ella's mouth dropped. "How do you know about the baby?"

"I heard you and Papa talking. C'mon, let's go see Miss Hattie." He grabbed her hand.

"Isaiah, wait."

The child paused. He looked up at her. Ella struggled for words. Jonah joined his brother on the floor. Both boys had heads tilted, eyes questioning. She cleared her throat. "You called us Mama and Papa."

"Yeah." Isaiah shrugged. "I don't wanna be different anymore. 'Specially with the baby coming. It's a sister, right? Addie needs someone to play with."

Ella laughed. She scooped her sons into her arms. They shrieked and giggled. She planted a kiss on each little cheek. "I love you, boys."

"Wuv you, Mama." Jonah returned her cheek kiss.

Isaiah just grinned and hugged her again. Then he paused. "Are you leavin' now too?"

"I am. That's why Miss Hattie is here."

"You'll be back soon, right?"

"Of course, sweetie. I have some things to pick up in town, then I'm having lunch with Aunt Cassie. After that, I'll be home."

Isaiah sighed. Jonah stuck out his lower lip. "Stay home, Mama."

She leaned toward them. "Can you keep a secret?"

They both lit up and nodded.

Ella put a finger over her lips. "I'm getting some things for Papa's birthday on Saturday. It's a surprise, so you can't tell him, okay?"

"We won't tell." Isaiah's eyes widened. "Can we make him something with Miss Hattie?"

"I'm sure you can. Shall we ask her?"

"Yeah!"

The boys raced downstairs. Ella followed at a more sedate pace. Her hand rested over her belly.

She paused at the bottom of the steps. Wonder filled her. To think that she carried a tiny child inside, part of her and part of Cody. Incredible. She rubbed her stomach gently. *What will this little one be like?*

With one more caress over her unborn baby, she headed for the kitchen to say goodbye to the kids.

～

*A*t a corner table in Cassie's café, Ella wiped her lips with a napkin as she finished her meal. "Lunch was delicious, Cassie. Thank you."

Her sister-in-law smiled. "Glad you liked it. I've been recipe testing."

"The roasted beets were perfect. Cold soup was never my favorite, but this one is tasty."

"I should make you my cucumber soup sometime. It's a customer favorite." Cassie refilled their water glasses.

"I'd like that."

They chatted a little longer before Ella stood. "I need to get going. Isaiah wanted me to come home sooner rather than later."

"It's wonderful that he's calling you Mama now. I wonder what sparked that change?"

Ella and Cody had agreed to keep news of her pregnancy quiet until a doctor could confirm it. Though she knew deep down she was with child, Ella understood the need for caution. It wouldn't do to spread the news only to have to announce a false alarm. So she chose the simple answer.

"He said he didn't want to be different anymore."

"Good for him." Cassie smiled. "I'm happy for you all. It's been wonderful watching your family come together." Her smile turned mischievous. "Now all we need is a baby to complete it."

Ella blushed. "Oh, you. We'll be happy to welcome a baby when God blesses us with one." *Hopefully by the end of this year.* She wasn't sure how she'd feel if she wasn't truly pregnant. "Until then, we'll be happy to welcome your little one."

Cassie put a hand on her small baby bump. A sappy smile tugged her lips. "I can't wait."

The women said their goodbyes. Ella loaded her things in the wagon and climbed into the driver seat. Before she could slap the reins, the postmaster exited his building across the street. "Mrs. Brooks! You have a letter."

A letter? A surge of excitement slid through her. Perhaps her sister had finally written. Mail traveled slowly across the country. Tori might have sent a missive weeks ago and it would only now be finding Ella. Mr. Johnston jogged over to the wagon. He handed her the letter, and she thanked him with a smile. A glance at the direction told her it was indeed from Tori. Eager to read what she had to say, Ella climbed back into the wagon and opened the envelope.

My dear Ella,

I wish this letter bore good tidings, but I'm afraid I write with a warning. I hardly know what to say. Last night, Father and Howard argued terribly in our study. Howard threatened Father with financial and social ruin. I dare not put all the details here. But you need to know that you are in danger. Both of them are determined to get you back. I believe they have someone in Harmony Springs to sabotage your new family. Be careful. I will come myself when I can to explain more. Until then, stay safe and be on your guard.

Love,

Tori

Ella's gaze flew to the date. Her sister posted it two weeks ago. She must have paid extra to have it mailed express.

A tingling sensation crept down Ella's spine. What could Father and Howard have argued about? How did it relate to her? She glanced around, uneasy. They might have caught Jacobson, but did it end there?

A train whistle made her jump. Ella exhaled. She tossed the letter into a bag. Maybe there was nothing to worry about. After all, the remainder of the planned attacks had failed. From all appearances, Jacobson was working alone in Harmony Springs.

She guided the wagon around a large carriage sitting near the stables. The move took her close to the train station. The disembarking passengers reminded her of her first day in town, when she had no idea what she was doing. God had taken her fear and turned it to joy.

Breathing a prayer of thanks, Ella lifted the reins to urge her horse into a trot, then paused. A woman stepped off the train. Sunlight glinted on her red hair. She wore a tasteful blue hat that matched her dress—a traveling outfit Ella recognized.

Tori!

Ella squealed. She hopped down from the wagon and led Carter to a nearby hitching post. How delightful it would be to surprise her sister. Once the horse was secured, Ella turned to the train station.

As she passed the stables, she tripped. Someone grabbed her from behind, dragging her into the shadows. Her scream was silenced by a damp cloth clamped over her nose and mouth. Something sweet and pungent filled her senses. She struggled. The immovable person held firm.

Ella's limbs grew heavy. Her eyes drooped. She fought for consciousness...and lost.

CHAPTER 24

*C*ody gave the new fence in his south pasture a firm shake. It didn't budge. Satisfied, he plunked his hands on his hips and looked around. Cows munched on the growing grass, their happy moos interspersed with the bleats of calves. So far, fifty cows had given birth. While their numbers were still much lower than before the harsh winter, he thanked God for the growth in his herd.

His thoughts wandered to his wife. Heart warming instantly, he grinned. How had he been so blessed? A few short months ago, he'd been so sure his life would never be the same —and he was right...just not for the reasons he expected.

Hank laughed beside him. "You've got that dopey look on your face again, Boss."

"That so?" Cody chuckled. "A common occurrence these days."

"It's good to see ya happy," Eddie said from the other side of the fence. "You were too serious before."

"Yeah," Joey chimed in. "If that's what family life does for a man, I should think about gettin' a wife. You're a changed man."

Another chuckle shook him. "Glad you've noticed, boys."

He clapped Joey's shoulder. "I highly recommend marriage, my friend." Looking around at his fellow cowboys, he winked. "For all three of you, in fact."

Hank held up his hands. "Oh, no. Ain't no woman gonna tie me up. I like the freedom of bein' by myself."

"Ya might change your mind someday," Eddie said. "If the right woman comes along."

"Nah. I'm good."

The cowpokes continued their good-natured teasing. Cody turned back to the fence with a smile.

A gunshot reverberated in the air. Cody's body tensed. All humor fled. His gaze shot in the direction of the house. Moments later, another gunshot sounded.

Ella!

"Hank, take charge!" Cody jumped onto his horse. He galloped off, urging Preston ever faster.

The ride to the house felt like ages. When he finally reached the front yard, Cody was out of breath. He swung down. Strong relief coursed through him when he saw Ella on the porch, rifle still in her hands. He ran to her, taking the steps two at a time. "Darlin', what's the..."

He halted dead in his tracks. The woman on the porch wasn't Ella. She looked like his wife, but there were distinct differences. Instead of a beautiful green, this woman had deep brown eyes. Her brows knit in a frown, the V reaching deeper than Ella's ever did.

The stranger pointed the rifle at him. "You'd better be my sister's husband."

"Tori?" Cody blinked. "What're you doing here?" He looked over her shoulder. "Where's Ella?"

She lowered the weapon and swallowed hard. "I don't know. Miss Hattie told me about the two-shot signal. I have a bad feeling something happened to Ella."

Hattie bustled onto the porch. Her face tightened. "There

you are, young man. Ella went to town this morning. She should have been back two hours ago. I'm doin' all I can to keep the kids from worryin', but Isaiah is right scared. It's rubbin' off on the other two."

A horse whinnied. Preston returned the greeting. Cody looked over his shoulder. Travis raced toward them, a cloud of dust kicking up behind him. He jumped from his horse before the stallion stopped moving. "Cody! You need to come with me. We found..." He stopped, mouth gaping. "Tori?"

With a little cry, the newcomer threw herself into his arms. "Travis! You're here. Thank God."

He steadied her as he pulled back after a brief hug. "What brought you here, Tori?"

Her spine straightened. "Howard went mad. I've never seen him in such a state. He and my father had a horrible argument. It seems Ella was meant to be insurance for some deal they made. I didn't hear all the details, but I do know that Howard isn't as wealthy as he likes people to think. And Travis...he's obsessed with Ella. He caught me listening outside the door and screamed with a wild look in his eyes. He said he'd get Ella back if it was the last thing he did. That's when I got scared. I had to come here, to warn her. Mail travels too slowly." Her throat bobbed. "Am I too late?"

"I don't know." Travis rammed his fingers through his hair. He turned to Cody. "Cassie came running into my office a little while ago. She said after lunch, Ella headed home, but your wagon is hitched to a post by the stables. I looked but couldn't find Ella anywhere in town." His jaw briefly clenched. "A bystander said they saw a well-dressed man carry an unconscious woman into a fancy carriage, one they'd never seen before. He said the woman had red hair and was wearing a blue dress."

Cody's heart plummeted. Fear clutched him in iron talons.

He could barely force words past his tight throat. "Ella wore blue today." He'd told her how lovely she looked when she came down for breakfast this morning. And she was one of just three redheads in Harmony Springs.

"Let's ride. We can discuss next steps in my office."

Cody started for his horse, then stopped. He turned to his sister-in-law. "I wish we could've met under better circumstances, ma'am. I promise you I'll do everything I can to bring Ella home."

Tori stared at him for several beats of his heart. She slowly nodded. "I believe you."

His eyes rose to Hattie. "Would you mind…"

"Of course, I'll watch the young'uns. You go get that wife of yours."

The children. Cody ran into the house. He found them huddled in a circle in the parlor.

Isaiah saw him first. "Papa!"

Cody had no time to enjoy the new title. He knelt and gathered all three children into his arms. "I have to go find your mama. Miss Hattie will stay with you until I get back."

Isaiah's lips trembled. "You'll bring Mama back?"

"Yeah." No hesitation faltered his words. He'd bring her back. End of story.

He rushed back outside. By the time he and Travis reached town, Cody's nerves were shot. He soon paced Travis's office like a caged animal. "Did your witness see which way the carriage went?"

"North." Travis unrolled a map of the territory. "Assuming the kidnapper is someone working for Howard, he'd probably head to Helena."

"Why a carriage? Why not the train?"

"Next train doesn't leave for the East until noon tomorrow. There are more trains running in Helena. The perpetrator wouldn't want to remain in Harmony Springs that long, not when he could get to Helena tonight and catch an early-morning train."

And Ella would be lost to them. Cody refused to think on that. He'd travel to Boston if necessary to find his wife. "How far to Helena?"

"Forty miles."

A pregnant silence grew. The kidnapper had a several-hour head start on them, and forty miles was a long journey for a horse. They would have to ride hard into the night to catch up. Cody exhaled. "Let's go. We can figure out a plan as we ride."

~

Blinking open heavy eyelids, Ella groaned. Her head throbbed. A burning sensation assaulted her nose and throat. Her hands tingled with sharp numbness. She tried to relieve the pain, but something kept them bound.

She struggled to see in the dim light. Where was she? Why couldn't she move? As her eyesight came into focus, more awareness trickled in. She lay on her back, arms raised above her head. Her hands were tied together and fastened to a bedpost. Terror took her. She thrashed her legs and pulled hard at her bonds.

Taunting, familiar laughter came from the corner of the room. Ella stilled. Her panic intensified. *No! Not him.*

Howard rose from a padded chair and walked in a deliberate manner toward the bed. "Good evening, Ariella." Reaching out, he ran a finger down her cheek. She flinched away. He sighed. "It seems you did not miss me as much as I missed you. I'm disappointed." He lifted one perfectly groomed, dark brow. "You married a rancher instead of me? Your standards have lowered, my dear."

Something sparked inside of her. "Don't call me that. I'm not yours."

Both brows hiked. "My, we've grown some confidence, have we? Can't have that."

She knew what was coming well before his hand hit her cheek. The slap bit hard, stinging pain radiating down her face.

Howard leaned toward her with a hiss. "I need my meek Ariella back."

Ella swallowed a retort. If he got angry, he might beat her. She needed to think of her baby, protect the little life within as best she could. She schooled her features into a blank mask. "I'm sorry."

His lips curved into an evil grin. "Not yet, you're not. You caused me quite a bit of trouble, my dear. You owe me." His eyes raked over her. "I've a mind to finish what I started the night you ran off."

Ella recoiled. "I'm a married woman."

"Not for long. When we get back to Boston, you will file for an annulment and send it to your rancher. It will be a minor inconvenience while we wait for it to go through, but once it does, we'll marry immediately."

"What makes you think I'd agree to such a plan? I love my husband."

Howard's eyes glittered. "You will marry me because your family will be ruined and disgraced if you don't. Including your precious sister."

"Tori doesn't care about status."

"You'd reduce her to poverty and shame for your own happiness?" He shook his head. "And I thought you cared about her."

Ella lifted her chin. "You don't have that kind of power over my family. My father…"

"Cheated the wrong people. Oh, they might not know that yet, but I do. I have the documents to prove it. If he doesn't pay out a handsome sum to refill my unfortunately low coffers, I will release the information to the authorities. Your father will be jailed and your family ruined."

"Low coffers?" Her mind spun. "You have more money than most families in Boston combined."

Howard chuckled. "Appearances are a beautiful thing. I picked up a little gambling habit a few years ago. The games didn't go my way. Hence my need for money." He loomed over her. "Marrying you assures I'll get that."

"You're already blackmailing Father. Why can't he just pay you the money?"

"My dear, you're forgetting that alliances between families are of utmost importance. Your dowry would pay off my debts and leave extra beside. And that's not counting the money your father owes me to stay quiet about his business exploits."

"Why me?" Ella hated how her voice shook. "There are other women with more impressive dowries."

"Ah, but they don't have the same submissive will as you. Something I prize highly in a wife." His eyes gleamed. "And your beauty is unparalleled. That alone makes possessing you...desirable."

He lowered his face to hers. Just before his lips made contact, Ella turned her face to the side. The lingering kiss he left on her cheek turned her stomach. The rough press of his mouth felt like domination. Tears stung her eyes as she thought of Cody and his gentle love.

Howard lifted his head. Lust burned in his gaze. He ran a hand along her side, sending disgusted shudders through her. When he leaned close once more, she froze. "I'm going to the saloon for a few games. It seems there's a lot of money to be won in this town. Quite a few millionaires, from what I've heard. But before I go, I want to leave you with some antici-pation." He sneered, pressing his hand against her hip. "When I get back, we're going to get to know one another *very* intimately. We'll see if your cowboy wants you after that."

Bile rose in her throat. Howard laughed again. He forced a piece of cloth into her mouth and tied the ends around her head. "See you soon, my dear."

As soon as the door shut behind him, Ella struggled against her bonds, her movements jerky and frantic. The fabric refused to give. The more she fought, the tighter it got.

Tears rolled down her cheeks. Howard would be back, and she had no doubt he'd make good on his threat. She had to get away. But how?

~

*W*ind whipped Cody's face as he and Travis galloped down the trail. Just an hour before, they'd swapped out their horses in Clancy for a fresh pair. As much as it chaffed to leave Preston in strange stables, Cody knew the prudence of not pushing too hard. So now he rode a horse whose name he didn't know but who flew swiftly over the miles.

How much longer 'til we reach Helena?

Cody swallowed hard. Moisture burned his eyes. His stomach turned each time he thought of Ella alone and afraid with some villain. He pressed his thighs into his horse. The animal responded with a burst of speed.

Tense silence was broken only by the pounding of hooves. Travis kept pace with him. On and on they rode. Stars winked above them, creating an illusion of peace.

Cody's horse made a strange sound. He slowed his mount. The horse's sides heaved.

Travis halted beside him. "Let's give them a rest by that stream." He jerked his head to the left.

Cody balled his hands into fists. Travis was right. They

needed to rest the horses. But every minute they lost was another minute something bad could happen to Ella.

"You won't do her any good if the horse gets injured and we can't continue on."

Blowing out a breath, Cody swung down to the ground. "You're right." He led his horse to the stream and patted it. The animal lowered its head to drink.

Cody paced near the bank. His mind filled with images of his wife. He'd failed to protect her. Heavy weight settled in his chest. Was that his lot in life? To fail the women he loved?

No. He could almost hear Ella's voice whispering in his ear. Bad things happened in life. He couldn't stop them all. But that didn't prevent the hurt from crushing him inside.

Travis squeezed his arm, jolting him from his thoughts. "Just a little longer, Cody. These animals will be ready to push hard the last miles."

"We're running out of time."

Steel glinted in Travis's gaze. "We'll find her."

Cody nodded. He exhaled a long breath, moving a little ways upstream. Raking his hands through his hair, he closed his eyes. "Please, God. Be with my wife and our unborn child. Keep them safe, I beg You. I can't lose them." His voice hitched. "You brought Ella into my life. Please keep her there."

Words clogged in his throat. He sank to his knees, silent prayers welling in his heart. Cody didn't move until Travis's hand landed heavy on his shoulder.

"C'mon. Let's head out."

He didn't need to be told twice.

～

*E*lla worked feverishly to loosen the material holding her captive. The gag had slipped the tiniest bit, but not enough for her to call out. Anxiety welled in her gut as time passed. Every minute was a minute closer to Howard's return. How had she ever fallen prey to his charm?

God, help me!

A tiny whisper sounded in her soul, one that calmed the frenetic rhythm of her heart. *Focus.*

Ella drew in a long breath. She slid her fingers back along her bonds as far as she could. There! The knot was within reach. Slowly, she wiggled a finger into the middle. Her hands bent at an awkward angle. Ella pushed through the discomfort. She slipped another finger into the underside of the knot.

Sounds came from the hallway. She froze. Her lungs cramped as she waited for the door to open, but it never did. Instead, she heard two women in conversation. They were so close. Ella shut her eyes, said a prayer, and screamed into her gag.

The conversation stopped. She yelled again. The handle jiggled. A woman's voice called out. "Hello? Is someone in there?"

"Help me!" Her voice sounded muffled. Ella tried again and kicked her feet against the base of the bed. A loud thump reverberated through the room. She kicked again and again and continued to scream.

The handle moved frantically, matching the pace of Ella's heart. If Howard came back before the door could be opened…

No. She refused to think of the repercussions. If he was bent on winning big at the gambling tables, she still had time.

Hopefully.

The woman called through the door again. "My mother-in-law is getting assistance. Hold on."

Why did minutes feel like hours? An eternity passed before a key grated in the lock. The door pushed open to reveal a bellhop and the ladies. All three gasped when they saw Ella tied to the bed. The older woman rushed forward in a flurry of skirts. "My dear girl!" She untied the gag with deft fingers. "What on earth happened?"

Tears flooded Ella's eyes, relief pulsing through her body. A thread of fear still remained. "I was kidnapped. The man is at the saloon. He...he's trying to take me back to Boston."

The woman's gray eyes hardened. She turned to the bellhop. "Notify the authorities at once, young man."

"Yes, ma'am." The wide-eyed boy backed out of the room. Ella silently blessed him for his immediate action.

The woman pulled a hatpin from her hair. "Let's see about getting you freed." She fiddled with the knot binding Ella's hands. "I'm Dorothy Jefferson." She nodded at the raven-haired beauty standing at the foot of the bed. "This is my daughter-in-law, Lydia."

"I'm Ella Brooks. Thank you both." Her chest rose and fell in rapid bursts. "I don't know what I would have done if you hadn't showed up."

"Think nothing of it." Moments later, the fabric fell away from her wrists. Ella sucked in a sharp breath as feeling flowed painfully back into her hands and arms.

Lydia sat beside her, muslin gown billowing, hands out. She nodded at Ella's arms. "May I?"

Ella held them up. The young woman rubbed firmly with brisk motions. "Come to our room. You'll be safe there. When the authorities arrive, you can tell them your story."

Dorothy peered at her. "What happened to your face, Ella?"

She swallowed. "Howard hit me." Touching her cheek, she winced. "It's bruised, isn't it?"

"It is." Dorothy's lips set in a thin line. "Lydia, take Ella to our room. I'll wait in the foyer for the police."

"Yes, Mother."

Lydia led Ella out of her prison. When they were safely situated in the Jeffersons' room, two doors away from Howard's, Ella started to relax. She opened her mouth to ask Lydia where she was from when a loud crash sounded down the hall. Angry shouts accompanied the racket. Ella couldn't hear the words, but she recognized the voice.

Howard was back.

She sank into a chair, her legs refusing to hold her up any longer. Lydia clutched her hand in silent support. Ella shook, her mind on the danger still at hand. She closed her eyes and prayed the authorities arrived soon.

CHAPTER 25

It was past midnight by the time Cody and Travis rode into Helena. Cody took in the surprisingly well-lit town. Raucous laughter and music came from the saloon down the street, and several buildings shone with gas lamps. People roamed the streets in packs. A patrol wagon sat outside a large hotel.

"That's our destination," Travis said, pointing to the inn. "Looks as though someone will be available to talk."

Cody's stomach sank. Why would a patrol wagon be outside such an establishment at this hour? The hotel looked respectable. Dread pulsed through him. If Ella was here...and the authorities...

Please, Lord, I can't lose her!

It might have nothing to do with his wife. Still, worry gnawed at him like a ravenous wolf as they directed their weary horses to the stable. A boy came running to meet them, eager for the coins Travis placed in his hand with instructions to brush down the two steeds and give them water and hay. As soon as the boy had the reins in hand, Cody strode for the hotel.

Travis grabbed his arm before he could barrel into the building. "Hold on. We need to go slow. Observe our surroundings before making any hasty decisions."

Cody plunked a hand on his hip. "Why're you always right?"

His friend chuckled. "It's a gift." Travis's focus sharpened. "In we go. And let me lead, okay?"

"Fine."

They walked into the hotel. All looked calm. The only person in the foyer was a sleepy-eyed bellhop standing behind a counter. Travis led the way to the young employee. He flashed his badge. "Howdy. We're from Harmony Springs, looking for a woman who may be at your hotel. She would've been brought here against her will."

The kid straightened. His eyes sparked with recognition. "Yeah, she's here. Some jerk had her tied up in one of the upstairs rooms. I got the marshal while a couple ladies freed her. They're still here."

"She's safe?"

Cody's voice sounded rough in his relief. The bellhop's eyes widened.

Travis waved a hand. "He doesn't mean to growl. That woman is his wife. He's been understandably worried."

"Oh." The kid relaxed. "Yeah, mister, she's safe. The marshal is with her and the other ladies in the tea parlor."

"And the man who kidnapped her? Is he…"

"Cody?"

Ella's voice spun him around right quick. His legs ate up the distance between them until she was wrapped snug in his embrace. Cody wasn't sure he'd ever let go. Judging from how tightly she held him in return, she felt the same.

When at last they pulled back, Cody cupped her cheek in his hand, keeping his other around her waist. "I was so worried. When Travis said he found our wagon…" He broke off suddenly, taking in the right side of her face. "Someone hit you." Anger flared. "Who took you, Ella? Was it one of Howard's cronies?"

"No." Her throat bobbed. "It was Howard."

Cody fought to control the anger turning to fury. He traced the mottled bruise on her fair skin. "Did he do anything else?"

A tremor went through her body. "He threatened to. Thank God Lydia and Dorothy found me before he could."

"Who?"

Ella pulled out of his arms. Cody wanted to grab her back, but he settled for taking her hand. She smiled at two women who approached from what must be the tea parlor. "Cody, meet Dorothy Jefferson and her daughter-in-law, Lydia. They rescued me from the room Howard locked me in."

"Ladies." Cody reached out to shake their hands. "Thanks for saving my wife."

"Our pleasure, young man." Dorothy patted his arm. "Always happy to do a good deed for another."

While Travis was deep in conversation with a man in a uniform, Cody moved closer to Ella. "Was Howard caught?"

Her face dimmed. "No. He went into a rage when he discovered me missing. Lydia and I could hear him from her hotel room."

"And I saw him when he stormed into the foyer." Dorothy frowned. "Then he disappeared. The authorities haven't been able to find him."

Travis joined them with the officer. "This is Marshal Quincy. He plans to help us find Howard."

The stocky man looped his fingers around his belt. "My guess is this man will try to get on an outbound train. We'll put a watch on all of 'em and see if we can flush him out."

A shiver of uneasiness glided down Cody's spine. "He could be anywhere."

Travis crossed his arms. "That's why I'm keeping watch

tonight. You and Ella get a room for yourselves, and I'll station myself by the door."

"We can't do that," Cody protested. "You're just as tired as I am after that ride. You need rest."

"I'll rest tomorrow." Travis's tone left no room for argument.

Ella hugged him. "You're a good friend, Travis."

"Excuse me." The bellhop appeared, the young stable hand with him. He looked at Cody. "This boy claims your horse won't settle, sir."

The boy nodded. "He don't seem to like his stall."

"I'll see to him. Thanks." Cody squeezed Ella's hand. "For now, can you get my wife and me a room?"

The bellhop nodded. "I've got a couple ready. Upstairs or downstairs?"

"Upstairs," Travis replied. Under his breath, he muttered, "Less chance of Howard breaking in through a window."

"Good thinking. Take care of Ella. I'm gonna head to the stables now."

Ella clung to his hand. "I'm coming with you."

Cody nearly resisted. Howard was still out there. He couldn't risk Ella's safety.

Before he could protest, Travis stepped in. "I'll come along too."

"As will I. Someone needs to keep a watch out." Marshal Quincy motioned for them to follow him.

That calmed Cody's fear. Ella would be well protected.

The Jefferson women said goodnight and headed up the stairs. The others stepped out into the street. The stable boy ran ahead of them, soon disappearing from sight.

Ella looked around, eyes wide. "Why are so many people still awake?"

"It's the territorial capital, ma'am. It expanded rapidly once the railroad came a few years back." Marshal Quincy shrugged. "The town never sleeps."

Cody pulled Ella close. There were too many people prowling the streets. At least the area was well lit. He'd never seen so many gas lamps in one place.

Quincy kept them away from shadowy corners and dark alleys. He walked on Ella's free side while Travis stayed behind, a protective barrier around her. Between the three of them, she should be safe.

When they approached the stables, the marshal held up a hand. "Let me check inside." He went in. Cody stayed with Ella while Travis stood like a sentinel, his eyes methodically sweeping back and forth. Quincy came out after a few minutes. "All clear. I'll watch from here while you care for your horse."

The stables were as bright as the rest of the town. Cody shook his head. "How does anyone get any rest with all this light?"

Travis chuckled. "You should see Boston."

"Oh, yes." Ella nodded. "This is nothing in comparison."

Cody couldn't wrap his mind around that. "Thank God for country life."

His wife smiled at him. "Indeed."

They stopped in front of the stall with Cody's nameless horse. Ella cooed at the animal, then looked at Cody. "Who's this?"

"I don't know his name. We switched horses in Clancy so Preston and Blaze didn't injure themselves." He opened the stall. "What's the matter, boy?"

The horse held his left foreleg aloft. Ella watched from outside the stall as Cody bent the leg to look at his hoof. "His shoe is loose." He shot a glance over his shoulder. "Where's the stable boy?"

"Here, sir!" The kid slid down from the loft, landing with a thud outside the stall.

"Can you find me strips of cloth? I need to wrap his hoof."

"Yessir." The boy skidded off.

Ella leaned into the stall. She patted the horse's muzzle. "What's the cloth for?"

"I'm gonna bind his hoof so the shoe doesn't fall off. In the morning, we'll need to take him to a blacksmith to get it nailed on again." He sighed and patted the steed. "Sorry, boy. I pushed you too hard."

The horse nickered, nudging Cody's shoulder with his nose. The stable boy returned with strips of white cotton. Cody wound the cloth under the shoe, then wove it around the horse's leg and tied it securely. "There you go."

Once the stall was locked again, he looked at Travis. "All well with your horse?"

"Yep." Travis handed Cody a sugar cube. "The kid provided a couple of these as a treat."

With a chuckle, Cody fed the cube to his horse. It snuffed his hand, searching for more. "I'll bring you another one in the morning, okay?"

Ella covered a yawn.

Travis nudged her. "A little sleepy?"

She smiled, but lines creased around her eyes.

Cody slipped an arm around her. "Let's head back. You need a good night's sleep."

"So do you," she countered, leaning her head against his shoulder. "I can't imagine how fast you and Travis must have ridden to get here so quickly."

"It was fine."

Her lips quirked. "Such a man thing to say."

Cody opened his mouth to retort, but Travis halted suddenly and held up a hand. "Where's Quincy?"

The man was nowhere to be seen. Cody's gaze darted about. People walked all over, but the marshal had disappeared. His body tensed. Cody pushed Ella behind him even as he came up behind Travis.

A moan sounded on the other side of the stable door. Travis

pulled his gun. They looked around the door. Quincy lay on the ground, a gash covering much of his forehead. Travis hollered for the stable boy. The kid didn't come.

Premonition sliced through Cody's heart. He gripped Ella's hand. "Should we find the doctor?"

Travis knelt at Quincy's side. He pulled a handkerchief from his pocket and pressed it to the wound. Quincy groaned but didn't wake. Travis looked up at them. "Yeah. And hurry."

Ella jogged to keep up with Cody's long strides. "Where will we find the doctor?"

"The bellhop at the hotel should know how to locate him."

They'd almost reached the hotel when a shout went up from the saloon. Two men crashed through the swinging door, landing in a tangle of fists and blows. A crowd quickly formed. People rushed past Ella and Cody, jostling them in the process. He tugged her to the side of a large building to protect her from the fray.

Gunshots rang out.

Cody looped an arm around his wife. He gaped at the crowd. "They're not even batting an eye."

"It's unsettling." Ella nestled closer as they reached the corner of the building. "This looks like something out of a dime novel."

"Except it's real." He shook his head. "At least we know someone'll be awake to point us to the doctor."

Ella opened her mouth. Her words were cut off as she was yanked from his grasp. She screamed, disappearing into the alley.

Cody's heart plummeted. He ran after her. "Ella!"

A shot cracked through the night. He stumbled back. Red-hot pain poured into him. He grabbed his shoulder. Sticky, warm blood seeped through his fingers.

A man emerged from the shadows, Ella pinned to his side. The gun in his hand pointed directly at Cody's heart. "Mr.

Brooks. You didn't heed my warnings." He *tsk*ed. "All you had to do was return Ariella to me, and no one would've been hurt. Now, you've forced my hand."

Ella's face shattered Cody. Her body trembled. Tears shone in her eyes. "I'm sorry, Cody."

"Don't apologize, darlin'. This isn't your fault." His eyes bore into the man's. "I'm guessin' this is Howard."

The man sneered. "I suppose you're not as dumb as you look."

Ella bristled.

Howard turned a slow smile on her. "Ah, you don't like insults aimed his way, do you?" His expression hardened. He cocked the gun. "You promise to come with me, my dear, no attempting to escape, and I'll let this"—his eyes raked disdainfully over Cody—"cowboy live. Your choice."

Despair filled his wife's eyes.

Rage ignited in Cody. He wasn't about to make Ella choose between him or freedom. His muscles coiled and tensed. The pain in his body faded. He'd tangled with a few steers over the years. An arrogant Boston businessman couldn't be any worse. Gun or no gun.

With a harsh yell, he sprang forward.

~

Gunfire rang in her ears again. Ella screamed as her husband's body jerked, but he continued his lunge at Howard. Cody hit him with his full weight. Howard's hold on her broke. Both men plummeted to the ground. The gun flew to the side.

Footsteps raced into the alley. Travis appeared, weapon drawn. Cody and Howard wrestled for the upper hand.

Travis took her arm and pulled her back. He thrust the gun

into her hands. "Hold this." His eyes bore into hers. "And Ella, if necessary…use it."

A stone settled in her stomach. Travis reached the men just as Howard sent a punch at Cody's face. It knocked her husband onto his back. Blood soaked his shirt. Ella cried out. She dropped to her knees beside him. "Cody!"

He groaned. His eyes opened into slits. "Ella. Travis came?"

"Yes. He's here." She looked behind her in time to see Travis haul Howard to his feet. "He has Howard."

Cody's eyes closed. "Good." Another groan seeped out of him. Moments later, his body went limp.

"Cody?" Ella shook his arm, panic threatening. "Cody!"

He didn't move.

Agony ripped through her. "No!"

Howard's maniacal laughter grated in her ears.

Travis jostled him. Anger lined his face. "Shut up."

"Of course." A sly smile tilted Howard's lips. "Actions speak louder than words, no?" He slammed his head back into Travis's face.

Stunned, Travis loosened his hold on him.

Howard ripped away. Turning, he planted a fist first in the side of the sheriff's head, then his gut. Travis stumbled back. Another punch sent him careening to the ground. Howard swept up the gun he'd lost fighting Cody. He pointed it at Travis. "Looks as though you'll be going the way of your friend." He sent Ella a grin full of malice. "Two men you care about, gone in one day. All because of you."

Pain threatened to swallow her, but she pushed to her feet. The cold metal in her hand felt heavy. But if Cody had a chance of survival, if Travis could be saved—she had to do something.

Ella lifted the gun. Everything Cody taught her flooded back. She took aim. "Drop your weapon, or I'll shoot."

Surprise flashed over Howard's face. He quickly masked it

with a scoff. "You've never shot a gun in your life. Put that down and admit you've lost."

"No." Fire pumped through her veins. Her hand held steady. "I'm an excellent shot. I won't miss."

Howard sneered. "I don't believe you. We're both about to see the truth." He turned back to a stunned Travis. His finger tightened against the trigger.

Ella pulled hers first.

CHAPTER 26

Two days later, Ella sat by Cody's side in one of Helena's hospitals. The staff were considerate and caring. Even so, a pall hung over her as she held her husband's hand, waiting and praying that he would wake up.

Extreme blood loss. That's what the doctor said. Between the shot to his upper chest and the one to his side, Cody had bled enough to faint after his fight with Howard. Then it had taken another half hour to get him to the hospital to begin the treatment that might save him.

Now all they could do was wait.

Marshal Quincy had revived after a full day in the hospital. The gash on his head looked worse than it was. They'd found the stable boy asleep in a stall, having given in to exhaustion right after providing sugar cubes for the horses.

Howard lay in an adjoining room. Ella's shot had proved true. She hadn't aimed to kill, but to disarm. The bullet passed through his right shoulder, disabling him. He'd cursed her—loudly—as Travis found his footing and arrested him. Later that day, the jailer brought Howard to the hospital. The wound had gone putrid. Shortly after, he lost consciousness.

Ella didn't dwell on his situation. She was too concerned with her husband's survival. Reaching out, she smoothed a hand down his arm. "Happy birthday, Cody." Tears stung her eyes. She sniffed. "It feels wrong that you're spending such a wonderful day fighting for your life." Leaning closer, she placed a hand on his chest. "Please wake up. Our children need you. I need you." A tear dropped onto his shirt. "We've only known each other for three months. We have a whole lifetime ahead. But you need to get better."

Two hands came to rest on her shoulders. Through hazy eyes, she glanced up to see Travis standing behind her. His face looked mottled, but otherwise, he'd survived the scuffle with Howard unscathed. He squeezed gently before sitting beside her. "Any change?"

"None." Her jaw worked. "He's going to be okay, right?"

Travis took her hand. "Cody's always been a fighter."

"That's not an answer, Travis." Fresh tears burned her eyes.

He sighed. "I know. I wish I had an answer, Ella."

She rested her head on his shoulder and let her tears fall. Travis wrapped his arm around her. They sat silently, keeping watch over Cody.

After a while, Travis stood. "You haven't eaten all day. You need sustenance."

"I'm not hungry."

His brow twitched. "If not for yourself, think of your baby."

Her gaze shot up. "How'd you know about the baby?"

"Cody prayed aloud whenever we stopped to rest the horses. Usually I couldn't hear him, but at one point, I grabbed his canteen to refill it, and I heard him mention the baby."

"It's a suspicion at this point. We don't know for sure." Ella's hands went to her stomach.

Travis's gaze followed the motion. "But you have a feeling, don't you?"

"Yes."

"I thought so." He gave her a half smile. "I've learned to never discount a woman's intuition."

Someone knocked at the door. They turned to see Lydia standing just outside, a covered box in her hands. "I brought some food from the café down the street. I figured you wouldn't want to leave his side."

Gratitude swept through Ella. "Thank you, Lydia. That's very kind."

"And timely." Travis shot her a look as he stood. "I'll leave you ladies to talk. There's some business I need to discuss with the deputy marshals."

Ella's brow furrowed.

A faint smile tugged at Travis's lips. "Later, Ella. For now, focus on Cody." He motioned for Lydia to take his seat.

Ella turned her attention to her new friend. "I'm glad you're here."

Lydia handed her the box. "Eat. I'd wager you haven't had anything yet."

Sheepish, Ella said a blessing over the simple fare and picked up the provided fork. "I haven't." Her stomach rumbled as the scent of roast beef and potatoes filled her nostrils. "It seems I'm hungrier than I realized."

"I know the feeling—so invested in someone's condition, you forget to eat."

Lydia's hazel eyes took on a faraway glaze. Ella touched her arm. "Are you all right?"

Blinking, Lydia shook herself. "Sorry. Lost in a memory."

"Did you...lose someone?"

Sadness flickered on her face. "I did."

"I'm sorry to hear that." Ella put her fork down. "Would you like to talk about it?"

Lydia produced a sad smile. "Maybe some other time."

They wouldn't see each other again after parting ways. Ella

didn't say it, but Lydia must have seen the sentiment on her face.

Her smile grew soft. "It seems we might have the chance to become good friends. Sheriff Doyle tells me you're from Harmony Springs. That's where my mother-in-law and I are headed."

Ella gasped. "Truly? Are you visiting family?"

Another uncertain expression crossed Lydia's face, but she quickly hid it, twisting a black curl over her gloved finger. "No. We're settling there."

"Oh! That's wonderful news."

Lydia grasped her hand. "I hope you and I shall see each other often. It would be nice to have a friend."

Something in her tone told Ella this woman had suffered much in her young life. Perhaps one day, they'd build the kind of trust that led to sharing confidences. Until then, she would happily accept an offer of friendship. "Cody and I will have you over once we return home."

If he returns home. Ella swallowed hard, pushing the thought from her mind.

Lydia nudged the fork closer to her. "You need to keep up your strength, Ella. Wasting away won't help your husband."

Ella finished her food, then drank a cup of tea one of the nurses brought her.

Though they'd just met, Ella felt comfortable with Lydia. She sensed they could be good friends. Lydia asked how she came to be in Harmony Springs, and the story poured out of Ella. By the end of an hour, she realized she'd done just about all the talking.

"I'm sorry. I don't usually talk this much," Ella said, a hint of heat touching her face.

Lydia smiled. "I don't mind. You needed the distraction." She glanced at the clock. "My mother-in-law will be expecting me. I should go." She stood, putting a hand on Ella's shoulder.

"Please let me know if you need anything. Sometimes it helps just to have someone present." The sadness glimmered again.

What was this woman's story? Some hidden pain lurked in her past. Ella said a prayer for Lydia as the woman departed, then turned her attention back to Cody.

He remained unresponsive. Without anyone else there, she sank into grief. What if he never woke up? Fear slithered up and down her spine. She banished the thought. He *had* to wake up.

"Did I ever tell you about my hopes for my own fairytale prince?" Ella combed her fingers through his hair. "Before I lost faith in love, I was a romantic. I dreamed of a knight in shining armor coming to rescue me from my dreary existence, sweeping me off to a faraway kingdom and showering me with all the affection no one else would give. We would talk for hours. He'd love poetry and be as much of a romantic as me." She blinked back the moisture that welled in her eyes. "Do you know what he looked like in my dreams? Blond hair. Blue eyes. Tall and strong. Capable of protecting me and someone I could love with all my heart.

"When Miles began courting me, I thought he could be my knight. He looked and acted the part. When I found out he only wanted my money, it broke something inside of me. I became disillusioned and cynical. After a while, when Howard showed interest, I thought the fairytale might be possible after all. He didn't fit the mental image of my knight, but he played the part well. He charmed me thoroughly and made me believe in love again. I was so naïve. His abuse beat me down until I was a shell of myself, frightened of my own shadow."

Her hand came to rest against his cheek. She stroked his skin gently. Three days of beard growth scratched her fingers and palm. "Then you swooped in and literally rescued me. You frightened me and growled like a bear, but underneath that gruff demeanor, you showed a patience and gentleness that broke through my walls. You protected me, loved me, sheltered me. Because of that, I believed in love again. And the best part?" She rested her forehead against his. "You showed me that real life is so much better than a fairytale."

"I agree, darlin'."

Ella's head flew up.

Cody's eyes were closed, but he wore a small smile. Slowly, he blinked them open.

A sob ripped through her throat. Ella flung her arms around him, careful to avoid his injuries. She buried her face in his neck. "You're awake!"

His hand came to rest on her back, rubbing in small circles while she cried in relief. She struggled to regain a semblance of composure. When she did, she lifted her head and cupped her husband's face. "How do you feel?"

"My body hurts like the dickens. What happened? Where am I?"

"St. John's Hospital. You've been unconscious for two days." She gave him a quick explanation of the events leading to his hospitalization. As she spoke, recognition sparked his eyes.

"Howard." His gaze darkened. "He's been arrested?"

"Yes."

Cody relaxed. "Good."

Ella debated telling him about Howard being down the hall but decided against it. When Cody regained some strength, she'd give him the whole story.

A doctor came in. When he saw Cody awake, the man's brows flew up. "Well, this is a happy turn of events. Let's check your vital signs, young man." He turned to Ella. "Would you mind waiting in the hall?"

She stood, ready to comply, but Cody grabbed her hand. "I want her here. Please."

The doctor glanced between them. A slow smile spread over his face. "True love, eh?"

Ella melted at the look on Cody's face.

He gazed into her eyes as he answered. "Yeah. We're living our very own fairytale."

She blushed. "Exactly how much of that story did you hear?"

He grinned. "All of it."

~

The morning after he regained consciousness, Cody sat up in bed, thankful to be alive. He sipped water as Ella held a cup to his lips. When he had enough, he leaned back. "Thanks, darlin'."

She set the cup on a small table. "The doctor says we should be able to go home tomorrow. Dorothy and Lydia are headed to Harmony Springs as well. They said they'd rent a carriage to take us all back."

"That's mighty kind of them. We're practically strangers."

His wife smoothed the blanket over his lap. "Perhaps for now. I have a feeling we'll get to know them well over time." She stood, pressing her hands against her back while she stretched. "It'll be nice to get home. I miss the children."

"Me too. And it's a relief to know we won't have any more incidents now that Howard's been caught."

"Yes." Ella released a long sigh. Did she still blame herself for the events of the past months? He started to ask, but she gave him a gentle look. "No, I don't blame myself."

"How'd you know that's what I was gonna ask?"

She chuckled. "It was written all over your face."

"Humph."

Ella's chuckle became a laugh. "Don't growl, love. It just means I can read you."

He shook his head. No one had ever been able to read him

before, not even Cassie. "You've done a number on me, darlin'. I used to have a tough reputation."

"All a cover for that tender heart beating in your chest."

He grunted. "Let's not go spreading that around."

She laughed again.

Cody reached for her hand, pulling her to his side. "Are you excited to see your sister?"

"Oh, yes." Her eyes lit up. "I've missed her dearly. It'll be wonderful to catch up. And I can't wait for you two to get to know one another."

One side of his mouth turned up. "Anything will be better than her pointing a rifle at me."

Ella gasped. "She didn't!"

"She sure did. In her defense, she didn't know who I was, and she'd just fired the signal for help. I could've been the ruffian, for all she knew. By the way, I'm glad we told Miss Hattie about the double gunshot summons. She's the one who told Tori."

"Thank God for that."

A familiar voice chimed in. "Glad to see you looking so well, my friend."

Cody's gaze swung to the door, where Travis leaned against the frame. His brother-in-law's face held a smile, but something serious lingered in his eyes. Cody frowned. "What's wrong?"

"You've never been one to mince words." Travis smirked and came into the room. "Nothing's wrong, necessarily. It's just..." His glance darted to Ella. "Howard's dead."

She sucked in a sharp breath. "Dead?" Her teeth came down hard on her bottom lip. "Is that...did I...kill him?"

"No." Travis emphasized his words with a shake of his head. "The infection killed him. He was alive and kicking when I took him to the deputy marshals. We don't know why his wound festered. There are a hundred possibilities. But I do know this —it wasn't your fault. Your actions saved all our lives."

Cody squeezed her hand. "He's right, darlin'. Howard made his choice. You did what you had to do." He smiled, tipping up her chin. "And just so we're clear, I'm downright impressed with your shooting skills."

Ella blushed, but it was accompanied by a smile. "I had an excellent teacher."

Blast his injuries. He wanted nothing more than to pull her into his arms and hold her tight, but that could reopen his wounds. Cody settled for kissing her hand. "We make a good team."

Travis coughed. "Not that either of you remember I'm in the room—but please, save the lovey-dovey stuff for private."

"The door is that way," Cody said, jerking his head to the side. "And might I remind you how many times I had to suffer through you and Cassie being exactly that?"

Travis laughed. "Point taken." He hitched his thumbs in his belt. "I need to be going, anyway. I'll take our borrowed horses back to Clancy and pick up Preston and Blaze. Just gotta finish up my business with the authorities here, then get home to my wife."

"Does that business have to do with Howard?" Ella asked.

"Yeah. That's why I've been at the station so much. At first, it was talking about how to try him since he committed crimes in Montana Territory. Now it'll be what to do with his body. Does he have any family in Boston?"

Ella shook her head. "Not that I know of."

"Well, that'll make it easier. We can just bury him here." Travis tipped his hat. "See you both back home."

Once he left, Ella pressed Cody's hand to her chest.

He studied her for a moment. "Are you sure you're all right, Ella?"

She didn't answer right away. Her teeth sank into her lip again, and she stared out the window for a full minute. But when she turned back to him, her eyes were clear. "Yes, Cody,

I'm fine. It's a bit of a shock that Howard died. But if given the chance to do it over again, knowing the outcome, my choice would be the same." She kissed his cheek. "We can finally put fear and uncertainty behind us. I'm ready to see what the future holds for our family."

Cody ran his fingers over her palm. "Me too." He tugged her closer, lowering his voice to a whisper. "From what I can tell, it's gonna be a bright one."

CHAPTER 27

The Jeffersons hired a comfortable carriage for the ride back to Harmony Springs. Ella watched their interactions with interest, wondering anew at their history, but she kept her questions to herself. Prying wasn't her style.

Cody's comfort mattered most. He struggled to move without wincing and was clearly in pain, but he insisted on walking to the carriage himself, refusing the proffered wheeled chair. Ella shook her head but respected his wish for some independence.

After several hours in the carriage, Ella experienced a nausea she'd never before known. She tried to ignore it. It pushed back with a vengeance.

"Stop the carriage!"

Dorothy pounded the roof. The vehicle soon came to a halt.

Ella stumbled out. She dropped to her knees and lost the contents of her stomach on the dusty roadside.

Someone crouched beside her, a hand on her back. "You all right, darlin'?"

She glanced up, her husband's blue eyes looking at her in

concern. "Cody, you shouldn't be out of the carriage. You need to rest."

"I'm not about to let you be sick out here by yourself. Not when I'm responsible for your condition."

That made her smile. She put a hand on his cheek. "It could simply be motion sickness. I felt some nausea on the train ride from Boston too."

He helped her stand. Ella caught the grimace as he turned to their conveyance and told him firmly, "You stay inside if I need to stop the carriage again."

"Hopefully, we won't need to."

She climbed in after him.

Lydia gripped her hand. "Are you ill?"

"Just some motion sickness. I'll be fine."

Thankfully, no further incidents occurred during their trip. As dusk fell, they reached the ranch. Ella thanked the Jeffersons for their generosity. "Are you sure you won't come in for a cup of tea or some other refreshment?"

Lydia smiled. "Thank you, Ella, but we need to settle into our new home. We'll call on you before long."

"Please do. I'm happy you're both staying." She hugged each lady. "Thank you for everything. I don't know what I would've done if you hadn't heard my cry for help."

Dorothy patted her hand. "I firmly believe the good Lord intended us to be there for you. And He brought us together for a reason. More than just being in the right place at the right time."

Ella tilted her head. "What do you mean?"

The older woman's gaze fluttered to her daughter-in-law before going back to Ella. "Let's just say friendship is something we all need. Some more than others."

"What—?"

Lydia took Dorothy's arm. "We should let them get to their family." She smiled at Ella. "See you soon."

Ella stood beside Cody as the carriage drove off. "I wonder what happened to Lydia. I get the sense she's been deeply hurt."

He slipped an arm around her waist. "I'm sure you'll find out when the time is right."

The front door burst open. Isaiah flew out of the house. "Mama! Papa!"

He made a beeline straight to Ella. She knelt down to catch him as he careened into her. Sobs shook his little body. "I thought you weren't coming back."

Ella held him close. "I'm sorry I scared you, sweetie."

"Did the bad man get caught?"

"Yes. He won't bother us any longer."

Isaiah sank into her. "Good." He squeezed her again, then started for Cody.

Ella put a restraining hand on his shoulder. "Be careful, Isaiah. Your papa is hurt."

Their son paused. "Hurt?"

Cody smiled. "I'll be fine, buddy. Just need you to hug me on this side for a bit." He pointed to his left.

Isaiah complied. "Why're you hurt, Papa?"

He was saved from answering by a shriek from the front door. Tori stood there, hands over her mouth. "You're back!" She raced down the steps and enveloped Ella in a hug. "I kept imagining the worst."

Ella threw her arms around her sister. "All's well now."

Their embrace lasted a long time. Cody mumbled something about checking on Preston, and he and Isaiah headed for the barn. Tori pulled back first, her eyes following Cody. "Is he all right?"

"He will be." Ella led her sister to the house. "I want to hear all about medical school."

"In time." Tori squeezed her arm. "First, I want to know what happened."

Ella gave a brief explanation of the events that led to Cody's injuries. By the time she finished, Tori's eyes were wide.

"My word, Ella. You've been through a lot in a few days."

She nodded, suddenly exhausted.

Tori slipped an arm around her waist. "Why don't you say hello to your other two children? Supper will be ready soon."

Ella blinked. "You cook?"

"Oh, goodness, no. I'm hopeless when it comes to that. Cassie brought over a large pot of stew." She smiled. "I like her. Travis found himself a wonderful wife."

"Indeed." Ella glanced around. "Is Miss Hattie here?"

Tori shook her head. "Her grandson had an emergency, so I told her to go home to help. The children and I have been getting along famously. I felt comfortable taking care of them myself, though Miss Hattie did promise to come back as soon as the situation at home was resolved."

They entered the kitchen. Addie and Jonah sat on the floor, playing. Jonah saw her first. His eyes grew large. "Mama!" He jumped up and ran to her. She wrapped him in her arms, kissing his forehead. Addie crawled over and tugged her skirt. Ella lowered herself to the floor so she could hold both children. She cuddled them close, basking in their sweet innocence. When her eyes finally opened again, she saw Tori watching her with an intense expression.

"What is it?"

Her sister shook her head. "You, my dear Ella. I wasn't sure how you'd survive in the wilds of the West. But it's obvious you've found your place. All I heard while you were gone was 'Mama this' and 'Papa that.' These children love you and your husband." She wiped a tear from her cheek. "It's the opposite of what we experienced as children. It...it gives me hope." She sat on the floor beside Ella. "I do have one question."

Ella rested her head against Addie's. "Go ahead."

"I can tell Cody loves you. His reaction to Howard taking you was telling. But you—how do you feel about him?"

A smile curled up her lips. "I love him too."

Cody poked his head around the corner. "I'll never get tired of hearing that. Or of saying it to you."

Tori jumped, a hand over her heart.

Ella chuckled as Jonah wiggled out of her arms. "Papa, Papa!"

"Careful, Jonah!" Isaiah stood like a guard in front of Cody, pointing to his uninjured side. "You need to hug him here."

Jonah plunked his hands on his hips. "Why?"

"'Cuz he's hurt. C'mere."

Isaiah guided his brother to the right spot. Addie bounced in Ella's lap, one arm straining toward Cody. Ella stood and waited for Jonah to finish his hug, then slipped to Cody's uninjured side and let the baby rest her head on his chest.

Cody put one hand over Addie's back and used the other to draw Ella closer. He let his head drop against hers with a sigh. "It's good to be home."

∾

The family insisted on celebrating Cody's birthday the Saturday after their return from Helena. Besides Ella and the children, Travis and Cassie, Tori, Miss Hattie, and the ranch hands all crowded around the kitchen table for a special dinner. Cody tried to help his wife serve dinner, only to be shooed to the table by a plethora of women.

Tori steered him to his seat. "From what Ella tells me, you are always trying to help. Let us show you some care today."

He dug in his heels. "I've been doing nothing but lying around all week."

"To recover. And this is a day celebrating you. Now sit!"

Her tone raised his brows. He looked over her head at Ella. "Is she always this bossy?"

Ella laughed. "Pretty much."

"And proudly so." Tori tossed her red curls, shooting Cody a wink. "Best get used to it, brother."

He chuckled and allowed her to push him into the chair.

Joey crossed his arms, a twinkle in his eye. "I don't recall you ever takin' orders from anyone. Family life changed you, Boss."

"For the better," Eddie injected. "You smile more."

"And you spend as much time with them as you can."

"And—"

"Okay." Cody held up a hand, cutting off the twins' praise. His face felt unnaturally warm. "Point taken, boys."

Ella served him a plate of chicken pot pie. The savory aroma of gravy and vegetables made his mouth water. His wife rubbed a hand against his back, leaning close. "I, for one, am grateful you're a family man."

Cassie and Tori brought over more plates. When everyone was served, they joined hands for grace. After a simple but heartfelt prayer, Cody looked up with a smile. "Amen."

"Amen."

Chatter ensued. Cody's knee bounced while his hand drummed against the table.

Travis eyed him with a grin. "Not used to being the center of attention, huh?"

Cody chuckled. "Is it that obvious?"

His friend laughed. "Oh, yeah."

Taking a bite of his meal, Cody forgot his trepidation. "Ella, this is wonderful. You make the best chicken pot pie."

She flushed with pleasure.

Cassie arched her brows. "Hey, now. What about me?"

He shrugged. "What can I say? You've been usurped."

"Well, since it's Ella, I won't complain." Cassie grinned at his wife. "I don't mind taking second to you."

Travis engaged him in a good-natured argument over their wives' cooking. The meal flew by. Tori and Hattie served dessert. Ella had made his favorite—caramel cake. He smiled, remembering the first time they'd had dinner together at Travis and Cassie's. He'd been impressed with her baking then, and she'd only improved over time. Somehow, the cake tasted even better now. He complimented her extensively, making her ears rosy.

"Present time!" Isaiah hollered, bouncing in his seat.

Cassie rose. "Let us get the dishes done, sweetie. Then your papa will open his gifts."

"Awww." Isaiah slumped back. "Why do we have to do so much waiting all the time?"

Cody tapped his shoulder. "That's life, buddy. How about we build a tower while we wait?"

"Yeah!"

He ushered the kids into the parlor. They got out the blocks and spent the next fifteen minutes on the rug making a tower that fell down over and over, much to the children's delight. By the time the rest of the adults trickled in, the three kids were laughing so hard, everyone else caught the amusement.

When the hilarity died down, Addie crawled into Cody's lap. She stuck her thumb in her mouth, looking around as people found places to sit. Cody eyed the couch but decided to remain where he was. Ella settled beside him on the floor. One by one, his family and friends presented him with gifts.

A new tool belt from his ranch hands.

A saddle he'd had his eye on from Travis and Cassie.

Cookies in a decorative tin from Hattie.

Artwork from his children—directed by Tori.

Ella handed him her gift last. It was wrapped in brown paper with a simple string tied around and looped into a bow.

He undid the bow. Addie reached for it. Cody dangled the string in front of her before letting her play with it. With her occupied, he removed the paper.

A frame sat in his hands. Inside, a sheet of white paper looked up at him. It was filled with beautiful cursive. A combination of watercolor and pressed wildflowers decorated the edges. The familiar words of his favorite poem came to life on the page. *How do I love thee? Let me count the ways…*

He caught his breath. His gaze found his wife's. "Did you make this?"

"I did." Her green eyes searched his. "Do you like it?"

Cody placed the frame on the floor. He cupped Ella's cheek and drew her close, pressing his lips against hers. "I love it." He grinned. "But not as much as I love you."

A chorus of laughs sounded throughout the room.

Hank groaned. "Sheesh, Boss, you're getting soft."

Ella's fingers trailed over his face. "He's always had a soft heart. He just didn't show it."

"I need to keep some secrets, darlin'."

More laughter rang out. Ella leaned against him, lowering her voice until only he could hear. "I thought you might like a reminder of your mother. We can hang it wherever you want."

He kissed her again, heedless of their audience. "It's a thoughtful gift, Ella. But it no longer just reminds me of Ma." His hand curled around hers. "It reminds me of us. How we married for practical purposes but found our way to love in the simplicity of everyday life." Their eyes met and held. "I thank God every single day that He saw fit to bring us together."

Ella melted into him, her eyes bright. "Me too."

EPILOGUE

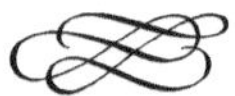

The sun rose slowly over the horizon. Pink and orange splashed the landscape. Ella watched from the parlor window, sipping her morning tea and enjoying the peaceful quiet. These early-morning moments were some of her favorites, time to gather her thoughts for the day ahead before her family woke up. All was still.

It was broken by a tiny coo. She smiled, her gaze moving down to where her infant daughter nestled against her chest. Almost two months old, Rosie added so much life to their family. She'd had her brothers' love from the start, and while Addie wasn't sure about the newcomer for a week or two, she eventually came around.

"Hello, sweet Rosie. Are you feeling more awake now?"

Sunlight glinted off the baby's red-blond hair. She yawned, her pink mouth forming a perfect O. Ella chuckled. "I suppose not. You're probably going to be hungry soon, aren't you?"

Strong arms wrapped around Ella from behind. She smiled, peeking over her shoulder. "Good morning, Cody."

"Mornin'." He kissed Rosie's petal-soft cheek, then slid a finger down it. "How's our baby girl?"

Ella loved watching her husband with their daughter. She turned around, placing Rosie in his arms. "She's ready for cuddles with her papa."

He accepted the precious bundle. Rosie gazed up at him, her blue eyes wide and alert. Cody rocked her back and forth, singing a lullaby quietly the way he did every morning. Ella sipped her tea, content to watch them together.

A few minutes later, Cody shifted Rosie to one arm. He reached into his pocket. "I have something for you."

"For me?"

He presented her with a box. Curiosity piqued, Ella opened it. She gasped. Two golden rings reflected the sunlight. Tiny diamonds encircled one of the bands. She stared up at her husband. "I forgot! It's our anniversary."

He plucked the diamond ring from its place with a grin. "Happy anniversary, darlin'. You never got a proper wedding band. Since our herd recovered, we made good money this last year. I wanted to get you a special gift now that we can afford it." He held it up. "Look at the engraving."

She squinted at the small words. "'By sun and candle-light.'" Blinking rapidly, she put her hands over her heart. "That's beautiful."

"It's on my ring too. Considering the significance of that particular part of the poem—to us, at least—I thought it appropriate."

A soft smile lifted her lips. "It's perfect. Thank you."

He placed Rosie on the sofa. Reaching for Ella's left hand, he removed the old borrowed ring from her finger before taking his off as well. He offered her the box. Ella took the shiny golden circle out and slipped it on his finger. "Happy anniversary, Cody."

A grin lit his face. He took his turn, sliding the diamond

ring into place. "Happy anniversary, Ella." Pulling her close, he nuzzled her nose. "I pray we have many, many more."

"So do I."

They shared a kiss. Ella wrapped her arms around his neck, getting lost in the moment. Little footsteps sounded seconds before a voice broke through her happy haze.

"Oh, gross. They're kissin' again."

Ella and Cody drew apart a couple inches. Their children stood in a semi-circle around them. Isaiah's nose scrunched, Jonah grinned, and Addie stared up at them curiously.

Cody laughed and tapped Ella's nose. "I guess it's time...to play!" He roared, lunging at the children. They shrieked and started running around the room. Cody gave chase, rumbling like a bear and raising his arms above his head as if they were paws.

Rosie fussed, so Ella sat on the sofa and picked her up. The baby's mouth worked as if searching for something. Ella took up a blanket on the side of the couch and draped it over herself. Adjusting her clothing, she held Rosie to her breast so her daughter could eat.

"Mama, save us!" Jonah dove onto the sofa, burying himself in the side of Ella that was baby-free.

She laughed, looping her arm around him. "I don't know, Jonah. The bear looks ferocious."

He blinked up at her. "What's fe'ocious?"

"It means fierce."

"Oh." Jonah giggled. "Yeah. Papa's fe'ocious!" He vaulted off the sofa as quickly as he'd got on.

Addie shot by next, waving at Ella as she ran with a giant grin. Isaiah also waved, his smile sporting two missing front teeth.

Cody growled, though it was belied by his laughter. "I see children who need eating!"

That ignited a new chorus of squeals and chortles. Ella took it all in with a full heart. Cody had blossomed as a father. With each passing day, he seemed more natural and at ease. He'd only needed practice and patience to become a man just as capable as his own father. Ella loved how he played with their children. She loved the tender way he held Rosie. He'd taken on the role he was given with strength, determination, and grace.

The children, too, had come a long way. According to Cody, Isaiah had become the child he was before his parents' death. Happy and loving, he always wanted to help with the younger children. Jonah and Addie were carefree, full of joy and life. Ella was amazed at their resilience.

Breathing hard, Cody plopped onto the sofa beside her. He scooped Addie into his arms as she blazed by. The little girl playfully fought his hold before snuggling into his arms and resting her head against his shoulder. She put a hand on Rosie's, and the baby responded by clenching her finger and holding it close.

The boys continued to play, laughter bursting from them every so often. Ella felt warm inside as she listened and watched. This family she had found providentially became so much more than a convenient escape from Boston. They were her true family. She looked at Cody. It still amazed her how much she loved this sometimes gruff, always gentle giant of a man who loved with everything in him.

He turned and met her gaze. The soft look in his blue eyes melted her heart. She smiled, slipping her hand into his.

This was home.

THE END

∿

Turn the page for a sneak peek of The Reverend's Second Chance the next book in the Second Chances in Harmony Springs series!

SNEAK PEEK: THE REVEREND'S SECOND CHANCE

Don't miss the next book in the Second Chances in Harmony
Springs *series!*

NOVEMBER 1888
MONTANA TERRITORY

Grief always hit at the most inopportune moment.

A lump formed in Lydia Jefferson's throat as she watched a group of her students work on their science project. The classroom boasted plenty of windows, letting natural light into the small one-room schoolhouse that provided education for the children of Harmony Springs. She faced one of those windows and drew in a long breath. Wind blew through the straw-colored grass, long dried up for autumn. The sky had turned gray, matching her mood. With a sigh, Lydia turned her attention back to her students. Their happy faces, so bright and innocent, tugged on a piece of her heart she tried to keep hidden. Most days, it worked. Today, though...

"Mrs. Jefferson?"

Lydia fumbled with a piece of clay before dropping it to the table. She found a smile for the child in front of her. "Yes, sweetie?"

Ruby Calhoun blinked up at her with wide hazel eyes, so like Lydia's own. Many people had marveled at the way the two of them resembled each other. Both with black curls, hazel eyes, and porcelain skin. Ruby had been mistaken for her daughter many times.

And she looks so much like...

Lydia clamped down on the thought. It would do no good to remember now. Not when she was in class.

Ruby held up a tangle of dried grass and sticks. "I made a nest."

"It's perfect, Ruby. Where are the clay birds to go with it?"

"Isaiah and Alice have them." Ruby smiled shyly, then made her way to the other youngsters in class.

Isaiah Brooks grinned as his classmate approached. Alice giggled and waved. The two girls were six and Isaiah seven, the three youngest in her group of twenty-five students, and they'd bonded over their similar age.

Lydia followed Ruby. She knelt beside the small children. "Isaiah, Alice, Ruby tells me you made the bird."

Alice nodded, her blond curls bouncing with each shake of her head.

"Uh-huh." Isaiah pointed to a lump of clay on the table. "It's a robin."

Look, Mama! The first robin of spring.

Stabs of pain radiated from Lydia's chest. She rubbed a hand over her heart, hoping to dull the ache. Not now. She couldn't fall apart now.

Isaiah stared at her, his little brow furrowed. "Mrs. Jefferson, what's wrong? Are you sad?"

She gave him a smile. Maybe it appeared less weak than it felt. "Nothing's wrong, Isaiah. You made a wonderful robin. Shall we put it in Ruby's nest?"

Isaiah's brown eyes remained on Lydia as if he knew she hid something. She'd learned quickly last year that her student possessed a keen understanding of people. Unease settled over her, as much from the child's gaze as from the fact that she was indeed hiding something. She abhorred lying—and yet here she was, lying to a student.

With a small sigh, Lydia looked Isaiah in the eyes. "Actually, something is bothering me, but I'll be all right. Especially with sweet students like you who care."

He darted forward and threw his arms around her neck. She pressed her toes against the floor to remain upright, then hugged him back. This sweet innocence, the pure affection of a child, was the best part of her job.

"Can we put the birdie in now?" Ruby's voice piped up.

Lydia smiled, surreptitiously wiping a tear from her eye. "Yes, we can."

Ruby put the nest on the table and arranged a few sticks

that had come loose. Then she peered up at Isaiah. "Can I help put him in?"

"Sure."

Isaiah took Ruby's palm in his before placing the bird in hers. They lowered it into the nest and spent the next minute arranging it just so. He then did the same with Alice. Pride swept over Lydia as she watched their careful movements. These children were more meticulous than she'd have thought possible in ones so young.

"Mrs. Jefferson, can you help me?"

Another student called for her attention. Lydia rose, but not before smiling at her young charges. "Wonderful work, you three. I'm impressed."

Isaiah and Alice beamed while Ruby blushed and ducked her head. Lydia pressed a hand to Ruby's shoulder in a silent show of support before heading to her other student.

By the end of the school day, Lydia almost forgot her lingering sadness. Almost.

One by one, her students filed out of the small schoolhouse. Each of them said a polite goodbye. Isaiah waved with a smile before bounding outside. Lydia followed at a more sedate pace, hoping to say hello to his mother.

Her friend grinned when Lydia came out the door. Ella Brooks's red waves were pinned up under a pretty bonnet. She held her eleven-month-old daughter in her arms. Isaiah had found his other two siblings, and the three were engaged in a game of chase around the yard.

Ella shook her head. "How those children have so much energy is beyond me." She turned her gaze to Lydia. "Did Isaiah behave himself today?"

"Always."

A flash of amusement crossed Ella's face. "I'm glad he's so well-behaved for you. At home, he has a stubborn streak the size of Montana."

Lydia laughed. "I have yet to see that."

Isaiah raced up to them, breathing hard. "Mama, ask Mrs. Jefferson if she's okay. She was sad today." With that declaration, he darted off again.

Ella tilted her head, a frown creasing her brow. "Lydia?"

All the grief crashed into her again. So much for trying to keep it at bay. Traitorous tears burned her eyes. She swallowed hard. Twice.

A comforting arm slid around her shoulders. Ella hugged her close, not saying anything. Twin trails of moisture worked their way down Lydia's cheeks before she swiped them away. She drew in a ragged breath before attempting to speak. "It's just...today is a hard day."

"Today as in the present, or because of something that happened in the past?"

Ella's tone held warmth and compassion. Lydia drew strength from that. She fidgeted with the sleeve of her dress, keeping her gaze down. "Something that happened in the past."

"Do you want to talk about it?"

"I..." Lydia shook her head. "Thank you for asking, Ella, but I'm not sure I want to dredge it up."

Her friend opened her mouth, then snapped it shut. She touched Lydia's shoulder. "You know I'm always here if you need to talk."

Yes, she knew. Ella had been a steadfast friend ever since Lydia moved to Harmony Springs eighteen months ago with her mother-in-law. So why did she still find it hard to confide her deepest pain to Ella?

"I know."

Maybe someday.

Little Rosie began fussing in her mother's arms. Ella bounced the baby. "We should get going." She put a hand on

Lydia's arm. "Will you and Dorothy like to join us for supper on Saturday?"

Her mother-in-law would love a visit with the Brooks family. Lydia nodded. "That would be great."

After saying farewell to Ella and the children, Lydia walked back into the schoolhouse. She stopped short at the sight of Ruby still at a table. "Ruby! What are you doing here, sweetie?"

The little girl had a thumb in her mouth, but she pulled it out to reply. "Granny didn't come yet."

Odd. Pearl was never late. Though the woman had to be in her seventies, she always came down the mountain to pick up her great-granddaughter.

Oh, Lord, please let nothing be wrong.

Even as the prayer welled up inside, Lydia's chest constricted. Her instincts buzzed with trepidation. Fighting it down, she found a smile and held out her hand to Ruby. "Would you like me to take you home?"

Ruby bounced up from her chair. "Yes, please." She slipped her hand into Lydia's, looking up at her with total trust.

Lydia tried to ignore the anxiety rising inside. Pearl had to be all right. She'd taken on custody of her granddaughter after Ruby's parents and baby brother died of cholera.

Ruby couldn't lose anyone else.

"Next stop, Harmony Springs."

The conductor's loud proclamation jerked Samuel Allen out of a restless sleep. He yawned and stretched as best he could in the cramped seat. A few minutes later, the train slowed its pace. Another few minutes and it came to a stop with a creaky groan.

He waited for the family seated beside him to disembark. The mother gathered up her four children while the father gave Samuel a tired smile, hoisting several bags. "Pleasure meeting you, Pastor Allen."

"The pleasure was mine. Enjoy the visit with your in-laws."

The man grimaced, but his lips tugged up in a smile. "Pray for me."

"Of course."

Once most of the car had emptied of passengers, Samuel stood and reached for his luggage. One bag held all his worldly possessions. He considered it a blessing, seeing as his vocation as pastor provided him with a home and a flock. This town was his first assignment on his own. He'd spent the past few years assisting his mentor, John Rivers, at a parish in Chicago. Now, he was to shepherd the people of Harmony Springs, the first permanent pastor the town had seen.

He didn't feel ready. But, as John often said, God would lead the way.

A rush of nerves tightened his belly. Samuel pushed them away. It wouldn't do to be swept away by emotion. He was all too familiar with that sensation.

Memories tried to rise in his mind. Samuel deliberately ignored them, turning his attention to getting off the train. John said he'd be met by the town's sheriff. Apparently, that office was the highest position of governance in many small towns of the American territories.

As he stepped off the train, his gaze landed on a tall, broad man in a cowboy hat with a star pinned to his vest. Dark hair peeked out from under his hat. Samuel walked forward confidently. "Sheriff Doyle?"

The man nodded with a friendly smile. "Pastor Allen?" His voice carried a familiar brogue.

Samuel's brows rose. "You're Irish."

"That I am. Parents came over from the old country before I was born, but I grew up among Irish immigrants." He pointed at Samuel's bag. "You got any more of those?"

"No, sir. This is everything."

The sheriff chuckled. "My name's Travis, young man. Unless we're in formal situations, feel free to call me by that name."

Young man? Samuel tilted his head, studying Travis. He couldn't be more than five or so years over Samuel's own twenty-six. Maybe they could become friends.

The thought lightened Samuel's heart. He loved making friends. His parents always said he'd need an occupation that involved getting to know people. Becoming a pastor had been perfect for that.

"And you can call me Samuel."

"All right, then. Let's get you to the parsonage."

Travis headed toward the street. Samuel fell into step with him. Wooden buildings lined the dusty main street, fitting his image of a small western town. Horses stood tied to hitching posts outside many of them. People milled the streets, the men in cowboy hats, the women in bonnets. Several noticed Samuel and offered polite smiles or tips of the hat.

He had a feeling he was going to like it here.

Ruby's great-grandmother wasn't well.

That became clear within moments of entering the small cabin where the only remaining members of the Calhoun family lived. The old woman lay in her bed, a cough wracking her frail body.

Lydia knelt by the bed and took the woman's hand. "Pearl?"

Pearl opened her rheumy eyes. "Mrs. Jefferson." She inhaled sharply, leading to another coughing fit before she wheezed out, "Am I late pickin' up Ruby?"

"I'm here, Granny." Ruby climbed onto the bed. "Mrs. Jefferson brought me home."

Confusion swirled over Pearl's face before she relaxed. "Thanks, ma'am. I'm sorry I missed pickup today."

Lydia eyed the throbbing vein in Pearl's throat. "Do you know what ails you?"

The woman shook her head, leaning back against her pillow with a tired sigh. "It's been comin' on slowly but surely. I probably need a doc, but we ain't got one no more."

Fear slithered through Lydia's heart. With Doc Grady having retired and gone farther west to be with his eldest daughter, Harmony Springs was left without a physician. A traveling nurse came through on occasion, but without a doctor in residence, emergencies had become a true problem. And this could become an emergency.

"Is there anything I can do for you?" Lydia asked.

Pearl smiled and gave Lydia's hand a pat. "No, thanks. I just needed a little rest." The elderly woman pushed back the covers and struggled to sit up. Lydia reached out to help, but Pearl waved her away. "Now, young lady, I've done this thousands of times before. I'll be fine soon enough." Her eyes flickered to Ruby. "Sweetie, can you fetch Granny a cup of water?"

Ruby squeezed Pearl's hand and dashed off. Pearl fixed her eyes on Lydia. "There is one thing you can do for me."

"What's that?"

Pearl nodded toward Ruby. "If something should happen to me, take care of my girl. It's only a matter of time before the Lord calls me home. I don't want her goin' to an orphanage."

Only a matter of time? Lydia stared at Pearl.

The other woman held her gaze, her mouth set in a firm line. "Please, Mrs. Jefferson. Ruby adores you. I know she'd be in good hands."

The woman talked as though her death was imminent. Chills made gooseflesh rise on Lydia's skin. "Pearl, is there something you're not telling me?"

Pearl dropped her gaze with a short exhale. "I'm seventy-eight, Mrs. Jefferson. I've already lived longer than most folks in these parts." She lifted one shoulder in a half shrug. "This sickness could do me in."

How could she say those words so factually? No despair marred her tone, no regret evidence in her words. She looked at Lydia with a calm steadiness that said Pearl had thought this through.

"I..." Lydia swallowed a lump in her throat. Her gaze found Ruby. How could she say no? She didn't *want* to say no. But could she raise a child on her own?

Pearl gripped her hand. "Please."

The single word broke through Lydia's reservation. If it came to that, she'd figure something out. She gently pressed Pearl's hand and took a breath.

"I will."

Did you enjoy this book? We hope so!
Would you take a quick minute to leave a review where you purchased the book?
It doesn't have to be long. Just a sentence or two telling what you liked about the story!

Receive a FREE ebook and get updates when new Wild Heart books release: https://wildheartbooks.org/newsletter

ABOUT THE AUTHOR

Lauralyn Keller loves to combine history and romance in stories that touch the heart. She lives in beautiful Colorado and is a member of American Christian Fiction Writers. When she's not writing, she enjoys cooking, hiking, and reading.

AUTHOR'S NOTE

Thank you so much for reading Cody and Ella's story! It was a joy to tell it. You readers are the reason I write, and I'm so thankful for all the support and encouragement through the process of getting this book published. If you liked the story, would you please take a moment to leave a review on Amazon and/or Goodreads? Reviews help authors immensely, and I'd be very grateful if you wrote one.

History and writing were two of my favorite subjects growing up. I much preferred essays to tests and history classes to math. Being able to combine those two loves is a dream come true. Diving into the world of 1880s Montana taught me a lot about the Wild West. It was like time traveling while sitting in my living room. How fun is that?

If you haven't already, please join me on Instagram (@lauralynkellerauthor) and sign up for my newsletter to receive updates on the next books in the series and future projects. Signups are on my website (lauralynkeller.com).

ACKNOWLEDGMENTS

Writers generally rely on the help of many people to help their stories shine. Most important is the support of those around them. For me, that's my family. Thank you to Mom, Dad, and my siblings for always believing in me and encouraging me to follow my dream of writing.

Thank you to my sister Christine, a fellow writer, for being there to talk through plots and characters and story elements.

Thank you to Misty and Denise at Wild Heart Books for publishing this story and taking a chance on a new writer. I will always be thankful for this opportunity! And another thank you to Denise for editing the manuscript.

Thank you to those in the ACFW critique group who went through each chapter of this story and helped make it better: Tamelia, Joe, Barbara, Jim, Susan, Taylor, Aveline, Doc, Michael, Nicole, and Paul. I appreciate all the comments, suggestions, and edits.

Thank you to Lynn, Candie, Heather, Erin, Anna, Katie, Dawna, Eileen, Gayle, and Emmy for helping determine the course of this book when I couldn't decide between two different versions. I appreciate you ladies taking the time to read those early chapters and give input.

And finally, thank you to the Lord for the ability to write and tell stories. As the Author of Life, He is the one who wrote The Story of all creation, and I am thankful to have a tiny role in mimicking that creative endeavor.

WANT MORE?

If you love historical romance, check out the other Wild Heart books!

Rescue in the Wilderness by Andrea Byrd

William Cole cannot forget the cruel burden he carries, not with the pock marks that serve as an outward reminder. Riddled with guilt, he assumed the solitary life of a long hunter, traveling into the wilds of Kentucky each year. But his quiet existence is changed in an instant when, sitting in a tavern, he overhears a man offering his daughter—and her virtue—to the winner of the next round of cards. William's integrity and desire for redemption will not allow him to sit idly by while such an injustice occurs.

Lucinda Gillespie has suffered from an inexplicable illness her entire life. Her father, embarrassed by her condition, has subjected her to a lonely existence of abuse and confinement. But faced with the ultimate betrayal on the eve of her eighteenth birthday, Lucinda quickly realizes her trust is better placed in the hands of the mysterious man who appears at her door. Especially when he offers her the one thing she never thought would be within her grasp—freedom.

In the blink of an eye, both lives change as they begin the difficult, danger-fraught journey westward on the Wilderness Trail. But can they overcome their own perceptions of themselves to find love and the life God created them for?

A Heart's Gift by Lena Nelson Dooley

Is a marriage of convenience the answer?

Franklin Vine has worked hard to build the ranch he inherited into one of the most successful in the majestic Colorado mountains. If only he had an heir to one day inherit the legacy he's building. But he was burned once in the worst way, and he doesn't plan to open his heart to another woman. Even if that means he'll eventually have to divide up his spread among the most loyal of his hired hands.

When Lorinda Sullivan is finally out from under the control of men who made all the decisions in her life, she promises herself she'll never allow a man to make choices for her again. But without a home in the midst of a hard Rocky Mountain winter, she has to do something to provide for her infant son.

A marriage of convenience seems like the perfect arrangement, yet the stakes quickly become much higher than either of them ever planned. When hearts become entangled, the increasing danger may change their lives forever.

~

Lone Star Ranger by Renae Brumbaugh Green

Elizabeth Covington will get her man.

And she has just a week to prove her brother isn't the murderer Texas Ranger Rett Smith accuses him of being. She'll show the good-looking lawman he's wrong, even if it means setting out on a risky race across Texas to catch the real killer.

Rett doesn't want to convict an innocent man. But he can't let the Boston beauty sway his senses to set a guilty man free. When Elizabeth follows him on a dangerous trek, the Ranger vows to keep her safe. But who will protect him from the woman whose conviction and courage leave him doubting everything—even his heart?

www.ingramcontent.com/pod-product-compliance
Lightning Source LLC
Chambersburg PA
CBHW070411310726
48977CB00003B/647